A Perfect Love

International Billionaires VI: The Greeks

Caro LaFever

Book cover: Kim Killion
Interior design: Caro LaFever

Publisher's Note: This is a work of fiction. Names, characters, places, and incidents are a product of the author's imagination. Locales
and public names are sometimes used for atmospheric purposes.
Any resemblance to actual people, living or dead, or to businesses,
companies, events, institutions, or locales is completely coinci-
dental.

.

A Perfect Love/Caro LaFever -- 1st ed.
ISBN 978-1-945007-14-9

For my dad, who taught me to love Shakespeare.

I walk to find a true

love; and I see

That 'tis not a mere

woman, that is she,

But must or more or less than woman be.

JOHN DONNE

evenge was not sweet.

It burned in his mouth and gut like acid.

It seared his throat and lungs.

Long ago, the need for it had charred his heart.

Raphael Vounó stood in front of the business that harbored his foes. The business he now owned, as well as the crumbling building it was housed in. London's icy rain slanted against the skin of his cheek and jaw. The chill did nothing to lessen the burn inside.

Time to settle the score. Finally.

He pushed open the hotel's battered steel door and strode in. The foyer was empty, but the low sound of a radio slid under the door behind the lobby desk. He didn't glance around. He knew exactly where everything was in this cramped excuse of a building. His investigation had been thorough. Nothing was left to chance. Not this time.

Striding past the front counter, he didn't hesitate. His hand slapped open the office door.

There he was. The first of his two enemies.

The man had aged during the last ten years. Yet he still lived, unlike Raphael's father. Loukas Vounó had not been as lucky as this old man.

Whose luck had just run out.

The old man lifted his head from the papers strewn across his desk. His gaze was blurry and tired. His skin drooped in grey flaps along his jaw. The years had not been kind, and today this enemy would find out his remaining years would be even worse. Who are you?" he muttered.

Leaning against the doorway, he gave the older man a mocking smile. "You don't recognize me, Drakos?"

The hazy eyes slowly cleared. The man straightened. Then, the curses flowed.

Raphael ignored them all. There was nothing this man could do or say that would hurt him. Not any longer. He'd spent the last ten years planning and plotting for this moment. Unlike his father, he took nothing for chance, trusted no one. He'd purposefully built a wall of protection around himself, his family, and his business. No one, certainly not Haimon Drakos, could ever touch him or his again.

"You're not welcome here." The old man glared at him. "Get out."

He laughed and prowled toward the desk. "No."

"I will call the police and have you thrown out." Drakos's words were edged with forced bravado as he uneasily reached for the ancient phone.

"The police are now your friends?"

The seated man gripped the phone in his shaking hand. "They will come and enforce my property rights. I own this place and I demand you leave."

"Demand?" Raphael slid his leg onto the wobbly wooden desk. Crossing his arms, he smiled. "You will no longer be making demands. Not here. Not anywhere."

"What do you mean?" Drakos' voice quivered.

Bending forward to stare into the man's eyes, he delivered the first blow. "I own Viper Enterprises."

The old eyes widened in horror. "No!"

"What's going on?" The voice came from the open doorway. The familiar lilt, the unique slur at the end of the words, the husky edge to the vowels...all unmistakably her.

Enemy number two.

Rafe forced a deep breath into his lungs. Finding his formidable control, he turned to confront the girl who'd cut out his naïve heart with her betrayal. "Tamsin."

She was no longer a girl.

Her bright-blonde hair had turned golden, impossibly more beautiful than before. Her green eyes no longer flashed with innocent joy; instead they had darkened into mist and mystery. Her body, the body he'd hugged in his arms when she laughed and clutched to his chest when she cried, the body no longer was a young girl's.

His reaction to her was the same.

His skin heated, his muscles tightened, and his groin stirred. Precisely as it had in the past, in that long-ago summer when he'd thought he'd found his soul mate. Thought he'd found his love. Over the years, when he'd allowed a thought of her to cross his mind, he'd shrugged off his reaction to her as youthful folly. He labeled it for what it must have been—merely a young man's hormones. In the last ten years, he'd had women when he needed them. None of them had elicited more than a night's interest.

None of them had made him sweat.

He twitched his shoulders and felt the trickle slide down his spine. The bitterness inside him churned into anger at himself. Lusting after an enemy wasn't part of the agenda.

"Raphael?" Her eyes went wide, her arms wrapping around her in useless defense.

Dóxa to Theó. His enemy didn't sense the lust running through him. The element of surprise, the ele-

ment he'd planned so carefully for this situation, saved
him from revealing anything she could use against him.

"*Nai.*" *Yes. Oh, yes. Tamsin. Did you think I would
forget? Forgive?* He stood with a jerk, ignoring the old
man's snarl behind him. "It's me."

"I can't—"

"I'm here." He stared right into her eyes so she
would know. Know what was in store for her. "Did you
think I would forget you and your family, *kardiá mou?*"

She flinched.

An exultant flare of acid triumph whipped through
him. She remembered. She remembered what he'd
called her. Which meant she remembered everything.
The loving nickname. Her betrayal. His anger at the
very end.

My heart.

What a foolish, stupid boy he'd been to give her
those words. To give her any power over him at all.
Now, though, she would know everything was different.

Her hands dropped to her sides and her jaw tightened. A familiar glint of defiance flashed in her green
gaze. "What are you doing here?"

She'd given him this same bold scowl when they'd
met for the first time. Sure, he'd been a cocky twenty-
one-year-old, full of himself, surly about having to
spend time with his younger sisters and a girl too
young to be of any interest. All because his father had
business with Drakos and wanted the families to know

each other. He'd slouched into the unfamiliar house, knowing he'd be bored out of his mind. And then it had happened.

He'd gazed into these green eyes and fallen.

Completely and utterly fallen.

Did she think she merely had to give him a defiant look and he'd be a fool once more?

"I'm here," he forced himself to stroll to her and stare into those dangerous eyes, "because I now own this place."

His claim slammed into her. He could see it in the taut, tense thrust of her jaw. See it in the way her head went back, as if slapped. He tried to focus on these telling details which told of his victory, but...

But the effort was futile.

These eyes. *Theós.* He'd truly forgotten. Her eyes had always reminded him of the laurel leaves his mother used in her cooking, the green glistening pure and clear in the heated water. There was no hint of blue or brown to lessen the impact of flawless color. In his fanciful youth, he'd dreamed her gaze had shone with a perfect love, with a belief in his ability to make all his dreams, and hers, come true. He'd fallen asleep in his lonely bed knowing someday these green eyes would look at him as he slept, watch over him and caress him and bless him with the crown of her love.

What a complete and utter fool he'd been.

The fringe of her blonde eyelashes whisked across her fair skin as she blinked. When she opened her eyes once more, they no longer reminded him of his lovesick days. They reminded him of the last time he'd stared at her. Then the green had turned dark and dirty, dulling into dismissal.

Exactly as they did now.

"We own this building." Her mouth twisted, turning the lushness of her lips into a rejecting curl. "We have for years."

The old man rustled some papers behind him. The noise shot through Raphael like a poisoned arrow. As soon as this woman had entered the room, he'd forgotten. He'd forgotten the old man. His plans. His revenge. He'd forgotten everything but her.

Damn her.

Turning around, he glared at the old man. "Tell her, Drakos."

The skin under the man's eyes looked like splotches of tar compared to the pale sickliness of the rest of his face. The scent of fear mixed with alcohol wafted off his fat body as he slouched down into the creaking hull of the plastic chair, still cradling the phone. The last puff of smoke rose from the chewed cigar lying in the ashtray among the waste of paper.

Theós. The realization struck Rafe. He'd come just in time.

How cruel would fate have been if he'd left his revenge too late, moved too slow, let this man escape into death before being punished? He could not have lived with himself if he hadn't fulfilled the pledge he'd made over his father's dead body. He could not have looked at himself in the mirror if this final revenge had not been delivered.

Yet luck and fate had been with him all through these past ten years.

The man before him still lived and would still suffer.

"Tell her," he demanded once more.

Rafe felt her behind him. She didn't move, didn't make a sound. Yet, he felt her. Like a burn in his blood, like a venomous snake sliding on his skin. He sensed her zigzagging thoughts. He tasted her growing unease. He knew what was inside of her. Just as he'd known the moment he'd first seen her.

The fact this connection still existed between them stunned him. He'd thought his reaction to her would be entirely one of bitter anger and harsh judgment.

He didn't like this trace of lust in his blood.

He didn't like this connection, this *feeling* of her.

However, he couldn't deny both were there inside him.

Haimon Drakos glanced at his stepdaughter. His eyes said everything his mouth would not say. Defeated. Dead. Two black holes of despair.

"What have you done?" Her whisper, soft and stark, sifted through the hushed silence.

The scent of her sudden fear wrapped around Rafe and he reveled in it. His impulse was to turn. Turn to see the fear in the green, green of her gaze. But he didn't want to stare into those dangerous eyes and chance losing his focus. Right now, he wanted to stare at this man before him who had tricked and scorned his father.

He glared at the old man who'd caused his father's death.

"Tell her."

Raphael.

Here.

Close enough to touch.

The reality was so intolerably unreal, Tamsin could barely breathe. She'd dreamed so many dreams of this moment. Dreams of ecstatic cries of love. Dreams of walking into his strong arms and crying out the years of pain and misery. Dreams that followed her from her bed every morning and swirled around in her head throughout the day.

Raphael.

He was so *him* and yet so very different.

He no longer had the lanky posture of youth. Years ago, he'd seemed more legs and arms, had always walked and moved as if he still were learning how to handle the growth spurt into six-feet-plus of male. Now his shoulders were no longer bony and lean. They were heavy with muscle. His body moved with fluid masculine grace, confident in its supremacy, filling the tiny, dingy room with its power.

Raphael.

She stared at his broad back, turned against her. Then her gaze took in the way he held his head. The proud tilt told her he no longer had any of the shy charm she'd found so irresistible when she'd been sixteen. His hair had been longer too, a mass of ebony curls. Curls that had clung to her fingers as they lay together in the sunlit vineyards of her stepfather's Greek estate. Curls that had given him a boyish beauty she'd fallen for within seconds of meeting him. Now those curls were ruthlessly suppressed, the cut emphasizing the symmetry of his ears, the elegance of his jaw line.

Rafe.

"Tell her."

His voice was different too. No longer warm and fun and full of laughter. Of love. Now his voice slashed into her like a cold slice of steel. His voice hacked through all her old memories and yearnings and brought her back to the reality of what stood before her.

A threat.

She had no doubt of this. None. She'd heard the voices and known immediately something was terribly wrong. Haimon rarely had anyone visit him anymore. He did all his dirty business by phone and she ignored what was going on because she couldn't do anything about it. As long as he left everything else alone, she was content to let him play his games from his seedy, shabby office.

"Don't involve the boys," she'd warned him.

"Of course not," he'd assured her, puffing on his ever-present cigar.

She'd chosen to believe him because she'd had no other choice.

Yet when she'd heard the voices today, she'd known with gut certainty this wasn't one of Haimon's customers surprising him in his office. This was worse. This was far worse. But not even her usually keen instincts had prepared her for what she saw as she walked into disaster.

Her past walking into her present.

No longer a ghost of regret and pain. No longer a memory she'd hidden in her heart all these years as she'd lived with her choice and her sacrifice. No, her ghost of past love now stood before her. And as soon as she'd seen his expression, she'd known.

He was a threat.

To Haimon, surely. Maybe with some justification. But not only to him.

To her home. To her.

To the boys.

"What have you done?" She managed to push out the words through the horror leaching into her belly. Her stepfather had promised her, promised he wouldn't touch what she'd created here. He'd assured her this place she'd hobbled together to make a home for the boys would stay safe. Stay apart from his dirty games.

Raphael Vounó suddenly threw his head back and laughed.

The sound jarred her. So different, so different and sad and horribly wrong compared to how he used to laugh. How many memories had she stored inside her soul, memories of the joy of his laughter as he'd swung her around in his arms? Memories that had sustained her through her terrible decision and the ugly after-math.

This laugh told her everything about him.

A lethal, deathly threat to everything she held dear.

With a swift jerk, he turned to face her one more time. The grief for all she'd lost and he'd lost swept through her again as she stared into his black, pitiless eyes. The eyes that had once danced with a bright glow. As a girl, she'd never been able to describe in her journal the way his black eyes were not dark but light. Not deep but open. She couldn't communicate in words how the very blackness of his gaze highlighted how brilliant the love shining from them was.

Yet now, like everything about him, the black had changed.

"He's too much of a coward," he snarled. "So I have the pleasure of informing you, *kardiá mou.*"

The nickname was too much. "Don't call me that."

The black gaze blazed, flared with unholy delight. "You don't appreciate irony, Tamsin?"

She tried to wrestle her brain into working order, tried to find her way out of this nightmare, but it was no use. His presence and hate swallowed her whole. His terrible, treacherous threat. What could be worse than this? What could be worse than confronting her old dreams arising from the ashes of her past as a menace?

But she'd absorbed a hard, bitter lesson at sixteen. One she'd learned again and again over the years. There was no way to win when confronted with disaster. The only thing a person could do was survive. "Tell me."

"Your loving father..." His accented drawl elongated the words, edging them with icy contempt.

Haimon wasn't her father. Once, when she'd been little, she'd hoped. Hoped he'd take the place of a father who'd abruptly disappeared from her life. However, her new stepfather wasn't the paternal type and she'd quickly accepted she was nothing more than a piece of her mother's baggage.

Raphael knew this.

He'd listened to her wistful dreams about her real fa-ther. He'd held her in his arms as she cried about some insult Haimon had thrown at her.

He knew. Too much.

"No more games." Tam reminded herself of what she'd become. She ran this hotel. She managed the small staff. She paid the bills. Moreover, she'd success-fully raised the twins for the last ten years. Two ram-bunctious, challenging, amazingly wonderful boys. She could handle anything.

She had to for the boys.

"Games?" Raphael's mouth turned grim. "I'm not playing a game."

"Then stop beating about the bush. Say what you have to say and leave."

His gaze sharpened. Was he surprised she challenged him? Didn't he realize she was different, too? She was not the loving, giving girl he'd known years ago. Her sacrifice to protect everyone, including him, had changed her forever.

"I'm not leaving," he stated. "You and your father are."

She didn't waste her breath denying Haimon as a fa-ther. Because she only had breath enough to deny his demand, deny a reality too horrible to contemplate. "We aren't going anywhere."

"*Nai*, Tamsin, you are going. Out onto the street." A confident smirk crossed his face. "I own this place, and I'm evicting you and your father."

This building wasn't merely a building. It didn't only house the cheap hotel rooms and struggling businesses which paid for the little they had. This building was their home. The top floor was where she and the boys slept, played, dreamed. This building was the only thing they had.

She peered past the horror standing before her and glared into Hamion's sunken eyes. "You told me you owned this place free and clear."

"I did." The shrug of old shoulders tinged the words with defeat. "Once."

"Not now?" She couldn't help the wail. What would she do? What would she do with the twins?

"He took out a mortgage a year ago." Raphael's voice was quiet, yet intense. "Which I bought."

"But...but..." None of the thoughts and emotions running through her brain made any sense. She couldn't seem to nail any of them down and put them in some comprehensible order.

"He's late with the payments." The deadly tone marched on.

"Not that late," Hamion blustered.

"The contract you signed, old man." The younger man appeared completely at ease, his arms casually crossed, his long legs planted solidly on the floor. The

floor he claimed he owned. "Didn't you read the contract? Were you as foolish as my father was years ago?"

The sharp tang of sheer rage filled the words. But
she detected something else in the flavor of his voice. A
hint of permanent, unbearable grief. All these years,
and he still mourned. And exactly like before, she
couldn't comfort him; she couldn't walk into his arms
and hold him. The stark thought brought unwilling,
unwanted tears to her eyes.

Raphael glanced her way and smiled. "Tears won't
do you any good, *kardiá mou.* They will not sway me
from throwing you out."

"I'm not—" She stopped. This man was no longer
her Raphael. He wouldn't believe a word she said. She
needed to understand right now: he was the enemy.
Somehow she had to find a way around this man and
his threats in order to protect the boys.

"In fact," he continued, his smile tight and taut.
"Tears will only make this more pleasurable for me. I
want both of you to suffer."

Just as my father did.

He didn't have to say the words. They lay in his eyes.
His dark black eyes.

She stared into those eyes and saw nothing of the boy
she'd loved. Clearly, that boy had died ten years ago
when his father had ended his life. Tamsin's grief billowed inside her. She'd thought she'd done the right
thing that long ago night. She'd been sure in her young

heart she was saving him. But saving him for what? Saving him only for him to lose any trace of humanity?

For a moment, something flashed in those black eyes. His big body flinched; his mouth tightened. And his eyes...For a moment, Tam thought she saw something.

Then it was gone.

Rafe swung back to Haimon. "Since you didn't read all the fine print, Drakos, I'll enlighten you. One late payment and this place is mine. One."

The old man sunk deeper in his chair.

"And you've missed three."

"We live here." Reality seeped into her skin like an oily claw of futility. "This is our home."

"Not any longer." He prowled to the door. "You were served with an eviction notice and today's the last day you can live here."

"I never saw any such notice." Tam clung to a last strand of hope.

Her tormentor stared over at her stepfather. Her gaze followed his and what she saw on Haimon's face cut any hope right out of her heart. "How could you keep this from me?"

"I have a deal in the works," he mumbled. "I'll have the money—"

"Too late." Leaning on the doorframe, Rafael crossed his arms. "I don't want your money, Drakos. I've got plenty of my own."

"If you'll give me some time—"

"I'll give you nothing." His words were like steel-edged nails. "I want you both out. If not willingly, then I will be glad to call the bailiffs in."

Fury and fear mixed inside her, making it hard to think. Only emotion shot through the mess in her mind. "The boys," she blurted.

"Ah, yes." He straightened, dropping his hands to his sides.

Her love for her brothers swelled, settling her emotions and letting her think. He remembered the boys. She saw the memories in his black gaze. The times he'd lifted them into the pool and played with them. The picnic they'd had with the twins one day. The fun he'd had, laughing and rolling with them in the fragrant grass by the river. If she had to plead and beg, if she had to use those memories, she would. She would do anything to save their home for them. "The boys live here."

"The boys." Sudden fury flashed across his face. "How could I forget?"

"They have a home here." Why did the memory of her boys make him angry? They'd only been three the last time he'd seen him. They'd done nothing to warrant any anger. She forced herself to continue, trying to find a foothold to negotiate with this man. "I'm...I'm their mother."

"Actually, you're not, are you?" The dark gaze pinned her to the floor. "Their mother was a whore, wasn't she?"

"Don't say that." Rage wiped away any impulse to negotiate. "It's not—"

"I speak only the truth." The long, elegant fingers of his hands tightened into fists. He glowered at the old man sagging in his chair. "The boys aren't yours, Drakos. Did you know that?"

The words blasted into the room like torches of fire. Her stepfather jerked in his seat, and if it were possible, his skin whitened even further. "What the hell are you insinuating?"

"I'm not insinuating anything. I'm telling you."

The fear in her blood raced, roared, and Tamsin thought she might faint. "What are you telling us?"

"The boys." Rafe looked right at her as he delivered the killing blow. "Are mine."

CHAPTER TWO

They were so young. So impossibly young.
The boys.

They lay in a jumble of gangly legs, gawky arms, slack mouths, together on the opposite plastic couch. Exhaustion had carried them away an hour ago as they sat in this sterile hospital lounge. Waiting for a report about their father's condition.

Their supposed father. Who'd collapsed at the news they were not his. Never his.

They are mine.

The words pumped in Rafe's heart. They were Vounós. They were not Drakos' or Tamsin's.

They were his. The last remnant of his brother.

And so very much like his brother Rhouben.

Ben.

Grief clutched in his throat. The grief he'd managed to suppress as he'd held his sobbing mother when the news had come two weeks ago. A grief he'd stifled when he'd made the funeral arrangements. Grief he'd crushed with the memories of how irresponsible and negligent Ben had been for years. In reality, his older brother had been lost to him at the moment of their father's death. He'd walked away from the emotional wreckage of their family, the collapse of the business, the destruction of the Vounó reputation. The companion of his childhood, the brother he'd adored and emulated, had deserted him as surely as his father had. As decisively as Tamsin had.

At the moment he'd most needed them all.

He'd dealt with it. Without letting emotion get in the way of what he had to do.

So it surprised him. This abrupt, overwhelming grief. This sudden sense he'd lost far more than his brother. This welling, gut-wrenching feeling he'd missed something important in his intense determination to make it *right.*

One of the boys grumbled in his sleep as he rolled over on the plastic couch.

The sound punctuated his grief like a straight pin stuck in his skin.

There was no time to grieve. There was far too much to do.

Rafe tore his gaze away from the slumbering teenagers. Glancing at his phone, he flipped through his messages. A message from his mother, who knew nothing of this trip. Not yet. Not until he had the twins in his hands would he reveal the startling, unbelievably wonderful news that Ben lived on in his children. A voicemail from his sister, asking if he could please stop by and talk to her husband about some new venture. Plus, a hundred messages from his business. Doctors pitching new medicines for his investment. Investors pleading to be brought in on the next deal. His PA wanting to know where he was and what he was doing.

He tried to focus. Focus on what needed to be done.

Yet, right now, in this silent room, inhabited by two boys who'd suddenly become the center of his universe, his usual responsibilities seemed so far away. Like a different life.

Theé mou, how thankful he was for the impulse that had driven him to go through his brother's belongings alone instead of shunting the work off to his grieving sisters. They would have been hysterical at the news of their lost nephews.

But no, it had only been his hands shaking as he'd scrolled through the long list of emails, shifted through the personal letters, scanned the texts—all written by the whore. Only his startled eyes had read her threats, her entreaties, her demands. Only he had gasped when he'd seen Ben's emailed response, admitting his paternal responsibilities, offering money for silence.

Memories had washed through him as he'd stared at the stark words.

The way Ben excused himself from the gatherings with the Drakos clan, even over their father's strenuous objections. The time Ben had abruptly walked out of the room when he and his mother had been talking about the young Drakos toddlers. The moment Ben's harsh voice had cut him off when he'd tried to explain how he'd fallen in love with...

Rafe clamped down on the old stupidity and instead, focused on who sat across from him.

The twins. Ben's twins.

Memories were the past and not useful in this situation. He needed to focus on the future and his plans for these boys. He owed it to his late father. To his dead brother.

The inside of his throat ached.

Jerking his head around, he pinned his gaze on the nurse's station at the end of the hall. He swallowed. Swallowed again. Breathed in deeply. The clang of a hospital cart rolling past the quiet room served as a needed distraction.

He breathed in once more.

One of the boys murmured, turned on the plastic cushion and subsided into sleep again.

Another breath in, the smell of antiseptic filling his nostrils with the bite of chemicals. Clearing away the buzzing in his brain and the aching in his heart. Satisfying him that he'd found his control.

His plan before he'd known of his nephews had been to continue to use stealth and secrecy in destroying Drakos. He held the mortgage, but this had not been enough. He'd been steadily adding information about the illegal deals the old man was making. Loan sharking. Bookmaking. He wanted the man in jail, not merely homeless. He wanted Haimon Drakos humiliated as his father had been. He wanted to drag out his revenge like a long, slow march of death, cementing the old man into a seal-tight, inescapable box one solid stone at a time.

However, the existence of the boys had changed everything. There had been no time to lose. He could not allow his flesh and blood to be tainted any longer by Haimon's influence.

Or Tamsin's. Certainly not hers.

Yet the knowledge of the boys' true paternity didn't mean he wouldn't continue to pursue Drakos. The police were interested in the information his security had provided them. Very interested.

Haimon Drakos had an arrest warrant waiting for him. If he survived.

"He's going to survive." Her silky, slurred voice reached him from the open doorway. The slight lilt she always edged her words with rasped along his nerves. He'd fallen for her husky voice, just as he'd fallen for her eyes. He'd relished the sexiness of it as she whispered in his ear. He'd dreamed endless dreams of what she'd say when he entered her body with his for the first time.

A first time that had never happened.

Maybe this was the whole issue. Maybe the fact he'd never taken her was the reason he still felt this unwilling lust for her. Maybe...

"Did you hear me?"

"*Nai.*" He looked up from his phone and managed an uninterested gaze. "I heard you."

She stood tall and straight, somehow projecting a calm, centered manner even though her clothes were wrinkled and her long hair rumpled. Staring him down, she no longer gazed at him with fear or regret. All he saw in those leafy eyes was determination.

Determination to get rid of him.

Why did this spark a flame of rage in him? Why, when he wanted the same thing?

To get rid of her.

"He's had a stroke, but the prognosis—"

His hand arced in a sharp move of rejection. "I have no interest in hearing the details. He survives. Good."

"Good?"

"Good because I'm not done with him." He straightened out of his slouch on the hard cushion.

"Haven't you done enough?"

"No." With an abrupt jerk, he stood. He was inordinately pleased when she took a step back.

"He's an old man." She glared, her eyes flaring with green heat. "Have some compassion."

"My father was a young man." Rafe found himself spitting the words at her. "Did Drakos show any compassion for him?"

His accusation punched into her, deflating the anger in her expression. A soft sigh spun out of her lush mouth, lingering in the air like wistful wisps of regret. "Their business dealings fell apart. It happens sometimes and years have gone by. Can't you let it go?"

"Let it go?" He laughed. "No. I will never let it go."

One of the boy's heads lolled, then straightened. Black curls slipped across his forehead in a thatch of ebony youth. "Tam?"

"Sssh, Isaák." With a quick step, she walked to the couch and brushed the boy's tangled hair aside. "Aarōn is still sleeping."

The kid curled his head into her palm like a kitten, not a man. Not a male Vounó. The woman had mollycoddled them; it was clear. It was also clear there was a strong attachment between the boy and Tamsin.

Both things needed to change. Immediately.

"May I have a private word with you?"

His clipped words hit her and the kid at the same time. She straightened, her back going rigid. The kid's eyes widened as he peered past her to pin his sights on Rafe.

Until now, there hadn't been time to properly introduce himself to the boys. Not as their supposed father had been raced to the hospital. Not as Tamsin had bundled them into a taxi, ignoring Raphael, and rushed behind the speeding ambulance. Not as the twins had huddled together on the hospital's couch, staring at their mobile phones, too dazed by events to take in their surroundings.

The curiosity in the boy's gaze was the opening he needed.

"I'm Raphael Vounó."

If it were possible, her back grew stiffer. She whipped her head around and opened her mouth. The green of her eyes darkened in instant dread. She knew. She knew instantly what he intended. Just as she always had.

Rafe slammed the thought, the connection aside. He spoke the words that would forever change everything for his nephews. Spoke them with clear, precise purpose. "Your uncle."

His claim crashed into the room like a comet. Exactly as he'd planned.

"What?" she gasped, turning to face him with a stare of blank astonishment. "You said they were yours—"

A biting surge of rage scorched his blood. "*O Theós na sas gamóto!*"

She flinched as his curse echoed in the room. The boy slipped behind her, his face pale with instant fear.

Rafe tried to stop, tried to control the billowing ball of anger and resentment and pure hurt pummeling inside. But it was too much, too ugly of an accusation to ignore.

"Did you think, Tamsin," he managed to breathe in a gasp, as fire roared through his lungs. "Did you really think I would sleep with your mother when I was seventeen and then four years later be with you—"

"No." She lifted one hand, as if ready to reach out and touch him. "I wasn't thinking straight."

Stepping away from her, he kept his body rigid, afraid of what he might do to her if she actually touched him and set him to flame.

"Rafe, I'm sorry."

He didn't want her apology. He wanted nothing from her. Nothing. Pacing to the long window at the side of the room, he stared out at the whispered beginnings of dawn.

"Then, who..." she stuttered to a stop. The boy murmured at her side.

"Ben." He forced himself to turn and confront her wide eyes and white skin. "Who else would I be talking about?"

She frowned as one of her arms wrapped around the silent boy standing at her side. "You can't be sure—"

"I'm sure."

The utter confidence in his voice shook her. He saw it in the way her shoulders tensed as if hit, the way her hand tightened at her side.

"What does he mean?" The boy glanced at Tamsin, confusion wrinkling his brow. "Who is this Ben?"

"Never mind." Patting the boy's arm, she gave him a tight smile. "He's lying."

"I don't lie." He stared at the boy. The one who mattered. "I never lie."

The statement came out of him as an accusation. Precisely as he meant it to be.

Tamsin got it. Got the message. *She and her mother and Haimon were the liars.* Her mouth tightened. "My mother—"

"Was a whore."

"Rafe." She placed a gentle hand on the boy's black curls as if to push him away from the horrible, true allegation. "She was their mother too."

Frustration at her interference, at the fact she was right in this case, pulsed through him. He'd been so consumed at throwing all of this at her like barbs, like knives, he'd missed the impact his words might have on the boys.

His boys.

"They need to know the truth, but first you and I need to get some things straight." He waved his hand at the doorway. "Privately."

Her gaze darted to the door and back to him. Reluctance was written across her face. Yet his stare and stance must have convinced her she'd rather hear what he had to say alone, than chance him stating whatever he had to say in front of the twins.

Time enough to talk to the boys. After he'd taken care of getting rid of her.

"Isaák, stay here with Aarōn. I'll be right back."

"But—"

She dipped down and placed a comforting kiss on his brow. "Everything will be fine."

Nai, everything would be fine. For the twins. Not for her.

She circled past him as if he was a live wire, and he felt like it. Charged with his mission. Electric intent zipping through his blood. He paced behind her as she walked down the hall, the low murmur of the nurses at the station doing nothing to break through the circle of awareness twitching around them.

He hated this connection. Hated it.

Still, he wasn't a man to deny what was in front of
him. Her measured pace, her baggy grey trousers, her
tense posture should have been asexual. There was no
swing of her hips or tight silk on her body or sultry
looks over her shoulder as he followed her. Nothing
that hinted at womanly favors offered which would
stoke a man.

None of it mattered. He burned for her.

Stopping in front of a red vending machine, she
turned to face him. The lights colored her blonde hair
pink, her pale skin rosy. She glanced at him and the
shock of those eyes shot through him afresh, torching
the fire inside him to instant inferno. He took the fire
and twisted it, tightened it around his hate for her.

"I'm taking the boys." He pitched his voice low, but
the steaming edge of his hostility colored each word.

He had to give her credit; she didn't crumble in the
face of his declaration of intent. She didn't cry or wail
or shriek. Or beg. She merely stared at him with a grim
determination of her own.

Damn her. He wanted to see her fall apart. He needed
to see it.

"Today."

She waved the word away as if it were a fly. "No,
you're not."

So stoic. So certain. So seemingly impervious to him.

"You can fight me, *kardiá mou.* Actually, I hope you
do."

She didn't even bat an eye at the nickname. Somehow, during the time she'd spent consulting with the doctors, the hours she'd guarded the boys from him, the minutes she'd taken inside the old man's hospital room...somehow she'd gathered herself. She'd built inner walls and barriers. The surprise of his appearance had been enough to crack her open for a while. Yet now the toughness and steely will he'd seen in her the last time, the time when she'd rejected him, had come back.

With a vengeance.

He hated these walls inside her. He would break through them somehow. He wanted to see her tears again and hear her wail once more and make her suffer. The compulsion wasn't reasonable or civilized. It was primitive, this seething mass of emotion roiling in him. It was barbaric.

Fight me, Tamsin. Fight me so I can conquer you once and for all and destroy the memory of you in my charred and broken heart.

"The boys will be going back home with me." She began to walk away as if he had no say and no claim.

Grabbing her arm, he yanked her to a stop.

"There is no home to go back to," he muttered into the pearled shell of her ear. How had he come so close to her? Too close to temptation?

"Take your hand off me." She didn't even glare at him or try and pull away. If he didn't feel the warmth of her skin beneath the white wool of her jumper, he'd swear she was some ancient Greek statue.

She shifted in his grip and a whisper of her scent floated around him, encircling him with memories. Fresh. Clean. Not soap or perfume or lotion. No, only pure Tamsin. When he'd been a fool, he'd allowed himself to breathe her in, imagining how her naked skin would smell on his. He'd spent hours by her side, satisfied with virgin kisses and soft, gentle touches because her scent and her skin had entranced him into wanting to keep her fresh. Keep her clean.

What a fool.

He dropped his hand and stepped back.

"Thank you." She held herself with rigid pride and began to walk away once more.

"Tamsin." He sucked in a breath of air that didn't hold her scent anymore. With the clear air came renewed determination. "I've evicted you."

Twirling, she glared at him. "I never saw any notices, any papers. I run the hotel. I should have been—"

"Drakos is the owner and he was served." He stopped himself from sliding into pity because this woman was now homeless. She didn't deserve pity. "It's not my problem he kept the news from you. I can order you out anytime I want to. And I want to. You're evicted."

He felt the hit inside her. She finally believed the words he shot at her. Accepting them, she knew her home was lost. Her face crumpled, and then she lifted one graceful hand and swept it across her eyes, hiding her anguish from him.

Unacceptable. He needed to see her suffer. She owed it to him. "Look at me."

Her hand dropped. She'd recovered with startling speed. The only thing he saw now was hardness in her gaze, like sharp shards of jade striking back at him. "All right. The boys and I will go somewhere else."

"I don't care where *you* go—"

Was that a tiny flinch? A microscopic gram of satisfaction for him?

"—but my nephews are coming with me."

"No." Pacing in front of him, resolve lined every inch of her body. "We'll take our things and find another place to live."

"Right at this moment, my staff is packing your belongings and the twins."

"You have no right—"

"I have every right. I own the building." He slipped a shaking hand inside his pocket. "You should be thankful."

"Thankful?" Stopping short, her sharp laugh filled the hallway with a harsh, rough noise.

"Thankful I'm delivering your belongings to you here instead of throwing them in the trash. The boys' belongings are being packed for the trip to Greece."

"You might own our home now. And you can do whatever you want with our stuff." The delicate edge of her jaw clenched. "However, you don't have guardianship of the boys."

"Not yet." He slid his mobile phone from his pocket and flashed the screen of emails at her. "But I will. One of these emails is from my solicitor."

"So what?" The curve of her shoulders shrugged, but he detected the tension in them.

"Who has prepared paperwork demanding a DNA test."

Her voice quivered. "If what you say about the boys is true—"

"I've said it before, I don't lie."

"Then you should have their best interests at heart."

"I do."

"They have a family. Me."

"No." He wanted to march over to her and shake her until she understood. Understood he won, all the time now. Yet he stayed away. She was too tempting, too treacherous. "I'm their family going forward."

"They don't know you." The paleness of her skin only highlighted the pure smoothness, the classic beauty of her features. "They don't know Greece. They don't know your mother or Rhachel or...Rhouth."

The slight pause before speaking his sister's name—her once-upon-a-time best friend's name—the pause did not escape him. "Ah," he said with a sneer. "You even remember Rhouth?"

"Of course I remember her." Her arms came up to hug herself, her hands tightening, shining white in the harsh overhead light.

"Then you will remember how sweet and caring she is." A picture of his sister flashed through his brain. The memory of her tears years ago. The memory of her questions about where Tamsin went. The memory of her sorrow at the loss of her friend. Every one of the memories crowded in his mind and if he'd had a heart anymore, it would have turned to cut stone. "You will remember how *loyal* she is."

"I remember." Her hands fell, leaving her unguarded. Her chin lifted and her eyes turned dark. "I remember everything."

Her actions and words disturbed him for some reason. The emotion filling her expression was not embarrassment or fear or regret. The way she lifted her chin gave him the sense she was proud, noble, had nothing to ask forgiveness for. The behavior and attitude enraged him, firing the torment inside. "Then you will know the boys will be fine with my family. They will be well taken care of. They will be loved."

"They will be lost without me." She kept going, kept kicking at the inevitable. "I'm the one who has taken care of them these last years. I'm the one who's loved them and fed them and taught them. I am everything to them."

The pride was evident in the clarity of her voice. For a moment, he let himself feel *her*. Understand *her*.

Iisoús. Jesus.

She'd been only sixteen. With two three-year-olds depending on her. Only her.

He'd had enough exposure to her worthless mother to know Skylla hadn't lifted a finger to help. Even in the sun-kissed summer of pretend love, when he'd been in a haze of passionate ecstasy, he'd noted the mother's inattention to her boys. But then, there'd been servants. There'd been a nanny and a housekeeper. Haimon had been riding high, successfully wheeling and dealing his dirty business.

But later? Later when the family had moved to London and their fortunes dwindled?

A slither of respect, unwanted and rejected, writhed in his gut.

His security team had spelled it out, the entire situation, before he'd ever entered the cursed building he now owned. He'd focused on what was important—destruction—not the reality of what the information had meant.

To Tamsin. To the twins.

"She takes care of everything." The head of his security said as he'd delivered his final report. "She runs the place and takes care of the boys."

At the time, the information had been mere spikes in the battering ram he was fashioning to destroy the Drakos family. Now the pieces of information came together to paint another picture. No longer a picture he relished of a family in decline, in desperation, ready to be destroyed. Now the information swirling in his brain painted a picture of a young girl spending ten years of her life taking care of everyone.

She takes care of everything.

The picture penetrated his gut and lay there, a sick brew of admiration.

"You have to see." Her voice shook for a moment before firming into a tight tone. "They belong to me."

Her words shocked the pictures right out of his head. Cold determination swallowed the sick brew in a wash of icy disgust. For a moment, she'd had him, hadn't she? For a second she'd managed to sway him off his course. However, he was no longer the boy wrapped around her female finger. No longer.

He took the chance of getting too near. Stepping right into her space, he glared into those pure green eyes. "What I see is two boys who look exactly like Vounós."

She held her place, did not back away. Yet her expression suddenly filled with a mixture of fear and acknowledgement. "Maybe—"

"No maybes." The blood in his veins pumped with lust. With hate. "Admit it. They are carbon copies of Ben."

"I—"

"Of me."

CHAPTER THREE

*C*arbon copies.

Of Ben? A memory of a young man whipped through Tamsin's brain.

Ben. Rafe's beloved brother. She'd met him only once, when she'd been invited by her love to his family home. She'd noted the bond between the brothers, although the elder one seemed a bit of a poppycock.

Raphael's older brother and her mother?

She stepped back, trying to push away the thought.

Still, the man in front of her was merciless. "Apparently your mother was not content to chase after my father—"

"Stop it." Embarrassment flooded through her body along with the memories she'd locked deep inside. The agonizing moments she'd endured when she'd watched her mother flirt and flutter around Loukas Vounó as he tried to politely ignore her. The way Skylla Drakos had thrust herself into tight dresses and paraded in front of the good doctor like she was selling her wares. Her mother's actions had been the one blight during the summer when she'd fallen in love.

Rafe had never said a word. Not until this moment. She'd naïvely assumed he hadn't noticed, that perhaps she'd been the only one to see. Yet he'd always been more aware than most, certainly most young men. He'd sensed many of her secrets and dreams and hopes even before she confided them to him. She'd been foolish to think he wouldn't have noticed her mother's behavior.

"Never mind." His mouth twisted, as if, incredibly, he regretted bringing the subject up. "None of that matters now."

It mattered. All of the events of ten years ago still mattered to her.

He took a step closer, leaning in to stare with determination into her eyes. "What matters is the boys are obviously Vounós."

His words hit her heart.

They are carbon copies. Of me.

The boys. Raphael.

Yes.

The truth of what he said, the undeniable, unacceptable truth, cut her breath from her throat. Cut her heart from her body.

Was this why she loved the twins with a fierceness which sometimes stunned her? At sixteen, she'd taken them on without a moment of doubt or a moment of anger. She'd taken them to her heart as if they were her own and she'd never begrudged a single minute of her time. She'd never ranted in private at the unfairness of giving her youth to these two small boys. She'd never once wavered when she'd watched kids her age going to parties and having fun.

Never. Never. *Never.*

Had she somehow intuitively known they were a part of Raphael? The only part she had left? Had her spirit connected with some unfathomable well of wisdom, running past her brain and her body to embrace two children with a love so wide and deep and long and vast she would sometimes sit in her bed at night and weep because she had them?

At least, she had *them.*

"The boys are *mine.*" The fervor in Raphael's tone matched her fierce love. Tamsin saw it in the black of his eyes. The commitment, the connection. The determination.

"What's going on?" A young voice cut through the electric current running between them. "Tam?"

She swung around. Aarōn stood in the doorway of the waiting room, Isaák right behind him. Both boys appeared wrinkled and tired and upset. And unbearably lovable. "I...we..."

"What does he mean?" Isaák piped in. "We're his? He's our uncle?"

"Who are you?" His twin frowned. "More importantly, what are you saying to our sister?"

The question shot at Rafe like a poisoned dart. Both of the boys suddenly bristled, hands fisted, shoulders hunched. She'd been amused during the last year as they'd started to walk from childhood into strutting youth. Aarōn had taken to dogging her steps, telling her she needed to be more careful when she went shopping alone. Isaák had announced only last week it was time he and his brother took on more of the work with the hotel so she could have some time with friends. Her non-existent friends.

The boys glared at Raphael Vounó as if he was a threat. To her.

He *was* a threat. To them.

"As I told your brother." The man standing before her didn't flinch from the boys' inspection. He turned and met their glares head on. "I'm your uncle. I'm Raphael Vounó."

"No way." Aarōn wasn't having any of it. "We only have Tam. She would have told us if—"

"She didn't know." He strode to the twins and stood right in front of them.

Seeing the three of them together, so close they could touch, stunned her anew. A huddle of maleness, a circle of resemblance, of family. It couldn't be denied. She saw it in the way they all held their stance—proud and masculine. She saw it in the sameness of the ebony locks; the way they tumbled on the boys' foreheads and were ruthlessly controlled on Rafe's. She saw it in the impossible, indefinable way they silently communicated with each other.

She didn't need a DNA test to know her new reality.

But she needed to demand the test to buy herself some time. Time to analyze how she was going to handle this new reality. This ugly, awful, new reality.

"That doesn't make sense. Tam knows everything."

A curl of a scorn appeared on Rafe's mouth.

Both boys straightened, anger flashing across their young faces at precisely the same time.

Their uncle wasn't intimidated. He sneered at her, the hate for her clear in his expression. "Does she now? Well, she didn't know about this. No one did. Not until two weeks ago when I went through your father's, your real father's, mementos."

"Mementos?" The word struck her, hard. "Ben's mementos?"

"Ben's mementos." Those black eyes never left her face, watching as she put two and two together.

"Ben is...dead?"

"*Nai*." The blackness of his grief swallowed her, sucked her under into his private hell.

"I'm so sorry—"

With a jerk, he turned to the twins, leaving her to stumble back from her attempt to console. Just once, she wished she could console him. Yet clearly, he wanted none of it, none of her. "Ben was my brother. Your father. He died in a motorcycle accident two weeks ago."

The boys looked stunned, not sad, but overwhelmed by the amount of information flying at them. Her motherly instincts kicked in with a wrench. "Enough. This is too much for—"

"Stop babying them." He didn't glance at her. Still, his words slapped her with a crack. "They are men, now. Not babies."

"They are not men—"

"Don't worry, Tam." Aarōn glared a challenge. "We can handle him and anything he says to us."

"Yeah." His twin backed him with a snarl.

"Good." Rafe's voice was smooth and satisfied. "I can see you are worthy to be Vounós."

"We're Tam's. Not Vounós." Aarōn's voice rang in the hallway like a call to arms.

"Whoever the Vounós are." Isaák would not be left behind.

At their declarations, Rafe stiffened. A warm wash of vindication ran through her. He couldn't take the boys from her. No matter how many DNA tests he took or how many solicitors he had.

The boys were hers.

Then, Rafe cut through her relief with a knife of hard, implacable intent.

"The Vounós are your family now. I will be taking you to meet them. In Greece."

"Wow!"

Wow was exactly the right word. Not that Tamsin would echo Isaák's exclamation. Not in front of Raphael Vounó.

The hotel entryway boasted soaring glass windows looking out on the bustling streets of London. The last few days of icy rain had turned into a brilliant late-spring day and the sunshine flecked the gold carpet beneath their feet with rays of light. Splashes of reds and blues in the art deco paintings brightened the arching white walls behind the lobby desk. A line of smartly dressed bellhops clothed in sleek grey suits trooped past her and the boys. In their wake rolled silver chrome luggage carts stacked with cardboard boxes and old, ratty suitcases.

Everything she and Aarōn and Isaák owned in the world. Stuffed onto four utilitarian carts being marched through an impressive hotel lobby towards a long line of swishing elevators. All because of the man standing beside her.

Who'd taken her home away and given her an ultimatum.

Either you and the twins come with me or I begin proceedings to declare you and Drakos unfit.

What choice did she have?

The boys needed to sleep. Somewhere safe.

And she needed time. Time to figure out how to handle this threat.

"Stay here," Raphael growled into her ear before he strode towards the concierge desk.

"He sure likes issuing orders, doesn't he?" Aarōn's surly tone snapped her gaze away from its slide down Rafe's long legs.

The boys' instant dislike of their uncle had not gone over well. Tam wondered if Rafe had been so clueless as to think he'd be able to bound into their life and take them away without a quiver of questions or a cry of complaint. Evidently he had because his reaction to their rejection had been one of blatant astonishment. If she hadn't been so exhausted and afraid, she would have been amused. True, when he'd announced he was taking them back to Greece the boys had been unwillingly intrigued. But when he had made the mistake of telling them about his plan to leave her behind, he'd been met with out-and-out rebellion.

He hadn't been happy.

"This is totally cool." Isaák's head jerked back and forth, trying to take in the details of an environment he'd never been exposed to. Extreme wealth. Unbelievable luxury. Something she hadn't been able to give them.

A pinch of regret tightened in her chest. Tam tried to ignore it. Money wasn't important. She'd given them what really mattered, love and attention. She'd given the boys good morals and taught them to be considerate. This, all this over-the-top elegance, was only a charade. This wasn't real life.

"It's okay." Aarōn shuffled to her side, his hands stuffed in his jean pockets. "If you like this kind of thing."

His twin snorted. "Who wouldn't like this?"

"No arguing." She watched the female concierge put a hand on Raphael's arm, the bright pink of her nail polish flashing in the sun.

"I wonder if this place has a pool."

It was Aarōn's turn to snort. "Of course this hotel has a pool, idiot."

"Boys."

They both grumbled under their breath at each other before subsiding in slouched surliness by her side.

They were tired. She was tired. After eighteen hours of waiting in the hospital, it wasn't a surprise the twins were grumpy and grouchy. They needed rest. A bed. And since the man striding toward them with a scowl on his face had evicted them from their own, she figured the least he could do was provide them with another one.

Temporarily.

She didn't have a plan yet. Once she got some sleep, though, she'd calculate some way to get rid of Raphael Vounó and start a new life for her and the boys. She'd have to find a new home, find a new job, evaluate how to take care of Haimon—

"The rooms are ready. Time to go up." Rafe's anger bristled from him, his dark eyes flashing, his big body rigid. Apparently, he wasn't used to any opposition to his wishes. The fact this opposition came from his nephews as well as her didn't seem to matter in his behavior towards her. In any other circumstance, she'd object to his arrogant command, the bite in his voice. However, all the fears and thoughts and emotions running through her swamped her ability to confront this man.

Later, she'd fight. Right now, she only wanted a bed and some peace.

"*Eláte.*" He waved at them impatiently as he marched past.

Come.

She hadn't spoken Greek in years. Speaking the language had been too painful, filled with memories of soft whispers and passionate promises which would never come true. She'd found it far easier to fall back on her native English tongue, the language of her natural father who'd faded in her memory to a blur. Unlike the sharp burr of the memories of Greece.

And the man striding across the lobby.

Eláte. Come.

The first word he said to her when they'd met. *Come with me*, as he led her onto his family's terrace, holding her hand in his, tugging her forward with a shy smile. *Come by me*, he'd said as he waved at her with a grin, organizing a team for volleyball in the pool. *Come to me*, as he opened his arms and took her into his grasp, giving her his kiss for the first time.

Eláte. Come.

"Tam." Aarōn touched her arm. "You okay?"

"Sure." She pushed the tears away, breathing through her nose. "I'm fine."

"Come, Tamsin." Rafe didn't even glance back, but he'd stopped in the middle of the lobby. As if sensing his displeasure, the other patrons and bellboys and even the flirtatious concierge gave him a wide berth. "Or don't come at all."

"Let's get out of here. We can find somewhere else to stay." Isaák's voice drifted into her ear like a siren call. "We don't need him."

The boy's suggestion echoed through the lobby. The words wafted to Rafe and his back stiffened. Then, he turned to face them.

He was so different. Achingly different.

Yet, she read him still. She knew what he thought and felt.

Hurt. Raphael Vounó was hurt by what her half-brother, his nephew, had said.

A mask of contempt and command came over his face, hiding what she knew, *she knew* she'd seen. "Well, Tamsin?"

"Come on, boys." Tightening her hand around her leather purse, she stepped forward. The decision to follow Rafe's rude demands was the wrong one. Surely it was. She should set down some boundaries and make some requirements of her own. Except she couldn't keep the thought of his hurt out of her head and heart.

Following him into the enclosed space of the lift felt like walking into a steel cage with a hissing, poisonous snake. But she did it. Because he'd been hurt and because she could not pluck another plan from her head at the moment.

The boys shuffled in behind them and the doors closed.

A dead silence filled the small space. Tam propped herself on the cold wall and shut her eyes. Bed. After sleep, she'd be back in fighting form and would have a strategy. A strategy to defeat this man and his determination to take the twins.

"Within the next hour, a doctor will be here to test the boys." The deep voice with its distinctive masculine edge and slight, sexy accent, cut through her thoughts.

No. *No.*

A shot of fear ran along her spine, causing her to stiffen in immediate rejection. She wasn't ready for a DNA test. She wasn't ready to confront what she already knew to be true. Couldn't this man give her a minute to catch her breath and figure out what her next step was?

He turned his head to gaze at her, his black eyes filled with determination.

No. *No.*

He couldn't. He wouldn't.

"I hate doctors." Aarōn was lying. He'd long ago become entranced with everything biological and had set his sights on going into the medical field.

"Whaddya mean, test? I hate tests." Another lie. This one from Isaák. A boy who thrived at school and couldn't decide if he enjoyed mathematics or geography more.

But she didn't care to enlighten this man about anything regarding the boys. Let him see how impossible it was going to be to take them over. Maybe he'd get discouraged after a few days of exposure. She loved them, yet they were absolutely a handful. Perhaps her anxiety and growing fear were for nothing and Raphael Vounó would eventually wash his hands of the situation in complete disgust.

She glanced over. Much to her regret, he didn't appear discouraged or disgusted. He stared at Aarōn as if he wanted to know the kid, wanted to understand him.

"That's too bad." His gruff words filled the lift, his accent slipping inside her and wrapping around her memories. "Your grandfather was a doctor."

Both boys straightened and their dark eyes, so like their uncle's, brightened with curiosity.

Tamsin's heart sank at their interest.

The tall man leaned against the silvered steel of the wall with negligent grace. His focus stayed on the twins, the edge of his mouth lifting in a tiny smile of satisfaction. "Your grandfather's name was Loukas Vounó."

Aarōn's eyebrows rose, a flash of surprise crossing his face. "What?"

"You have heard of him?" Raphael's dark gaze lit with a fierce light at Aarōn's reaction.

The boy snorted. Yet his eyes were just as bright. "Of course."

Before his death, Loukas Vounó had been known as one of the best cancer doctors and researchers in Greece and all of Europe. In the medical community, he'd been regarded as a master healer and inventor. He'd held patents for many therapeutic drugs and devices.

Which is why he'd come to Haimon's attention.

"Of course." The male voice softened into a slight smugness.

"Who's this Loukas guy?" Isaák's tone was dismissive as he threw a look of distrust at the man lounging in the corner of the lift.

"Only the most important cancer researcher of the last fifty years, idiot." Aarōn managed to appear both superior and disgusted with his brother at the same time.

"And your grandfather."

Raphael's words were not mere words. They were a claim, an inclusion of the twins into a long tradition of family honor and prestige. She felt the words impact on her own fear and saw the impact on the twins' faces.

They were no longer heirs to the sullied reputation of Haimon Drakos.

They were heirs to a Greek legend.

Heirs to this man standing before them as well, so clearly powerful and rich and important.

Her fear bubbled inside before bursting into a cold stream of wretched realization. How could she deny her boys this amazing transformation of their future? How could she hide them from what they were being offered? How could she hold them back from getting away from Haimon's ugly influence?

The lift doors whooshed open as the last of the questions echoed in her head.

Tamsin bolted out of the enclosed space, running not so much from the questions as from what she knew in her heart would be the final answer to those questions.

The long hallway was covered with golden carpeting; the walls done in cream, highlighting the brightly colored artwork hung between the dozens of doorways. The whole scene screamed wealth beyond her experience. Wealth Haimon in his glory days had certainly never achieved. Not even Loukas Vounó, with his influence and reputation, had ever climbed this high in the money stakes.

The thought stopped her cold.

"Trying to walk away from me once more?" Raphael's voice came from behind her, mock and malice mixed in the taunt. "Are you sure of where you are going?"

She'd been sure long ago. Sure of walking away.

Sure of what her sacrifice would give him.

You have a choice, Tamsin. Walk away from him and I will make sure there is enough money left for his medical schooling.

Haimon's ugly words slithered from the past.

A doctor, no matter how successful, would not drive in a limo. A doctor, no matter how many new inventions he created, would not stride into the lobby of this kind of hotel and receive the fawning attention Rafe had gotten moments ago. Plus, no doctor she'd ever met held such an air of confidence, arrogance, and complete command as Raphael Vounó had shown from the moment he'd walked back into her life.

She turned with a jerk.

He was close, too close, and the heat of his body scorched her skin. But the cold harshness of his face told her the heat came from anger, not passion.

"Did you go to medical school?" Her hushed tone carried through the hallway and the twins stilled behind them, for once stopping their ever-present ribbing and punching of each other.

His eyes went blank. "No, of course not."

"Of course not?" The cry came from her soul, the soul who'd done everything, given everything for this to happen. "Why not?"

"You?" His jaw clenched. "You of all people have to ask?"

"What?" Memories banged in her brain. Through these endless years, through the times she'd cried herself to sleep, she'd held onto the knowledge that Raphael would at least have this, this one thing she'd given him. His future. The glorious future he'd dreamed about his entire life.

His eyes were no longer blank. They were alive with hate. "You don't remember, Tamsin? You don't remember our last conversation?"

"Yes, I remember, but—"

"Then, please. Spare me these oh-so-innocent questions." He strode past her down the hallway.

Bewildered, heartsick, she stood and watched him walk away from her. Exactly as he had so long ago. Yet at that time, she'd had the solace of knowing she'd done the right thing.

Now?

Now she was lost. Her home lost, her plans for the future lost. And God help her, even her view of the past, of having done the right thing, even this was lost, too.

"Tammy?" The old nickname, the one the boys had used when they'd been toddlers, yanked her back from the edge of despair and defeat. Isaák's worried face peered into her own. "We can go away from here. He upsets you."

The boys.

Whatever had happened to Raphael in these previous years didn't matter anymore. What mattered to her more than her life were the twins and their future happiness. Raphael Vounó obviously had money, though she sincerely doubted he had a heart.

Somehow, someway she needed to rescue her brothers from this man's influence.

"No, I'm fine." Grief pooled in her throat. She pushed it away. "Come on."

The three of them, a family unit no one could pull apart, followed the man who was intent on trying. His spine was stiff with tension. Still, she couldn't help but notice how broad it was, how the bulge of his shoulders filled the silk of his jacket and how those long legs of his were lined with muscles.

He strode to the last doorway. "This is our room."

She stumbled to a stop, immediate outrage coursing through her veins. "We're not staying in the same room as you."

"No?" The edge of his mouth curled in sudden, surprising amusement.

Ignoring her sputter, he slid the silver card into the slot and the cream and gold door opened. Tamsin gasped. The boys crowded around her.

"Brilliant." Isaák whooped.

Aarōn humphed, yet she knew him well enough to know he was just as impressed.

This was not a hotel room. This was not a couple of beds with a dresser lining one wall. The lobby had been grand so she'd figured the rooms would be a bit on the nicer side, but she hadn't come close to imagining this.

The big room sported ceiling-to-floor windows looking out on a terrace filled with pots of flowers and shrubs. An ultra-modern couch covered in red-tinted leather was surrounded by several plush chairs of velveteen blue. A flat-screened TV hung right next to a series of black and white charcoal drawings which looked suspiciously like originals.

"There are three bedrooms in this particular suite." His amusement weaved through each word. "I hope the boys won't mind sharing a room."

"Oh, man." Isaák could not contain himself any longer. With another whoop, he hopped into the suite and across to the huge TV. "I wonder how many movies we can get."

Aarōn slouched on the doorframe. "I haven't shared a room with the idiot since we were seven."

"Well," the man beside her drawled. "I guess your sister and I could share a room."

She sucked in a deep breath. Memories washed over her in a tidal wave of regret and longing. Being held by this man, once a boy. Virginal dreams of what it would be like to be together. Soft, sucking kisses shared with him; the first and last kisses she'd ever experienced.

"Not a chance." Aarōn's harsh voice cut through her thoughts.

Rafe gave him a wry smile. "Then you'll have to share—"

"I have a better idea." The boy didn't back down. "Why don't you get your own room?"

"I'm afraid that's not on offer." The black eyes heated with a sudden flash of anger. "While I give you credit for your protective instincts towards your sister, I can assure you they aren't needed."

That was pretty clear, wasn't it? Raphael Vounó didn't want her at all. Not that she wanted him, either.

"We don't want you here." Aarōn's dark gaze was sharp with distrust.

The man beside her stiffened. Again, Tam felt him. Felt the hurt this rejection brought him. Even though he was the enemy, even though he threatened everything she held dear, she couldn't help her protest, her protection. "Aarōn—"

"Tough." Rafe cut past her attempted intervention. "I'm here to stay."

"I don't—"

"I'm in your life and your brother's forever."

Aarōn's mouth, so like his uncle's, twisted. "Tamsin's the only one in our life we need."

Her heart swelled, although exhaustion ate at her composure. Whatever happened going forward, the tie between the boys and her could not be denied.

Not by Raphael Vounó. Not by his family. Not by any court.

"Hey!" Isaák bopped into the conversation, cutting through the tense air with his thrilled excitement. "Come on, A. Help me figure out how to turn on the TV."

"You're such an idiot." His twin turned to throw him a scowl of disgust. "Can't you see—"

"Go on, Aarōn." She appreciated the boy's defense, but he was only a kid. He doggedly stood by her side, and yet she could tell by the tightness around his eyes he was tired. Also, she saw the one yearning peek he'd given to the TV. "Go help Isaák while I unpack our clothes."

"You're sure?" Her fierce teenage protector cast a narrowed gaze at the man standing beside her.

"I'm sure." Even though she was not. Not at all. Still, she couldn't let the boys become her warriors. She needed to win this battle on her own.

Aarōn slunk away to join his twin.

"Very smart." Long, masculine fingers nudged the door partially shut, leaving them alone in the hallway. "It would be mistake to put the twins in the middle of this."

"This?" She wanted to flee from him. She wanted to run down the hall to the elevator and escape. She wanted to forget what an awful man her first love had become. Aarōn and Isaák tied her down, though. Leaving the boys to this man wasn't an option and right now, she didn't have the weapons to drive Raphael away. Not yet.

"This disagreement between us on what is best for them."

Tamsin forced herself to look at him. Faint white lines of strain bracketed his mouth and his deep-set eyes were hooded, as if he had a hard time keeping them open. Long dark eyelashes brushed down and then up, bringing her attention to the smudges of weariness on his skin.

Her too-soft heart turned over.

"We're all tired." She offered an olive branch. Fighting him was inevitable, yet at this moment she didn't want the inevitable. At this moment, she wanted him to lie down and rest. "Let's table this until tomorrow."

"The doctor's going to be here soon." His mouth turned grim as he stared at his watch.

She already knew what the test was going to tell her, but she needed time. Time to evaluate her options, her weapons. "No. I'm not going to allow the boys to be tested just because you say so."

His head jerked up, his expression going fierce. "We can do this the easy way. Or the hard way. Either way, I will win."

She hadn't ever once let herself slip into trawling for information about Raphael Vounó. Never once had she allowed herself to Google him on the web or search for him on Facebook—it would have been too painful. She'd assumed he'd used the gift she'd sacrificed for and was somewhere in Greece being a pediatric doctor, fulfilling his life-long dream. There'd been many moments when she'd derived some comfort from the thought of him fulfilling his destiny.

Did you go to medical school?

No, of course not.

So this particular dream, like every one of her others, was dead. The reality was she knew nothing about him or the weapons he might hold to get his way. Yet look at where they were staying. Look at the sleek limo that had driven them here. Look at the silver Rolex watch on his wrist. More than anything, though, the deadly intent in his words told her what Raphael Vounó had become.

A man who wouldn't be a good influence on her brothers. A man who threatened all the hard work she'd done through the years to raise her boys in the right way. She just needed a few hours to take stock and strategize how she was going to save them from this man.

"I'm asking for a day." She pulled out the skills she'd used for years to try and keep Haimon in control. "A lot has happened in the last twenty-four hours. Is it too much to ask for a bit of time?"

"Don't wheedle or attempt to manipulate me. It won't work." His eyes went flat. "Not now. I'm immune."

The words hurt, much as he'd intended. She'd never wheedled or manipulated anyone, she wanted to yell. She'd loved. She'd cared. She'd sacrificed. Still, none of the protests slipped from her lips because she knew they would make no difference.

"The test is a simple swab of their mouth," he said. "We're not talking major surgery."

"The boys—"

"This isn't about the boys." His gaze bore into hers. "This is about stalling."

"I'm not—"

"You are. And I won't have it."

His arrogance fired her tired temper, snapping apart her attempt to find some common ground. "Forget it. I'm not going to try and reason with you anymore."

"Good." He took two paces down the hall before returning, closer this time, more threatening. "There's no whining, no weeping, no wheedling that's going to deter me from this."

"I can demand a legal summons."

"You can." Leaning closer, invading her personal space, his heat swept around her like a swath of danger. "And you'll get it."

"That's what I want." She stepped back, trying to get away from him and his heat.

"But you'll lose far more than you gain, *kardiá mou.*" Threat no longer merely edged his words, they were filled with it. "I will make sure of it."

CHAPTER FOUR

Rafe stared at his laptop and wrestled with his brain. He needed to answer the ten emails his PA had stated were most important. Then he had to Skype with the manager in charge of studying the potential of a patent they were thinking of acquiring. Finally, he must review and approve the quarterly budget within the next couple of hours.

He didn't want to do any of it. Not one single item.

"Throw it over here, A!" There was an adolescent squeak at the end of the shout, yet it didn't lessen the volume or the punch of the command.

He glanced at the boys.

The enclosed pool lay at the top of the hotel, surrounded by walls of glass looking down on the center of London. A line of potted palm trees mixed around the dozens of unoccupied lounge chairs. The pool was empty except for his two nephews. But by the amount of water splashing onto the white tile, the amount of screeching and yelling, the amount of arm-waving and leg-kicking, a man could think an army of a thousand had descended to make mayhem and cause destruction.

"My turn," Aarōn shouted loud enough to make Rafe's eardrums ring.

This morning he'd been confronted with two very different boys than the ones he'd met the day before. He supposed he should have expected this. They'd been tired; they'd been through a trauma. Naturally, they'd be more subdued than normal. He also had several nieces and nephews. True, they were younger than the twins, but he'd experienced numerous tantrums and several episodes of squealing and screaming.

He knew kids.

Yet he didn't know teenagers, did he?

He'd been surprised.

Aarōn and Isaák had burst from their hotel bedroom like rambunctious, runaway cubs. They'd devoured the breakfast Rafe had ordered in something less than nine seconds. They'd then proceeded to charge onto the terrace, running up and down its length as if they were competing in the next Olympics. Before he could voice some concern about their climbing on the railing, they'd swooped inside and began arguing about what movie they were going to order.

All before he'd managed to finish his coffee.

He'd admit only to himself he'd started to feel slightly overwhelmed. Slightly out of his element. However, before the thought had formed into a tight knot in the center of his chest, she'd appeared. With one single sentence from her, the boys had turned into docile lambs. And he'd been relieved.

Relieved.

His fingers tightened around the edge of the laptop lying on one of the glass tables strewn around the pool.

"You can't stop me!" Isaák's face filled with glee as he yanked the rubber ball from his brother's hands and dived under the water.

His brother roared in protest and lunged for the feet flapping in Isaák's wake.

They had ignored him from the moment they'd left their bedroom to the last hour he'd been supervising them here in the hotel pool.

Rafe snorted. *Supervised.*

He didn't think sitting here watching the boys splash all the water from the pool would be classified as supervising.

This whole situation had been her suggestion. Those devious green eyes had turned cunning as she suggested the twins might like to go to the pool. At first, he'd thought it a good idea. With this noisy, distracting crew out of his sight, he could get his work done.

He'd underestimated Tamsin.

Those lush lips had pursed and the lilting, slurred words that had come from her mouth had landed him here. "You can get to know one another."

The twins had scowled, obviously not in accord with their sister.

His pride had kicked out his agreement. Surely he could handle a couple of teenagers and win them over. She was right about one thing; he needed to get to know Aarōn and Isaák before he could tear them from her clutches.

A teetering fear tripped into his head.

Could he actually control these boys once he'd ripped them away from Tamsin's corrupting influence?

His logical brain kicked in. What did it matter? He'd eventually wrest Isaák and Aarōn from Tamsin's grip and deliver them to his mother and two sisters. All three of the women were entirely capable of raising two teenage boys. Once they were settled with his family, he'd be free to go back to work.

He'd see them, of course. He'd supervise their education.

Still, he wouldn't need to spend any time worrying about them. That would be his mother's and sisters' job.

Two dark heads popped out of the water at the same time. He took in a deep breath of relief—they had been under for quite awhile—then, Aarōn roared again and pushed his brother's head under the water.

Rafe found himself halfway out of his chair, but before he called a halt to the immediate death of one of his nephews, Isaák's laughing face appeared a cool yard away from Aarōn.

"Ha!" The crazy scamp egged his brother on.

"I'll get you." Aarōn lunged.

Isaák paddled away from his reach.

"Okay, fine, idiot." His brother jerked to a stop, his face tight with challenge. "Let's race."

Within seconds, the twin terrors were whizzing across the pool, arms arcing, feet kicking in exact unison. In superb form.

Rafe slumped back into his chair. A storming brew of relief clashed with a stunning realization.

They'd taken swimming lessons.

His dread that the boys had been allowed to run wild with no goals or training or purpose were unfounded. Even in this short amount of time with them, he'd figured out quickly they were bright, well-educated, and ready to take on the world. Now, add to this the knowledge that someone had paid for swimming lessons. What other kind of lessons had the boys been given?

He was sure, with every particle in his body; Haimon Drakos had nothing to do with any of the boys' achievements.

Someone did, though.

Which drew his mind back to her. The woman who was in their hotel room, doing what, precisely? The woman who'd landed him in this supervisory position. The woman who'd also landed him in the position of not being able to move forward with his plans.

She'd stuck to her rejection yesterday even after his threats had turned her face pale. The doctor had been sent away. The DNA tests had not been completed. Rafe had been left to seethe on the terrace while she blithely organized the boys' belongings and urged them to take a nap.

A nap. As if they were babies.

"I won!" crowed Isaák at one end of the pool.

"You cheated." His twin charged not only with his words, but his actions.

A splash of water washed over the tiled rim as the boys wrestled themselves into another perilous under-water engagement.

Rafe tried to focus his concentration on his work, yet the instinct to dive in and separate them was almost overwhelming. But the twins had managed to live for thirteen years without killing each other, so surely—

"They'll be fine." Her soft, slurred voice came from behind him. "Don't worry."

He hated, instantly, that she knew what he was thinking. He hated her, and even more, he hated this damned connection between them. "I hardly think a swimming pool is going to conquer two Vounó males."

She gave him a sniff and he was conscious of her moving behind him. A wicker bag plopped onto a lounge chair several feet away from his.

Before he could stop himself, he turned to look.

A hot pointed dagger of heat struck deep in his belly.

She was covered. Barely.

At first glance, the beach coverup appeared conservative, conventional. The thing covered her arms to her wrists and fell to almost mid-thigh. But then she moved and the fabric swung around her hips. White beads, laced along the seams of cloth, tinkled and sparkled.

The banked fire of need inside him burst into pure lust.

The coverlet was a woven mesh of tan weaving across her body. Standing still, she appeared decent. Moving, the artifice dropped away. The mesh flashed bare skin in between the trails of lace and beads.

Pale, ivory skin. Perfect.

The beads plinked and plunked.

Craving poured through his blood, hurling any thoughts of business or boys out of his mind altogether.

Once again, she appeared oblivious to his sexual desire. The connection he hated didn't seem to extend to her sensing the lust pumping in his blood. Turning her back to him, she eased herself onto the lounge chair without taking off the coverlet. He managed to catch a glimpse of the bathing suit underneath, though.

Green. As green as her eyes. A bikini. A bathing suit leaving little to his fertile and heated imagination.

"Come in, Tam!" Isaák's excited voice cut through the humid air.

"Come in with us and swim." Aarōn joined the chorus. Both of them lunged to the side of the pool, big grins on their faces.

The invitations to their sister were a blatant contrast to the ignoring he'd received. The flashing thought burned inside him along with the lust.

"In a bit." She flipped a blond braid over one shoulder and turned to stare across the chairs at him. "I have something I want to discuss with..."

She stuttered to a stop.

"Your uncle," Rafe filled in.

The boys went silent before the splash of their limbs signaled their retreat.

Tamsin's lips firmed and her gaze grew bright. With what? Anger? Curiosity? More likely thinking of wheedling something from him. She'd likely spent this past hour analyzing how much he was worth and what she could extract from him.

She was out of luck.

"I want to know." Pausing, she lowered her voice. "Why you didn't go to medical school."

The question was so unexpected compared to what he'd thought she'd ask, he stilled, completely stunned. He'd been so busy thinking about the twins, the DNA test denied, as well as the myriad of business problems he'd been forced to address from afar, that her question from yesterday had been forgotten.

"What has that got to do with anything?" he barked.

Her shoulders straightened and her jaw tensed. "I want to know."

Stark, sharp memories swamped him. The young Tam had appeared so soft and so sweet. Yet there had been a few times, times she'd held firm. A time when she'd chided him for making a joke about something important to her. A time when she'd argued passionately for a new law being fought for in the courts. A time when she'd chastised his sister when Rhouth had teased Rafe about his collection of wounded animals.

This was important to her.

Why?

He scowled, trying to understand what this was all about. "I don't get it. It was ten years ago. What's important right now are my nephews and their future. That's what we should be discussing."

She glanced away from his hard glare to stare at the pool and the laughing boys as they threw the ball back and forth. "We'll get to them soon enough."

"Now." Swiveling in his chair to face her, he clasped his hands in front of him. "I discussed my options with my solicitors this morning."

"Solicitors. Plural." The slurred ending to each of her words gave them a sinister taint.

"Correct." He wasn't sinister. He was claiming what was his. If he needed a phalanx of solicitors to get what he wanted, then that's what he'd do. "I've been advised getting a legal summons for a DNA is doable. Eventually, I'll win this."

"Yes, I suppose you will." She kept her focus on her brothers. "Eventually."

Rafe's hands fisted at his sides as he threw himself back in the chair. She was right, damn her. It would take weeks if she fought him over this. Fury at this woman and her stubbornness threatened to defeat his control. His solicitors had counseled him...*get her consent, it will save time, it'll be easier, don't alienate her, get her on your side*...but something about Tamsin's attitude eroded all his good intentions. "I have little time to spare here. I have work to do back in Greece."

"So, then." She turned back to stare at him. "Perhaps we can negotiate."

The look in her eyes lanced through him, striking him off his game plan. Her gaze was clear and keen.

Intelligent and sharp. This was not the sixteen-year-old young lady he'd known years ago. This wasn't a sweet girl who had turned out to be simply a teasing betrayer. This was a woman who knew what she was doing.

She runs everything.

The remembered words whispered in his ears as he stared into her green eyes. The Drakos clan might be full of liars and thieves, yet no one had ever said they weren't smart. And all about money. Always about the money. He and his family and his father had learned this the hard way.

She cocked her head, her eyes narrowing.

He could practically see the numbers running in her head.

He didn't want to negotiate with her. When he'd descended on the run-down hotel, he'd assumed he'd win, easily and handily. Haimon would be charged with numerous crimes and hauled off to jail. Tamsin would be thrown from her home and left in the dust. His nephews would be in his plane on their way to Greece.

His solicitors had counseled him before he'd arrived in London, and once more this morning....*she might ask for money, she might not give away the twins without some monetary settlement*...but he'd been too eager to deliver his revenge to take this into account.

He didn't want to give her money.

He didn't want to reward her.

He didn't want her to win.

Yet what were his options? He had to have the boys and he had to be in Greece. Soon. One of the biggest deals in his life was finally coming together and he couldn't afford to spend weeks and weeks in England fighting this woman.

"All right." He forced himself to lounge back and appear relaxed. "How much?"

She jerked as if he'd yanked her ponytail. "What?"

"I'm negotiating, exactly as you requested." The tang of fury coated his tongue with hot, hard hate. She was just like her lying stepfather and cheating mother. Still, if money was what it took, he had plenty of that. "How much?"

A furrow creased her brow. Then a flash of understanding lit in her gaze. The green turned to cold agate. "Are you suggesting I would take money to allow Aarōn and Isaák to take this test?"

"I'm suggesting far more than that." Rafe curled his lip in disgust. "I'm asking point-blank. How much for the boys?"

The muscles in her jaw went taut, her eyes glowed with a fiery heat, and her hands tightened into two small fists. For a second, he thought she might jump over the chairs to wrap her fingers around his neck.

He tensed, an explosive blend of excitement and anger flowing like lava in his veins.

"There isn't enough money in the world to get me to let go of my brothers." Her voice was hoarse, yet steady and steely. "However, we can still come to an agreement."

The commitment in her tone shook him. He'd known, deep down, the tie between Tamsin and the twins was strong. He'd had enough exposure during these last couple of days to note the powerful bond. Up to now, though, he'd convinced himself she'd ultimately cede to the new reality. He was here. The boys were Vounós. And she wasn't needed anymore.

Her words and tone shook his belief.

A hard knot settled in his stomach, his tension and anger curdling like a poisoned brew. "I'm supposed to believe you won't walk away from Aarōn and Isaák at some point?"

"Believe it." She held herself with confidence—her hands draped calmly on her lap, her shoulders relaxed. Her intent gaze never left his.

"I'm supposed to believe they can depend on you?" he snarled. "I think we both know I have ample experience to reject that belief."

A spark of something, some unguarded emotion, crossed her expression, but she didn't back down and she didn't look away. "As you pointed out, this isn't about ten years ago. It's about now."

Rafe gritted his teeth. She was right. She'd thrown his own words back at him and she was right. Damn her.

"I have something you want." The green of her eyes blazed into him, heating him, making him feel as if he were pinned to the wall. "And you have something I want."

He crossed his arms across his chest. A jolt of shock went through him when he realized his palms were sweating. In fact, his entire torso was damp. Not with anger or pain or fear.

You want.

I want.

Lust. He was sweating with lust.

She sat there: blond hair in a simple braid, no paint on her face, challenge in every line of her covered body. Nothing like the women he'd dallied with during the last few years. Women who spent hours in the salon. Women who dressed in gowns worth thousands. Women who drank in his every word.

Yet not one of those women ever made him sweat.

The woman before him, and yes, she'd become a woman not only in form, but in strength of mind, continued. Relentlessly. "I'll agree to the DNA test."

He narrowed his gaze, keeping his tense hands tucked beneath his arms.

"If you tell me why you didn't go to medical school."

CHAPTER FIVE

*T*amsin sensed when Rafe made his decision. The scowl on his face smoothed into bland disinterest. He stretched his long, naked legs out in front of him. His hands slid from under his arms to land on his thighs in a careless gesture.

He shrugged his big shoulders. The white of the T-shirt he wore emphasized the thickly muscled curve of his biceps. A quick kick of awareness rushed through her.

"I decided to go into business instead." His voice was all smooth, all solid dismissiveness.

"You dreamed of being a doctor." She couldn't stop the emotion flooding her words. "You never wanted to be anything else."

He gazed at her, his eyes blank. Then he shrugged again. "I changed my mind."

Tamsin didn't know why she kept pushing. Maybe it was because she wanted to understand why this one dream, among the other dreams she'd lost, this one dream had been denied. Perhaps if she understood this, she could make sense of the rest of the turbulent emotions this man's arrival back into her life had stirred inside her.

"You couldn't have simply changed your mind." She frowned at her clenched hands lying in her lap as if she could find a resolution there instead of trying to find it in eyes dark with disdain.

"Couldn't I?" His question was quiet yet biting. "But why not? You changed your mind about us."

She jerked her head up to meet his gaze. "That was different."

"Was it?" His voice twined around the words, hostility leaching into each vowel. "I don't see how. I discarded something I supposedly loved, just as you did."

His cynicism rolled through her, dragging her into a depressed funk. Except she knew. She knew. He was faking with his *supposedly* and his *changing his mind*. "You were going to be a doctor from the moment I met you. You talked about it all the time. Your father—"

"*Nai.*" The curt, brittle word cut her off. "And now you have reached the reason why I didn't attend medical school."

Sucking in a breath, she forced herself to continue. "Your father would have wanted you to go. Even after he..."

His words didn't stop her this time. No, it was the look in his dark gaze.

Brutal hate.

Bitter anger.

Unbearable pain.

"Rafe." A deep well of sorrow and compassion opened in the depths of her.

"Even after my father killed himself, you were going to say." His lips curved, but it was no smile he gave her. "However, this was when all hope of going to medical school ended, of course."

"You still had the opportunity—"

"No, I did not." One of his hands lifted in rejection before slashing down, as if trying to cut off the past. "There were far too many things that had to be done and not enough money to fix everything."

"There was money for you to go to school, though." Her throat tightened around each word until her voice cracked at the end.

He appeared startled for a moment, almost shaken. A dark frown furrowed his brow. "What the hell do you mean by that?"

Had she been fooled by Haimon? But no, she'd made sure. Absolutely sure. She'd even forced her stepfather to show her the wire, show her the bank account with her love's name on it, show her when the money had been withdrawn by Rafe.

"You had money." She had to know. Had to understand.

He stared at her hard for a moment, before leaning back, his eyes blank once more. "Whatever money that was left after my father died, I used to strengthen the family finances."

"I don't understand—"

"Don't understand what?" His long fingers splayed on his thighs, white and tense. "You don't understand your father left us broke after he killed my father?"

The accusation knifed into her, cutting through her determination to find out what had happened. "Are you talking about Haimon?"

He laughed. His ugly laugh. "Who else?"

The memories of years ago swept into her mind. The sudden announcement of Loukas Vounó's surprising suicide. The meeting with Haimon. Her decision, her wretched decision. And her last confrontation with Rafe. "Haimon had something to do with your father's death?"

A rough sound of male rage filled the air around them. "Don't play the innocent, Tamsin. Don't even try."

"I have no idea what you're talking about." She stared at him, willing him to believe.

His black gaze was as dark and empty as a wasteland. "You have no idea your father—"

"He's not my—"

"—stole my father's most important patent."

"No, I can't believe—"

"Driving my father to his suicide."

Horror filled her stomach. She knew Haimon played his tricks. This, though? This was far past anything she could imagine. "You have to be wrong."

"I'm not wrong." He lounged in his chair, yet his face was white and his eyes blazed with conviction. "Just as I'm not wrong about the boys, I'm not wrong about this."

The clear certainty of his words shook the horror in her stomach until it seeped into every inch of her body. "I'm sure there must be some mistake."

"There was one mistake made." His casual pose held, but she wasn't fooled. The tight line of his jaw told her; he was livid with remembered rage. "My father trusting yours was a mistake."

She glanced at her hands again, no longer willing to face his wrath. Because something deep inside told her, it was true. Everything he said. "I can't believe—"

"Believe." The one word was pitched low. Still, it hit her hard. "Believe me when I tell you there was no way I could go to medical school after what your father did to my family."

Medical school. Her mind whipped back to how this conversation had started. She'd asked one simple question and opened a Pandora's box filled with unbelievable evil. How she wished she hadn't even opened her mouth.

"Don't you understand my family almost lost their home?"

"What?" Her head came up in a sharp snap. She hadn't realized. Hadn't understood the situation had been so bad. "I didn't know—"

"You didn't know? Didn't know your stepfather stole my father's prized patent and then threatened him? Didn't know my father took his life because of this and our family was destroyed?"

Only the lap of the pool water on the tiles filled the deadened silence. The boys huddled at the end of the pool, whispering. Tam suddenly remembered what she'd never forgotten before. Her brothers. Their safety, their comfort, their needs. She took a quick peek over at them, wanting to make sure—

"They didn't hear," he said. "They aren't a part of this. All of this is in the past and unimportant."

In the past and unimportant. She pushed back the tears threatening to fall. She tried to collect herself, tried to put her old dream to rest. But her soul couldn't recover from its wretched realization that something had gone terribly wrong with the sacrifice she'd thought so terribly right years ago.

The clutch in her throat tightened until she couldn't breathe.

"There was a small amount of money left." He kept going, almost as if he'd tied himself to the tale and had to finish it. "I used it to pay off the mortgage on the house and start the business."

Her brain buzzed as her heart ached. "The business?"

"My business." The claim was stated with pride, though there was a hint of something else there, something distracted, even disturbed.

She couldn't wrap her head around the thought. Rafe hadn't ever been about business. He'd been about healing and loving and caring. "You started a business?"

Turning to inspect him, she tried to imagine. Even in a simple white T-shirt and casual blue shorts, he did exude harsh authority and complete confidence. Years ago, she'd seen the authoritative way he'd handled his menagerie of wounded creatures and she'd noticed his confidence about his university studies. Yet these qualities had been wrapped in a kind heart, a healing spirit.

"*Nai.*" His eyes blazed, now with arrogance. "A business I'm very successful in."

She assumed he was correct. The trappings of wealth were hard to ignore. "But it's not what you're supposed to do."

A disparaging sound came from deep in his throat. "Don't become trite."

"I know—"

"I know I have given you what you negotiated for," he continued. "And now it's time you gave me what I asked for."

Soul-deep and bruising, she hurt. She couldn't look at him any longer, couldn't look at the boys, couldn't look at his rejection of what he was without hurting.

"I'll call the doctor right now." He kept marching toward his victory.

"No." Laying awake far into the night, she'd come to some decisions. She knew in her heart what Rafe claimed was true. The boys were not Haimon's and the twins deserved to know their history. They deserved to know the family they had in Greece. Haimon wouldn't agree, but he was still unconscious and fighting for his life, and she was as much the boys' guardian as he was. So this man would get his DNA test, although not as quickly as he wanted.

"I should have known you'd go back on your word." The heat of his animosity radiated around her.

"I'm not going back on my word." She forced herself to stay calm. "They'll take the test."

"Then I don't see why I can't—"

"Not until I see my solicitor, though."

The *lap, lap, lap* of the waves filled the void between them.

"You?" he finally said, astonishment wrapping around the question. "Have a solicitor?"

Indignation surged past the pain. "Of course I do," she snarled, turning to glare at him. "I ran a business only a few days ago."

He stared at her, irritation now mixed with the lingering astonishment in his expression. "I don't see why you need a solicitor. It's a pretty simple process."

"I need to know my options."

"You have no options." A gentle, sinister tone came into his voice. "I'll win."

"Eventually."

He rustled in his chair, and she felt his frustration. Still, she knew from his non-rebuttal, she'd bought some time. "I've got an appointment with my solicitor tomorrow."

"Tomorrow." His one word was clipped and taut and filled with aggravation.

"Yes, in the afternoon." Braving a glance his way, she tried to make him believe through the sincerity in her voice. "That was the earliest appointment I could get."

He shifted in his seat, his eyes shining with distrust.

Why did she even care what he thought? Frustration boiled over. "Did you think you could merely swoop in and within a day or two take the boys away?"

"*Nai.*" He spat the one word out.

"Well, you were wrong." Folding her arms around her, she tried to hold the frustration in. "All I'm saying is you can have your test after I see my solicitor."

"A stipulation you didn't mention when we made our bargain." His long fingers tapped on his leg. "Yet why should I be surprised? I'm dealing with a Drakos."

"You'll get your test." She stopped herself from trying to defend against his slur. What was the use? "You can schedule the doctor for tomorrow evening."

"I have no choice, do I?"

"No, you don't."

He growled. *Growled.*

She jerked herself off the lounge, irked at his unwillingness to see her side. Turning to face him, she leaned over the chair and matched his glare with one of her own. "Can't you see how totally unfair you're being?"

"I'm not—"

"It's been less than two days since you arrived." She barreled past his outrage. "Two days ago the boys didn't even know you existed."

"That isn't my—"

"Two days ago I didn't know they weren't Haimon's."

"So you admit it." He shot forward in his chair, his expression alight with immediate victory. "They are mine."

"They are ours."

Her words fell into complete silence. Except the weight and impact of the claim echoed around them, filling her head with all the repercussions of what this one simple sentence meant for the boys and for her and for Rafe.

"Tam." Aarōn's tentative voice cut past her turmoil.

Jerking around, she met the twins' anxious gazes. Both of them had swum to the edge of the pool close to where she and Rafe had been arguing about their future. What had she been thinking? She didn't want the boys in the middle of this mess.

Yet they were, weren't they? They were directly in the center of this situation.

"Come into the pool and swim, Tammy," Isaák said in a soft, comforting tone. As if he and his brother should have any responsibility or need to take care of her.

She took care of *them.*

Still, the man sitting silent several chairs down was too much for her to handle for any length of time. She'd made her demands. She'd stated her plans. Now the only thing she wanted to do was swim away from all of it. Swim away from Rafe.

She flipped her coverlet over her head and dropped it on the lounge chair. With two swift steps, she launched herself into the water.

As the water swallowed her, she felt a part of her come apart.

They are ours.

CHAPTER SIX

"Tell me." Haimon's eyes were sharp, although his voice was rough and faint. "What is going on?"

Tamsin sat beside the hospital bed. The bright light above the bed cast shadows across his face, making him appear even older and sicker.

But he was alive. And after waking from a three-day coma, he showed no signs of being confused. Not with that familiar sly look in his eyes. The doctor said he'd make a full recovery and for this, she should be grateful.

Shouldn't she?

"Tell me." His gaze grew sharper, narrower.

This was the man who'd come into her life when she'd been six and had never left it, not even when her mother had deserted them. He'd kept a roof over their heads for those first few years all on his own. And although it had been several years since she'd taken on their finances, she felt as if there should be at least a modicum of loyalty inside her.

Shouldn't there?

"Tamsin."

The nurse had told her in no uncertain terms not to upset him, yet she could barely contain the bitter words and angry emotions from erupting. Haimon had promised her the hotel would stay safe. He'd promised her he wouldn't let his dirty business ruin what she'd created.

He'd lied.

Still, he'd lied so many times before. Even at sixteen she'd known she had to extract absolute confirmation he'd done what he told her he'd do for Rafe if she agreed to his demands. So why did this last betrayal surprise her? She should let it slide right off her back like she had so many other times.

Shouldn't she?

"The hotel is gone," she blurted.

He waved her words away, as if they meant nothing. "I know that."

Their home gone meant nothing.

A caustic accusation bubbled in her throat and before she could stuff it down, it burst out. "How could you?"

"I had some bad luck with a deal." He sighed. "I needed to raise some funds to cover the debt. You know how it goes."

"Bad luck?" Her hands shook so hard she stuffed them between her legs. "You promised."

The low murmur of the nurses standing at their station filtered into the room. The *click, click, click* of the monitors behind the bed pinged in her head and on her nerves.

"None of that matters now," he finally responded. "What matters is what we do going forward."

We.

Her hands fisted between her legs. All these years, she'd been part of this man's orbit because she had to be. The boys were his, and the boys were the only thing she had. So she'd stayed. No college or love life. Instead, she'd spent her time raising the twins, figuring out how to run a business, trying to keep Aarōn and Isaák insulated from Haimon and his filthy ways. She'd asked for only one thing. One promise.

"There's no *we* now." Her words shot from her with firm conviction.

"Don't be daft." He shifted on the bed, an irritated frown on his face. "We have a common enemy. Don't you forget it."

"Rafe is not my enemy." He hated her, but she didn't share the sentiment.

How could she hate him for being bitter and angry about what Haimon had done to their family? At sixteen, she'd known the Vounós would be devastated at their patriarch's suicide. Not until yesterday, though, had she realized how complete their devastation had been.

Last night, instead of sleeping, she'd again spent hours staring at the hotel's gilded ceiling, running Rafe's accusations through her head over and over. Like an endless drone those words of his had moaned in her brain, wafting around her perceptions of her life and her memories of the past.

When her stepfather had come to her ten years ago, he'd gone straight to the point. He'd been sorry about the news of Loukas Vounó's suicide, sad to see such a smart man do such a stupid thing, yet this changed everything. Without their patriarch, the Vounós would have no money coming in and no more status to lean on. Combine this loss of lifestyle with the disgrace of the suicide and they would no longer be welcome in society or Haimon's home. He would no longer tolerate any relationship with the remaining family—including hers with Rafe.

She'd objected, fought hard, but he'd held the winning hand.

We are moving to London, Tamsin. Of course, your mother and your brothers will need you there. Your loyalty to your family comes first.

At sixteen, she hadn't been strong or wise enough to strategize a way around the surprising announcement of the move. And then Haimon had dangled the carrot in front of her.

Break all contact with him, Tammy, and I'll provide the money for his schooling.

Insuring Rafe would be able to achieve his dream, even if his father was dead and his family's finances would grow increasingly precarious, had seemed paramount to her. Her stepfather had made it clear. There would be no money and no influence with Loukas Vounó out of the picture. Rafe's chances of achieving his dream wouldn't be impossible, but with her help, his dream would be assured.

She'd thought she'd done the right thing.

The only thing she could have done.

Now though? Now all of her justifications were thrown into turmoil. Because what she had done, it seemed, was side with this man before her. This man who, if Rafe were to believed, had done far worse than make her split with her boyfriend that long ago night. Far worse.

"Don't tell me you're falling for the guy again."
Haimon glared at her. "Don't be a foolish girl."

When was the last time she'd allowed herself to be a
girl? To have girlish dreams? When had she been given
a moment to think of herself? An unexpected rage
filled her, her nails biting into the skin of her palms.
"I'm not falling for anything or anyone. Not anymore."

At the fierce tone in her voice, her stepfather
dropped back on his pillow. His deep sigh reminded her
of the nurse's warning. He'd nearly died three days ago.
She shouldn't be talking to him this way.

Tamsin pulled her anger inside and stuffed it down.
"Let's not argue."

"Where are Aarōn and Isaák?" the old man muttered.

"They're safe." Reaching over, she forced herself to
pat the gnarled hand lying on the blue blanket. "Don't
worry."

Leaving them with Rafe had been her only real option. She might not trust him, yet she knew he meant
no harm to the boys. If she didn't believe this, she
wouldn't have left them in his care today to keep her
appointment with her solicitor. There was no way he
could leave the country with the twins without her consent. Plus, she'd come to accept he was now part of
their lives and they needed to get to know him. Even
understanding this, she'd wanted to race back to the
hotel as soon as she was done with her appointment.

The phone call from the hospital telling her Haimon had awakened had stopped the rush. Stepping out of her solicitor's office as she clicked her mobile off, Tam had known she couldn't ignore this. He was her stepfather and she was the only person he had.

"I'm not worried about them." Haimon brushed off her hand. "I want to know where they are."

"We took some rooms in a hotel." Now was not the time to upset him, she told herself. She wasn't lying. She was merely taking one thing at a time. "They have supervision."

"Who?" His grey eyes narrowed once more.

"Someone safe." She eased back on her padded chair, trying to appear nonchalant, trying to figure out how to change the subject. "I actually had an appointment this morning so I'd already made arrangements."

The memory of the meeting with her solicitor drummed in the back of her head. She couldn't quite wrap her mind around what she'd learned there, what she'd realized she had to deal with.

"What did you say his name was?" Mr. Kempler's crisp, clear tone had sharpened.

"Raphael Vounó," she'd said.

The meeting had gone well up until that point. She'd laid out her dilemma, the fear her brothers would be taken from her against her will if she allowed the DNA test. She'd been encouraged when Mr. Kempler had dismissed the very thought. He'd assured her no mere DNA test could match her years of caring for Aarōn and Isaák. No English court would side with a man unknown to the twins only days ago.

But then...then, she'd mentioned the name.

"Good God." Mr. Kempler had lurched from his leather chair and started to pace. "Viper Enterprises."

"What?" The thread of concern in his voice made her heart chug.

He whipped around to stare at her in surprise. "Didn't you at least Google this man? Do some investigation on him?"

A wash of embarrassment swept through her. She hadn't. Not once had she typed Raphael Vounó's name into her computer. Too painful, too bitter. And the last two days had been too overwhelming to dig out her laptop from their luggage and do any investigation. Or maybe, if she was honest with herself, what she might find frightened her. She'd stupidly stuffed her head into a hole. The heat of anger at herself made her flush once more. "I didn't."

Her solicitor sighed. Walking to his chair, he slumped down. "You have a problem, Ms. Drakos."

Fear tightened its grip around her throat. "I do?"

"You do." Mr. Kempler sifted through the papers on his desk until he found what he'd been searching for. A newspaper.

He pushed it toward her. "Take a look."

Tamsin cautiously drew the paper towards her. It was one of the financial papers Haimon sometimes read. She'd never had time. Between the boys and the hotel, she'd rarely had time to do any reading at all.

Viper Enterprises One of the Top 10 Stocks to Buy

The headline blared. She skimmed the article. The writer touted the company, the company's prospects, the new patents they'd acquired in the past year, the major patent for some kind of wonder medical device the company was currently bidding on. And the owner. Quite a lot of glowing prose on the owner.

My business.

A business I'm very successful in.

She glanced up to meet the worried eyes of her solicitor. Her heart sunk and her stomach began to churn. "He told me he had a business."

The solicitor scoffed. "A bit of an understatement."

Cold fear slid down her throat. The limo, the silk suit, the fancy hotel: all the clues combined into a sick sort of sense. "He owns a big business?"

A dry chuckle laced with irony was her response.

"How big?"

"Just the biggest global healthcare company in the world."

"What?" she gasped. Yet the horror at her solicitor's announcement blended with a shock of joy inside her.

Rafe hadn't become a doctor, but at least he'd founded a company that helped heal people.

"You have a formidable enemy, Ms. Drakos. A billionaire." Mr. Kempler eased forward, placing his elbows on his desk and his pointed fingers under his chin. "I'd advise you to proceed with care."

"I could lose the boys?" Her greatest fear broke loose in her heart, pounding in her brain and her body like an awful march of death. She couldn't lose the twins. Aarōn and Isaák were why she lived.

"Yes, if you're not careful." The solicitor's voice grew intense. "A man like Mr. Vounó has endless resources."

"He told me he'd talked with his solicitors. Plural."

Another dry chuckle. "I'm sure the man has many solicitors."

"What should I do?" she whispered, stark fear shivering along her spine.

"You could sue him for back child support. Still, that would be tricky." Mr. Kempler's gaze narrowed. "And costly."

"I don't want his money." The thought of accepting any more of Rafe's largess stuck like a stone in her gut.

"Then, I'd advise you to make a deal with the man. Quickly." Her solicitor leaned back in his chair, his mouth firming. "If you believe the DNA test will prove what he says is true, the best thing you can do is to come to some agreement with Vounó about the boys' custody."

"He wants to take them away from me." Chilled terror had run down her arms, giving her goose bumps.

"You've got a problem, Ms. Drakos."

"That's your problem." Haimon's voice ripped right through her recollection.

"What?" Tam turned her vacant gaze to meet the old man's keen eyes.

"You haven't heard a word I've said these last few minutes, have you?' He coughed, a harsh, deep sound. "Give me some water."

She stood and grabbed the glass of water on the side table. Leaning over him, she held the glass as he sucked down a small amount of the liquid.

"Enough." He pushed the glass away.

"I should go. You're tired."

"No. Not yet." He plopped his head back on the pillow, his face sallow, his breathing hoarse. "There's still some things I have to say."

"All right." Tamsin sat, wishing she could leave and never come back. But the strings of loyalty after so many years were too hard to cut. "A few more minutes."

"I need money."

Apparently, the subject of the boys had been forgotten, much to her relief. Or more likely, knowing her stepfather, the subject of money was far more important. She shouldn't be surprised. He always needed money. They'd never made a lot of cash with the hotel, yet whatever profit there'd been had been immediately seized by Haimon to fund one of his many schemes. Only by a deft slight-of-hand, had she been able to find the money to pay for the boys' clothes and lessons. "I hardly think you need money in the hospital."

"I'm not going to be here for long." The old man's eyes glittered. "I'm going to get well."

She should be glad at this show of determination, but all she could feel right now was a building panic.

I'm not done with him. Rafe's harsh voice echoed in her memory.

"You've gone pale." Haimon's ragged voice cut through her thoughts. "Did the doctor tell you something I don't know?"

"No." She plastered a smile on her face. "I only remembered something I have to take care of."

With a humph, he eased back onto the pillow. "I'm going to get well, I tell you. I'm going to get back at Vounó."

Tam stifled a moan. On the one side she had Raphael Vounó, who hated this man and *had plans for him.* Rafe, who if what her solicitor said was true, had more money than a Greek god. Rafe, with whom she had to make a deal to keep her in the twins' life. On the other hand, she had Haimon. A man who'd raised her. A man who wanted his own revenge against Raphael Vounó. A man who expected her loyalty and who she probably should warn...

"Did you hear me?" Her stepfather's hand fisted on the side of the bed and his jaw tautened. "I'll get back at Vounó for both of us."

"Don't drag me or the twins into this fight."

His hoarse laugh filled the small hospital room. "There's no way to make peace, Tammy. Not this time. You'll have to pick sides."

"No, I won't." She stood, every one of her bones and muscles aching with tension.

He sighed in clear disgust. "You can't leave until we talk about the money."

"Focus on getting well first." How was she going to juggle the needs of Haimon coming out of the hospital with the obvious hate Rafe felt for the man? How was she going to soften Rafe's attitude while still taking care of this old man? It was impossible to think about at this point. "For now, you don't need money."

"I do. I want you to sign over the money in the hotel account to me."

"You can't be serious." Years ago, she'd made another deal with her stepfather. She had control of the funds. She kept track of the bank account. In return, he could keep going with his businesses as she turned a blind eye. Foolishly, she hadn't demanded he sign off on his ownership of the hotel. An oversight she found beyond unforgivable.

"Completely serious." He shifted in his bed, yet his gaze never left hers. "You've clearly landed on the gravy train."

"What?"

"You didn't admit it, but I know. I'm not stupid. The boys are with Vounó, aren't they?"

"Yes." What was the use of hiding the fact their lives had irrevocably changed? "So what? He won't kidnap them. He can't leave the country without my consent."

"And mine."

His words hit her. This could be awful. If what her solicitor had counseled her to do was the only way she kept the boys, then her stepfather's demands would destroy any hope of her keeping Rafe amiable. "They aren't yours, Haimon. We both know that, don't we?"

The old man closed his eyes. "Your mother," he sighed.

Bittersweet emotion whispered through her. Her mother had never been much, but this man before her had loved her in his own way. "Haimon—"

"Never mind." His eyes opened and he stared at her. "Give me the money and I walk away from the boys for good."

Tam's hands trembled as she clutched them in front of her. That money, small amount that it was, was the only thing standing between her and complete poverty.

Losing her home because she'd been stupid was one thing. Losing the last of her power willingly was a whole other level of insanity. The boys would be taken care of by Rafe, come what may. Yet without any money of her own, how could she possibly keep pace with a billionaire? She couldn't pay her solicitor. She couldn't find another flat. She wouldn't even be able to pay for a flight to Greece.

She'd be totally defenseless. At the mercy of a man who hated her.

"Sign the money over to me, Tamsin." Haimon pursed his lips. "Or I make trouble for the boys."

CHAPTER SEVEN

*S*he appeared exhausted. Defeated.

"Tam!" Isaák hooted, jumping off the couch he and his twin had been slouched on and running toward where she stood at the door of the hotel suite.

"You won't believe what we did." Aarōn followed his brother, his voice rising excitedly.

Did with *him*. Their uncle. That went unmentioned, of course. Still, today, he'd made progress of a sort. The mention of tickets to Wembley Stadium to see a semi-final game of football had lit the twins' faces. All the gloom and grouching about Tamsin leaving them behind with *him* had disappeared in one flat second.

The boys hadn't become enamored of him, yet they hadn't ignored him either. The first trip ever to Wembley was met with wide eyes and excited talk. Overall, though, Rafe had kept a handle on them and the excursion was a success.

He'd been surprised. Not only because the twins hadn't gone off the rails in his care, but also because he hadn't enjoyed a football game as much as he had to-day...well, in a very long time. The twins' excitement had brought back memories of his trips to the stadium with his father and Ben. They'd brought back the joy of the game and being a kid. He'd clicked his phone off halfway through the match. Only when they'd returned to the hotel, had he turned it on again.

The boys combined voices rose as they competed to tell Tamsin of their day at Wembley.

"Did you really?" She glanced at Rafe, her green eyes shadowed. "How exciting. Did you say your thank yous?"

"Wait, I'm not finished." Isaák waved her question away and launched into another story about the match. Aarōn bounced on his toes next to his brother.

His nephews had not said their thank yous. Yet he'd had time with them and time was the key to winning them over. Time away from their Drakos relatives. Time with the Vounó family. Time was on his side. Rafe leaned back in his chair and watched as she slid her hand along Isaák's shoulder and swung her arm around to hug Aarōn.

His hand tensed on seat of the chair.

Mollycoddling.

Time enough to end that once and for all.

He'd been careful in his questioning. The boys were protective of her and he didn't want to stir a hornet's nest. However, between the treat of the tickets, the Cokes and hamburgers, and the roar of the fans, he'd figured a couple of things out.

Enough to know he'd already won what he wanted.

"What's Greece like?" Isaák had questioned as the crowd kept filing into the stadium.

"When are we going there?" his brother demanded.

Both pairs of dark eyes had stared at him expectantly. A wash of grief had ran through him at the thought of everything Ben had lost by not claiming Aarōn and Isaák as Vounós. At everything his family had lost by being deprived of watching these two grow. At everything the twins had lost by not knowing their heritage.

"Greece is..." How could he keep it simple yet communicate how important this rocky piece of land was to him and his family? "Greece is home."

Both boys gave him an identical quizzical scowl.

"Huh?" Aarōn finally blurted out.

He tried again. "Greece is where our ancestors came from. It is in our blood. You'll see when you get there."

"When's that going to be?" Isaák said.

"Soon."

"Not soon enough." Aarōn slurped from his Coke.

"You want to go." A surge of fierce joy swam through Rafe at the realization.

"Definitely." Isaák gave him a disbelieving look. "Who wouldn't want to spend the summer in Greece?"

"You won't be returning to London in the fall." He ventured out into shaky territory, but he didn't want the twins misled. "You'll go to school in Greece starting this fall."

In an eerily identical movement, both boys turned to gaze out at the beginning skirmishes of the match. They each appeared pensive, even sad.

Rafe's heart had wrenched.

He hadn't thought everything through when he'd charged into these boys' lives. He had been intent on saving them. Not hurting them. Yet he was tearing them away from everything they knew. Their home, their school, their family. An unexpected and unwanted emotion had surged through him in a split second. One he was unfamiliar with.

Indecision.

"So we're not going back home?" Isaák's voice cracked at the end.

"I don't care about that heap of a place." Aarōn frowned. "But what about our friends at school?"

"You'll make new friends in Greece." Rafe stuffed down the urge to plead. "Plus, you'll have a big family surrounding you. You have a grandmother. Aunts. Cousins."

"How many?" Aarōn appeared enchanted with the thought, the memories of school friends fading away.

"Half a dozen."

"Half a dozen cousins." Isaák piped in.

The boys both chortled at his play on words.

"That's so cool to think we have all these other relatives." A grimace turned Isaák's mouth down. "But...what about...our dad—"

"He's not our dad, idiot." His brother frowned once more. "At least I'm pretty sure."

His twin stared at the field below. "He never acted like our dad, honestly."

The wistful tone in Isaák's voice made the grief for what they'd missed well inside Rafe. He wanted to march into the hospital and choke Drakos until he died. Except there was another man at fault: his own brother. The knowledge ate inside him. Somehow, he'd make this up to the twins.

"I never cared." Aarōn had shifted in his seat, a dismissive look on his face. "We always had Tamsin."

"Yeah." His brother glanced at his twin, a sudden, sunny smile on his face. "We did, didn't we? And still do."

Rafe soaked in the harsh knowledge; Their sister was their lodestar and wasn't going to be as easy to get rid of as Haimon Drakos. Bitter anger swirled into his grief and regrets.

Aarōn crossed his arms in front of him. "Maybe he'll die."

"Tam says he won't die."

The indifference in both of their voices told Rafe everything he needed to know about their relationship to their so-called father. Yet indecision still hovered inside him. Perhaps he needed to ease them into this more slowly. He might need to acquire a home here so they could return and visit their London friends. Maybe he'd have to let Tamsin stay in their lives...

The thought choked inside him, like a tight hard fist.

He didn't want her around. Not only because of her corrupting influence on the boys, but her corrupting influence on him. Her soft, slurred voice kept bringing back unwanted memories. Her gentle demeanor continued to beat against his hate. Her pale, delicate skin and green eyes and golden hair lashed around his libido.

The last thing he wanted was Tamsin coming to Greece with them.

It could be he'd have to stay in London a bit longer. The boys were only thirteen and if this was what was needed, then he'd do it for them. "We can take it slower if you'd like. We can wait to leave for—"

"No, it's okay," Isaák stated, squaring his shoulders.

"We're fine with leaving," Aarōn said. It was as if the twins had silently communicated with each other and made a decision. "We want to see Greece and meet our new family."

"As long as our sister is with us, we'll be happy in Greece." Isaák took another sip of his drink, his face now smooth and complacent.

"Yeah," Aarōn threw a look across at Rafe, the communication clear.

Tamsin stays with us.

The beginning of the match had stopped the conversation, but it had told Rafe what he needed to know and didn't want to confront. Clearly, separating them from Haimon Drakos was not going to be a problem.

The problem was going to be Tamsin.

"Did you eat?" She smiled at Aarōn and Isaák, a gentle smile that brought back aching memories. That smile was exactly like the smiles she used to give him long ago. And he'd believed them—exactly as the twins believed in her now.

How was he going to separate her from them before she hurt them, too? How was he going to do this without damaging the boys permanently, like she'd damaged him?

There isn't enough money in the world to get me to let go of my brothers.

He lurched out of the chair, anger and indecision churning inside. "Tamsin. We need to talk."

Both boys jerked around and gave him the exact same look.

Protective. Of their sister.

Rafe realized with a sickening dread that this was going to be the hardest deal he'd ever make. A deal that had to be done with Tamsin.

Tamsin, with her husky voice and leaf-green eyes, bringing back unwanted memories.

Tamsin, with her clean scent and beautiful body, making him sweat with lust.

Tamsin, with her dogged demands and cunning mind, causing him to lose all battles.

CHAPTER EIGHT

*A*s Tamsin followed Rafe into his bedroom, exhaustion competed with fear. She'd done what Haimon requested. She'd signed over every pound to him. The moment her shaking hand had finished signing the last of the bank papers, she'd felt a profound sense of doom. She had no more resources. She was completely powerless.

The thump of a building headache beat in her head.

But what else could she have done? She'd had to in order to gain custody of the boys.

Anger bubbled beneath her fear and exhaustion. Anger at Haimon for letting the twins go so easily. He'd used them as a weapon to get his way. When she'd called him and told him what she'd done at the bank, that the funds would be released to his name as soon as he signed the custody papers, he'd readily agreed. He hadn't even asked about what the future was for the twins. It was as if he'd washed his hands of them.

Over the years, he'd rarely paid much attention to them, yet they'd been a family, hadn't they? The four of them had stuck together and she'd thought...she'd thought...

"The doctor's coming at seven p.m. to do the tests."

Closing the door behind her to shield the boys from this conversation, she turned to face the harsh, hard man standing close by. The man who now held every advantage in this war going on between them. The only weapon she had was the love of Aarōn and Isaák. Yet if she used this to gain her way, was she any better than Haimon?

A gurgle of ragged tears filled her throat.

Tam swallowed them down.

She had to stay strong. She had to remember the twins needed her. How could she possibly walk away from them and leave them in the care of this cold man?

She wasn't using them. She was protecting them.

"Did you hear me?" Rafe snarled.

"Yes, I heard you." Her anger at her stepfather rolled into indignation. Indignation at this man snarling at her. A man who relentlessly pushed her, pummeled her with his directions and demands. "I didn't agree to that."

"*Nai.*" He turned around to glare at her. "You did."

She had. If not literally, then certainly, figuratively. Still, resentment burned in her blood. Rafe just kept charging forward, running over everything and everyone standing in his way. If he had a heart any longer, he'd give her and the boys a moment to come to grips with the changes coming at them.

But he didn't have a heart any longer.

He'd proven that time and time again during the last few days.

"You did, Tamsin." He took a step towards her, outrage in every line of his body at her continued silence. "Admit it."

Pressing herself on the door, she met his gaze and shivered at what she saw. The black hostility in his eyes burned like hot coals. "Okay, I did. However, you should have checked with me before setting the appointment."

"Why?" Another sardonic snarl twisted his lips. "When you'd previously agreed?"

He was a mere foot from her. The heat of his body wrapped around her, making the cold shivers turn abruptly to hot. Catching her breath, she reeled from the punch of his presence and the taste of his smell on her tongue. The realization struck her that for all the innumerable changes in Raphael, in one way, he was the same as her memories.

His distinct scent.

She'd teased him about it long ago. She'd chuckled when he'd shrugged and waved it off and then blushed. He'd said maybe he should get some cologne, try some manly perfume like his older brother. Snuggling into the space between his neck and shoulder, she'd told him, "don't you dare."

Rafe had thrown his head back and laughed.

Tam tried to bring her thoughts together. This was too important, too vital to her very being. She needed to focus on her brothers, not on bittersweet memories. She needed to fortify her stand, her rights, not allow herself to be distracted by something that no longer mattered.

But she sunk deeper into his spell.

He surrounded her.

The dark richness of his natural scent filled her nostrils and despite her determination, she breathed him in. Chocolate and caramel and some indefinable salty sweetness permeated his skin like an overlay of sin. All the memories. Such a short time together, yet all the memories, like a flood of endless perfection, endless dreams, swirled around her and inside her.

For a moment, a flash of something crossed his face.

Some connection. Some emotion.

Her body went from burning hot to yearning warmth. Something prickled in her nipples. Something turned buttery at her core. "Rafe?"

With a jerk, he strode to an ultra-modern glass desk that stood by the open terrace window. Shoving aside one file folder, he drew out a piece of paper from another. "Sign this."

She wrapped her arms around herself, trying to stop the warm, prickly, buttery feeling from disappearing. "What is it?"

"You know what it is." A waft of spring breeze ruffled his dark hair, making him appear boyish, lovable. But there was nothing boyish or lovable about the scowl he gave her.

The warmth frosted away, burned off by her returning anger and frustration. She'd been dreaming when she'd imagined a connection. This was the man who threatened her position in the boys' lives. She had to remember that. "Something from your solicitors, I'll bet."

"You'd bet right." His tight smile held utter disdain. "You must have inherited the need for betting from your father."

Her hands tightened on her arms at the insult. "I'm not signing anything my solicitor doesn't review."

A solicitor who told her to sweet-talk this man. A solicitor who advised her to make a deal with this man before being run over by his money. A solicitor she could no longer afford.

"He doesn't need to review a simple consent form."
He waved a pen at her.

"I don't know—"

"Tamsin." His anger radiated through the room.
"We made a deal. Are you going to do what every
Drakos I know has done—?"

"I just need to think." Running her hand across her
forehead, she tried to soothe the pounding ache inside.
"Can't you give me a minute—?"

"You've seen your solicitor. Now sign the paper as
promised."

She thought of her past life. The one that had ended
mere days ago. The life where she'd controlled her surroundings. Where she'd been competent, looked to for
instruction, able to deal with any problems coming her
way. Now she felt as if she'd suddenly turned into a
weak, wilting leaf, swirling down this man's river, unable to catch a current into a secret eddy or hook herself
to a safe branch.

His voice came again, tough and curt. "I had hoped
your solicitor was a good one. One who laid out your
so-called options."

She laughed, a shaky, almost hysterical laugh. "My
non-existent options."

"Well, well. You do have a good solicitor."

This was not smart. She was arguing with him. Ril-
ing him. Admitting how weak her position was. She
needed to think with a clear head. Why was she argu-

ing about this DNA test? She'd agreed to it before, believing it was best for the twins.

There were far more important battles to be waged and won.

Pushing herself off the door, she walked to where Rafe stood. "Give it to me."

The consent was simple, easily understood. Grabbing the pen from his hand, she bent down and signed the form. "There. Happy now?"

She moved back, unable to bear being so close to the scent of him. Using flippant words to cover the awful need to reach out and wrap herself around him, which was silly and ridiculous. The last thing she wanted to do was get near this hateful man.

"Happy?" His laugh was hard and cold. "I'm not going to be happy until I see your father in jail."

"What?" Her lingering anger at her stepfather dropped away, leaving only horror. "What do you mean?"

"I told you." White lines bracketed his mouth. "I told you at the hospital I wasn't done with him."

"But jail?" She reeled away, trying to escape his threats and his presence. "What can you possibly have—?"

"I have plenty." He followed her, looming over her. "Did you think merely taking his filthy hovel would be enough for what he did to my father?"

"The hotel wasn't a hovel." Fury raged back. "The place was our home."

"No Vounó should live in a place like that." He dismissed her rage with a flick of one long finger. "Good enough, I suppose for a Drakos."

His sneer ratcheted up her pumping fury at his continued insults. "Then why not leave Haimon to it? Why do you have to put him in jail?"

"Come on. Don't play the fool." His hand slashed across his body, cutting her objection off. "You must have known the old man was dealing dirt."

"I didn't know—"

"Please." His rejection came with a swift edge. "Don't make me laugh again."

"He's sick. He's old. He can barely talk, much less fight you or survive jail—"

"What?" He stilled, black gaze instantly alert and sharp. "What did you say?"

She stood silent. She hadn't intended to tell him she'd visited Haimon. The revelation would only aggravate him further when she needed to make a deal to stay in the boys' life. Still, she hadn't thought of it as concealment, only a strategic decision. Yet by the look in Rafe's eye, this was another brick in the wall of *Tamsin can't be trusted.*

"I visited him after the meeting with the solicitor." She straightened her shoulders.

"Today?" He paced away as if trying to keep his hands from wringing her neck. "You visited Drakos today?"

"Yes." She stood in the middle of the room, feeling as if she were about to be called to the execution block.

"He's awake."

"Yes."

"Then he's going to try and escape." He grabbed his mobile phone off the desk. "I told the hospital to inform me immediately, dammit."

"What are you doing?" Without thinking, she ran to him and tried to tug the phone from his hands. "Why should the doctors inform you of anything? You're not next-of-kin."

He turned, jerking the phone out of her reach. "They know about the warrant for his arrest."

"A warrant?" She froze. "Already?"

"Several." His back to her, he dialed. "The police need to be notified."

"Haimon isn't going anywhere." A wash of dread ran through her. "He's too sick."

I'm not going to be here for long.

If she told him she'd given her stepfather the means to escape, the money to flee, she'd never, ever gain his consent to stay with the twins. But she hadn't done it for her stepfather. She'd done it for the boys.

Rafe wouldn't believe that though, would he?

His curt voice murmured into the phone. Tam stood on wobbly legs listening as he issued terse orders to his security. A welter of emotions fought inside her. Guilt that she'd let Haimon's waking slip. Anger at this man for being so bloody ruthless. Fear that he'd find out about the money at some point.

Rafe pivoted to stare at her as he dropped his phone on the desk. "That's taken care of."

"He's an old man." She tried one more time to reach the the wonderful young man she'd once loved.

"Let's not have the same argument." He grimaced. "You'll lose. Again."

Hate radiated from him. Tamsin realized with a hard ache that this emotion had ultimately consumed the boy she'd loved. Consumed the compassionate heart, the kind soul, the healing hands.

A wrenching grief swelled inside her, closing her throat.

"Good." He folded his arms in front of him. "No rebuttal. You might finally be understanding the new reality."

Anger blasted apart the grief, still, she kept her mouth shut. She needed to remember the bigger picture. Haimon would have to take care of himself. She had to take care of the boys.

Rafe eyed her, as if momentarily puzzled at her silence. "Let's get something straight," he said. "No more contact with Drakos. Ever."

"I have the right—"

"You. Or the twins."

A flicker of hope sprang to life inside her. He wasn't talking about her leaving anymore. He was dictating, which made her burn in anger, yet he wasn't telling her to leave. He was telling her what to do. "So you acknowledge the fact the boys and I are meant to be together."

He narrowed his eyes. "I acknowledge no such thing."

"Then why would you care if I see Haimon or not?"

"I won't have that man pollute the twins' life any longer."

"Or mine because I'm a part of the boys' lives." She could tell her words irked him, but he didn't deny them either.

"I don't care about you." A muscle in his jaw tightened.

"The boys do."

He stared at her, his mouth grim. "Do what I tell you to do or you'll be sorry."

"I'm already sorry about this whole situation." Her courage soared at the expression on his face. The trapped look. "A little more sorry isn't going to faze me."

He made an irritated sound deep in his throat. Turning away from her intent gaze, he stomped to the desk and began leafing through the files.

Ignoring her.

Or she should say, trying to ignore her.

Because his body language screamed recognition of the new reality. The taut line of his shoulders told her she'd won a battle in this war between them. The tense stance of his legs declared he knew she'd found a foothold in his life with the twins. Even the way he moved his hands, in a rough, edgy way, screamed the knowledge he couldn't get rid of her.

Not yet. Not now.

With a jerk, he turned to confront her. "*Entáxei.* I'll deal."

"Okay." She didn't want to overplay this win. Except the thrill of holding the upper hand for once threatened to overcome her common sense. "You first."

"You have joint custody with Drakos, right?" Stark pain flashed through his eyes, striking her straight through.

"Correct." Literally correct, if not in spirit. Until she got those papers back with Haimon's signature, though, she couldn't be sure.

Rafe dropped his head and his shoulders sagged. A heartbroken sigh gusted from him.

She tried to stop the stream of compassion threatening to well inside her. She didn't want it to drown this sure win. The only thing she needed to do was keep her wits sharp and her emotions dead and she'd have what she wanted. Continuing access to her boys.

He swiveled around, slamming his hands down on the desk. "All these years. *Anáthemá se!* I should have been with them."

The stream turned into a river. She wanted to swear too. Swear at herself. Swear at her too-tender heart. "Rafe—"

"Never mind." He kept his gaze turned toward the open window. "What matters is getting Drakos out of my nephews' lives forever."

These last few days she'd seen only the angry man, the man filled with hate. But now, before her stood a weary man, a man weighted down by regret. The urge to soothe swept through her. "I have already—"

"That means I need your help." He restlessly ran his hand through his hair, indicating he understood the underlying premise of what that meant. "So what do I have to give you to make this happen?"

She didn't want Haimon anywhere near Aarōn and Isaák either. Not anymore. He'd shown his true colors and as far as she was concerned, he'd never see the boys again. Admitting this to Rafe, however, would cause her to lose any bargaining power. Right now, this very minute, she could ask for the only thing she wanted, and get it. She saw the realization in his hostile black eyes. She had him backed into a corner. He knew it and she knew it.

I get to stay in the boys' life. For now.

She'd work on forever later.

Yet the words froze on her tongue. She tried to choke them out, but they wouldn't come. They refused to be said because she didn't want to force Rafe to do this. She wanted him to willingly acknowledge the bond between her and the boys couldn't be broken. Should never be broken.

"It's already done," she stuttered. "I've taken care of it."

"What?" His eyes widened and went blank.

Why was she letting this opportunity flit away? What she wanted lay right in front of her. She couldn't make herself claim it, though. Not in this way. "My solicitor is sending over papers now."

"Papers."

"Haimon has agreed to grant me sole custody." Her last chance to bargain wafted away with her words.

"Really." He shook himself, as if trying to wake from a dream. Never taking his gaze off her, he folded his arms across his broad chest and leaned on the desk. "How did you manage that?"

"The details aren't important." She wasn't stupid enough to tell him about the money. Or lack thereof. She'd given far too much as it was. "Just know he's out of the boys' lives."

"And yours." Implacable, insistent, his demand rang in the room.

She sighed. What did it matter if she, too, never saw her stepfather again? His actions today, his actions during the years, and his actions against Rafe and his family, had stolen any affection she'd ever had for the man. "And mine."

His shoulders relaxed. Silence descended while he examined her, and Tamsin had the silly impulse to duck her head like she'd done something wrong.

She *had* done something wrong.

She'd foolishly thrown aside a bargaining chip. One she desperately needed to fend off this man and his ruthless march to victory.

"Interesting." He tapped one finger on his arm; his face was smooth, yet his eyes were still sharp and pointed. "I wonder what your scheme is."

The unjustness of the attack drove every thought of bargaining chips and strategies straight out of her head. Her fists tightened in knots at her side. "Why do you always believe the worst in people?"

"I don't." The finger stopped. "I only believe the worst when it's been proven to me over and over again."

"You don't know—"

"I know all about the Drakos way of life." The tapping began once more. "For example, I know you lied to me ten years ago."

"I never lied to you." She wanted to race across the room and bang his head on the wall.

"No?" Gazing at her, his mouth went grim. "Not with your kisses? Your sweet promises?"

"I was sixteen!"

"Kisses and promises that disappeared as soon as my father killed himself."

She should tell him. Tell him the truth of her motivations all those years ago. True, she'd promised Haimon to keep their deal secret, but she had no loyalty to her stepfather anymore. She was free to tell Rafe she'd still loved when she told him to leave, that she still loved...

"Once a liar, Tamsin, always a liar." He thrust the words at her like a sheaf of knives.

He wouldn't believe her. Not a word. So why should she throw her heart in front of him only so he could march right over it? Something inside him had been poisoned and she'd be a fool to trust him with her truth.

"Nothing to say?" He smiled, another brutal thrust. "Then should I keep going on the Drakos way of life? I know everything about your father and his dirty deals."

"He's not my father." The flash of energy his unfair accusation had caused inside her dulled in the face of his relentless attacks. Staring at the floor, she imagined sinking into the thick rug, curling into a ball and sleeping this conversation away.

Rafe ignored her and kept going with his list. "I know what your mother did to my brother."

"What?" Jerking her head up from her contemplation of the dark blue carpet, she eyed him. "What are you talking about?"

"I'm talking about blackmail." His words landed like jagged stones on her heart.

"No." She had no love for her mother. Hadn't really mourned her passing nine years ago. As a kid, she'd tried to wrench Skylla's attention her way, but had never been successful. By the time she'd been a teenager, she'd stopped trying. Still, her mother wouldn't have—

"Your mother wasn't satisfied with concealing the twins from their true heritage. From their true father." Rafe's eyes blazed with the inevitable hate. "No, she went one evil step further."

"I don't know what you mean." The headache came back with a vicious bump. Tam lifted her hand once more, attempting to stroke away the pain.

His hands tightened on his arms as if trying to keep himself from physically ripping her apart. So he did it in words instead.

"I went through my brother's papers after he died." His voice dropped with the last word like he had to push it out. "All of them."

Staring at him, she knew immediately whatever he was going to say would be bad. But she couldn't find anything inside herself to stop him.

His mouth tightened at her silence. "There were pictures of the twins."

"Pictures?" A sharp, slashing cut across her heart made her gasp. Her mother hadn't spared her sons one visit after she left mere months after they'd landed in London. She'd been too busy with her new rich boyfriend, she'd said. Too busy for mewling babies. Yet bizarrely, she'd asked Tam to send her regular photos of the boys. "She sent your brother pictures?"

"*Nai.*" The finger tapped a staccato refrain on his skin. "Along with her blackmail letters."

"She wouldn't have." The protest held no punch, because deep inside, she acknowledged her mother might have done such a thing if she'd been desperate.

Rafe's smile had no life in it. Cold and icy, it sliced into her weak objection. "She wanted money. Or else she was going to tell his family about the twins. So Ben sent it to her."

"Why would he do that?"

Her question stopped the tapping finger and for a moment, she thought she detected a shadow of pain slip across his eyes. Then they turned black as death once more. "Who knows?" He shrugged. "But he paid her."

"So..." Her mind whirled. "Your brother didn't want the boys to know his family. Is that right?"

"Like I said, who—"

"I wonder why?" A deep well of rage opened inside her, wiping out the load of guilt she'd carried around since the moment this man had walked back into her life.

During these last few days, Rafe had thrown accusation after accusation at her. At first, she'd taken it because she'd felt guilty that the twins had been unfairly kept from the Vounós. Then, she'd felt guilt for the devastation Haimon had caused to Rafe's family. And finally, a tiny part of her heart still mourned and grieved for the pain she'd caused this man unintentionally, thinking she'd been giving a gift.

A gift he hadn't received.

"What does it matter?" He straightened from the desk.

"It matters." A Vounó, Rafe's brother, was as much at fault for this mess as any Drakos.

"He's dead—"

"So is my mother. Yet that doesn't stop you from judging her." Tam's head of steamy anger burst. "Maybe Ben thought your family wasn't worthy of knowing the boys."

He tensed, his hands fisting. "That's not—"

"Maybe Ben thought *you* shouldn't have any contact with the twins."

"Stop right there—"

She stood her ground when he prowled closer. "Maybe Ben realized what you'd become and didn't want his sons tainted with *you*."

"That's enough." Grabbing her arms, he yanked her to him. "Don't say another word."

She wasn't going to stop. She couldn't. "Maybe Ben knew the man you'd become—angry, hateful, ruthless—and didn't want his sons anywhere near you."

His mouth slammed onto hers, stopping the words that clearly seared him. She knew they had when she saw the flash of pain in his eyes.

Before she closed her own.

Because she couldn't take him in all at once. Not his pain, and then his hate and then his lust. Because the kiss wasn't only about punishment; it was about lust. She fought against the pull, the draw. Tightening her muscles against him, she pushed on his chest.

He ignored her. His lips were hot and hard. The heat of his body branded her, while his mouth commanded her unconditional surrender. And somehow, someway, her body responded.

The prickle of her nipples itched again.

The buttery warmth blossomed inside once more.

She opened her mouth to protest. To protest his demands. To protest to herself for her response. His tongue delved in before she could catch her breath. It swept over her objections and swirled them into a blend of lust and need. His tongue played magic on her own, filling her head with mindless desire. His hands moved to her back and hips, pushing her into his heat.

This was nothing like the kisses they'd shared years ago. This was a man's kiss, a man's demand, and hopelessly, Tamsin slid into him, gave to him.

All her muscles softened. All her emotions melted.

All her dreams reawakened.

She wrapped her arms around his neck and moaned, a husky, sultry call.

With an abrupt jerk, he yanked himself from her embrace.

Tam swayed, bereft and chagrined and shaken. The jumble of emotions inside made her want to retch. Or cry. Or fall at his feet in defeat.

Forcing herself to steady, she stared at him.

His back was to her. He'd walked to the desk and his hands were idly sifting through some papers as if what had just occurred was no more than a minor occurrence in a very busy day.

She couldn't say anything. Not without crying out in pain.

He took a breath in, his shoulders lifting then almost, but not quite, shrugging. "You can come to Greece."

Joy should have filled her, and yet, the only thing she felt swimming through her blood was dread. Because this man, this man was a threat to her in a way she hadn't realized until moments ago. A violent delight to her body. A infecting madness for her emotions.

A threat in a way that had nothing to do with the boys.

CHAPTER NINE

*T*he plane banked, the last lights of London twinkling brightly, then hazing with the first of the clouds sliding past.

The last of the life she'd known for ten years.

The last of the life she'd cobbled together from disaster.

The last of the life where she'd been the most important person in the boys' life.

Tamsin swung away from the window to stare at her brothers. Both dark heads were bent over the tablet Rafe held in his hands as he leaned across the low, ultra-modern table sitting between him and the twins.

She glanced around and once again, the reality of his wealth stunned her.

Scared her.

The limo ride to the airport hadn't frightened her. Not after several days of getting used to the ease of traveling through the city without battling the crowds on the Tube. No, the anxiety had started when they'd arrived at Heathrow and had been ushered into a private lounge.

"What's this?" she'd said, peering behind her as the door had closed, shutting out the masses of people waiting to check in.

"This is your private lounge, madam." The attendant had smiled.

Not hers.

His private lounge.

Aarōn and Isaák hadn't even blinked. But then again, they'd never returned to Heathrow since they'd been babies.

Yet she'd remembered. Remembered their arrival years ago. Her mother snarling at Haimon as they wrested luggage from the carousel. The boys crying in their carriers as they'd waited for the last suitcase. She'd remembered how overwhelmed she'd been with the bustling crowds, the dozens of shops, the Byzantine hallways.

This time there'd been only smooth service. A glass of wine in her hand while they waited. A smile as her passport was handed back to her. Another limo to the plane.

"My private plane," Rafe had explained to Isaák as they'd boarded.

Both boys had finally been appropriately dazzled.

She'd been filled with fear. It was one thing to be told Raphael Vounó had money. It was an entirely different matter to be faced with precisely what that meant.

The plane was huge, as big as a commercial airplane. However, size was the only thing comparable. The interior didn't have hundreds of seats smashed together in order to conserve space. Instead, it looked like something from a science-fiction movie. Silvered panels lined the walls, giving one a sense of being in a spaceship. Lush grey carpet covered the floor. Cushioned chairs and sofas were scattered across a vast living room.

"It's like so cool," Isaák had hooted.

Even Aarōn had been impressed.

The boys had explored the ultra-modern bathroom, the two bedrooms with the king-size beds, the galley featuring crystal glassware and porcelain china.

"This can't be yours." The protest had slid out before she could stop.

"No? Why not?" He hadn't even glanced at her. He'd been focused on the twins. Ushering them into chairs directly opposite his, he'd begun his continued campaign to win them over.

A campaign he was winning.

He was becoming important to Aarōn and Isaák.

During the last three days, as they'd waited for the DNA test to come back, Rafe had steadily undermined the twins' initial hostility. There'd been the ongoing chats about Greece and the big family awaiting their arrival. The family who now knew they existed and were ecstatic at the news, he'd told them. There had been the daily outings to various London attractions she'd never been able to afford either in time or money or both. Madame Tussaud's, the zoo, even a musical at a West End theatre. She'd come along to the events because the boys had wanted her there, but she hadn't enjoyed any of them.

She'd been sad. Sad she hadn't been able to do this for them. Which wasn't sensible. She'd given them many more important things.

She'd also been angry. Angry at Rafe that he'd given the twins something she hadn't. Which was churlish of her. She shouldn't begrudge him giving to the twins after so many years lost.

More than anything else, though, she'd started to be afraid. Afraid of the wealth this man obviously had and the power this gave him over her and the boys.

Yet it wasn't merely money that was winning the boys' attention.

It was him.

There'd been the mornings where Rafe talked about his father and the family legacy of brilliance. There'd been the times he had described Greece and its beauty with a boyish charm that reminded her of the past. There'd been the daily trips to the pool where he'd dived into the twins' play—at first meeting resistance, but soon, winning them over. Only yesterday, Aarōn had laughed as Rafe had twirled the plastic pool ball on his fingertips.

And Rafe had smiled.

That one smile had shafted into her heart like a torpedo. The memories of *that* smile had stayed in her heart for years. A balm to her pain and an ache all the same.

He'd turned at that moment, stared into her eyes, and the smile, *that* smile, had fallen away.

"Let me try." Isaák wiggled on the silver couch, his gaze never leaving the tablet in front of him.

"I want to try first." His twin reached for the electronic enchantment.

Tamsin gulped in a big load of guilt. She'd been able to provide food for the boys and a home. She'd managed to eke out enough money to give them some lessons. Still, she'd never been able to give them the extras other children received without even asking. She'd never been able to give them Wembley and the West End. She'd never been able to carve enough money from the budget to buy them first-rate computers. Much less tablets or e-readers or fancy PlayStations.

"You both get one." Their uncle slipped out another tablet from a side pocket of his ever-present leather briefcase.

This was too much. Way too much. She jerked forward in her seat, the bite of the seatbelt cutting into her shoulder. But before she could mount a feeble objection to this continued largess, both boys crowed with delight.

"You're spoiling them." Her hushed accusation slipped through the chortles and glee from the twins and hit Rafe. She could tell by his sudden tenseness.

He ignored her as he'd been doing quite successfully since the kiss.

The kiss.

The memory of the meeting of their mouths consumed her every night as soon as she slid under the silk bedcovers. He'd tasted of heat and hot. Of intent and intensity. She couldn't say the kiss had been anything except aggression wrapped in fire.

But she couldn't stop thinking about every moment of *the kiss.*

"Tam!" Isaák piped up, popping her thoughts and memories like a pin to a balloon. "Look at what we got!"

A small nod was the only thing she could manage.

"They'll use them in school." Rafe didn't turn to stare at her, although his cool words finally addressed her accusation. "Every child in their new school has them."

He'd informed her about his plans for the boys' schooling by email. *Email.* Tam had opened her laptop yesterday to find an abrupt message with an attachment. The school was top-notch, catering to international students. The fees were astronomical; far more than anything she could have possibly afforded. The class list and teachers were impressive. The opportunity for Aarōn and Isaák was undeniable.

The place was a boarding school.

Tamsin's hands fisted in her lap.

Glancing at her lap, she forced her fingers to splay out. Forced them to smooth across her simple cotton dress.

A boarding school.

What would she do if the twins went away in the fall? What would she do with herself? Yet how could she protest when the school would be such an amazing chance for her boys? The questions rattled in her brain exactly as they had since she'd received the cold, brutal email.

"Would anyone like something to eat?" The flight attendant came out from the galley. She was young and beautiful and looked like something from a futuristic movie herself, with the silver dress and metallic jewelry.

"Pizza?" Aarōn gave her a half smile, all adolescent charm.

"Pizza sounds great." Isaák grinned. "If you have it."

The attendant nodded. "Of course, we—"

"Wait." Tamsin had to put her foot down somewhere. "This is dinnertime and they should eat something healthier."

"Oh, come on, Tammy."

"Why not? This is so cool—"

"I don't think one meal of pizza will hurt." Rafe's words cut through the cluttered objections of the boys.

The voice of authority.

The attendant didn't even give her a glance. She walked away, her mission clear.

The twins stared at her, quiet all of a sudden. As if they could also sense what was happening.

She was losing control of her brothers.

A clutch of fear and anger surged inside. She whipped around to glare at the man sitting so negligently on the cushioned seat several feet from her. "It's dinnertime. They shouldn't eat junk."

Easing back on the leather sofa, his dark gaze never left her face. "Consider it a snack. We will be eating with the family once we land."

"But..." She stuttered to a stop. "But we won't land until after eight p.m."

"You've forgotten so much." He clicked his tongue, a disgusted sound. "Don't you remember Greece? We eat late."

She remembered. Too much. "Of course I do. However, the boys aren't used to the lifestyle. They'll need to go to bed as soon as we arrive."

"Come on, Tam." Aarōn appeared as disgusted as his uncle.

"We're not babies, Tammy." Isaák's voice was softer, yet still filled with disagreement about her dictates.

She felt the reins of her control slipping away. Panic edged her words. "You've had a lot to deal with during the last few days. You need to rest."

"The family will be gathered to meet the boys when we arrive." Rafe's fingers tapped impatience on the silk-covered arm of the sofa. "I'm sure they are gathering even as we speak."

"All of them?" Aarōn leaned forward eagerly.

"When I called your grandmother, what we call *giagiá*—"

"*Giagiá.*" Isaák tried out the word, rolling the vowels and consonants in his mouth.

"Correct." Rafe smiled. A genuine one. "You'll catch on very quickly."

Another billow of guilt went down her throat even though her choices had been solid when she'd made them years ago. The boys had been adjusting to a new home, the loss of their mother, a strange environment. Choosing only one language for them to learn had made things much simpler.

"No," she'd told Rafe when he'd expressed shock and anger at the fact his nephews knew no Greek. "I haven't taught the boys to speak their native tongue."

His glare had shot her way as if she'd personally insulted him. Had rejected not only Greece, not only her own heritage, but everything he prized in life.

Except he didn't understand. He didn't know how much it had hurt to hear the words that had only brought back bitter memories and the defeat of sweet dreams. Rafe didn't understand the yawning pain in her heart was the reason for her decision. As soon as she'd had some semblance of control over their London life, she'd forbidden Greek in their home. The boys need to learn English for school, she'd said, don't confuse them. In this, as with many things, Haimon had agreed.

Haimon.

Tamsin peeked across the plane to meet gleaming black eyes. She resisted the impulse to look away as if she had anything to be sorry for. Even though, she did. "What?"

He stared at her for one more moment, before glancing at the attendant who was bringing in platters of pizza.

Guilt at what he didn't know about Haimon clogged in Tam's throat, making it impossible for her to continue to fight about the food.

"You warned him, didn't you?" Rafe had cornered her the night after the kiss. The only time he'd come near her since. "You went to the hospital to warn him."

"What?" She'd skittered back from the angry accusation. "What are you talking about?"

"He's gone." As if he couldn't stand to be close to her, he wrenched himself away and began to pace back and forth in front of her. The echo of the TV in the other room joined by the boys' chatter competed with Rafe's harsh breath.

"Gone? From the hospital?" She couldn't imagine the old man having the energy to leave.

"Don't pretend you didn't know what his plans were." Swiveling around, he glared.

"I had no idea." Tam gazed at his face. A face filled with instant rejection. "Didn't you have security surrounding him?"

"Not enough, clearly." He paced again. "The police are searching for him. He can't go far without money."

Saying nothing had seemed the best choice. He apparently thought the Drakos clan had little money—and he was mostly right. But she'd saved some. Enough to give Haimon the chance to escape.

Something she hadn't confided to Rafe.

"Here." He reached over, breaking into her thoughts. A plate of pizza rested in his hand. "You have to eat something."

The air stilled between them. The simple act of giving her food was not so simple when coming from this man. A gift. An acknowledgement of her presence and her needs. Tamsin's brain whirred.

She took the plate.

Something sparked in those dark eyes. Then his mouth tightened, and he leaned back. "Or not. It's your choice."

Frowning at the pizza, she was amazed when her stomach growled. Even with the guilt and anger and fear surging in her, it appeared her body still wanted food.

A short laugh escaped him. "Eat."

The pepperoni spiced in her mouth and the gooey cheese oozed into her taste buds. Her stomach rumbled in satisfaction, and for a moment, she let herself focus on the delicious junk food rather than her worries.

The boys consumed the pizza within minutes, before bounding down the aisle to inspect the huge flat-screen TV, which looked like a big movie screen to her.

"Do you want more?" Rafe's draped himself lazily on the sofa.

"No." Unbuckling herself, she walked over to put the plate on the table. "I'm full."

He stared at her, his eyes carefully blank, his mouth easy, his jaw relaxed. Was this a truce? Was he beginning to accept her in the twins' life?

"We have some things we need to discuss before we land."

Her stomach knotted around the food she'd eaten. He might appear approachable, but his voice told another story. His voice was hard and determined.

Backing away, she sat with a thump. "What things?" she managed through the sudden burn in her throat.

"Once we arrive," he said, "my mother and sisters are going to want to spend time with the boys."

"Of course." She sagged into her chair, relieved. "I would never object to that."

"Yet they will object to you."

The bald statement hit her like a punch. "Why would they do that? They liked me when you and I were..."

His mouth turned into a sarcastic smile as she slid to a stop. "*Nai?*"

Grabbing her pride, she propped it up. "When we were dating. The point is, I always got along with your family."

"That was before. This is now."

"I can't think what's changed—"

He laughed. "Can't you?"

"Unless you've poisoned the well before I even step into your home." Her accusation flamed into him and set him to blaze. She could tell by the sudden tenseness of his shoulders and the way his eyes turned to black fire.

"You did all the poisoning yourself."

"I don't understand." She truly didn't. Previously, she'd been accepted into his family as a daughter and sister. Beyond her love for Rafe, she'd found in the Vounó villa the home life she'd never had. His father had been warm and charming. His mother had been loving and kind. Rhouth had promptly become her best friend with Rhachel not far behind. Though she'd rejected the family's son at the end, she'd never exchanged one bad word with any of the other Vounós. In fact, she'd spent months and months writing letters to Rhouth...

With no response.

"They hate me because I split with you? Ten years ago?"

He bent forward, his arms on his knees, his hands clasped before him. The pose projected ease and dismissal. His white fingers told her something far different. "They hate you because you are a Drakos."

"So are the boys."

"No." He shook his head slowly. "The boys are Vounós."

"The boys are mine, too."

"I'm working on that." Threat laced every word and her greatest fear raised its head inside.

He hadn't said what his phalanx of solicitors was working on now the DNA test had been done and Haimon had escaped. However, a person didn't have a phalanx of solicitors around to do nothing. "Don't threaten me."

"That wasn't a threat." His gaze blazed with intent. "It's reality."

"I won't let them go."

"Let's put this to rest for now." He eased closer. "What we need to do is come to an agreement."

"Why do I always feel like I lose whenever I make an agreement with you?"

A dark brow arched. "Lose? You've just spent a week in a very nice hotel—"

"You know that's not what I meant."

"You've been wined and dined. Taken to the theatre. Spent the day at the pool."

"I don't care—"

"You haven't had to spend a dime in the entire week—"

"I didn't want or ask for any of that."

"Yet you accepted the gifts. All of them."

He was right. And the thought of being beholden to him, of what this made him think of her, crushed her. He didn't know how capable she was, how much she could do. The only thing he saw when he looked at her was a parasite. She couldn't stand the thought. "You've made your point."

His hands loosened on his taut thighs. "Then the agreement I ask of you should be fairly simple."

"What?"

"Let my mother and sisters have their time with Isaák and Aarōn." His words were threaded with a wary distrust that made it clear he found it impossible to think she'd comply. "Don't mother them, stifle them. Don't make them choose between you and my relatives."

She stared across the aisle at him. Not only did Rafe think she was a parasite, he thought she was a control freak. He thought she was cruel enough to tear the boys apart with a demand for their loyalty. She was nothing like this. How could she possibly prove this to him?

By agreeing.

By getting her feet on the ground and finding a job once they arrived in Greece.

By showing him what she really was instead of trying to tell him.

"I would never do such a thing," she stated. "I want the boys to know their new family."

"Their only family."

"Hey, Tam!" Isaák rushed right between them, breaking through the awful tension. "Come and see what movie we're watching."

Tamsin let herself be led away, a dead weight inside her. By the time she returned to her seat, Rafe was on the phone, his laptop in front of him.

She didn't want to talk to him right now anyway.

She needed to reinforce her defenses before arriving in Greece.

During the last few days, as she'd reconciled herself to going back to Greece, she'd been worried, yes. And angry, true. But in the mix had also been a wistful happiness. The memories of Greece had washed over her: the blazing blue of the sea, the smell of the dry land, the heat of the sun. For years, she'd blanked Greece out of her mind as a necessity. Yet for these last few days, she'd let Greece seep into her heart.

Greece. Her old home.

Where, apparently, she was not going to be welcomed back with open arms.

Isolated. Rejected.

That is what she had to look forward to when this plane landed.

Her throat hurt from stuffing down tears for the rest of the flight. She wished with fervent, irrational hope the plane would never arrive. That they would fly and fly and fly until this wretched pain inside her disappeared.

The thud of the plane's wheels on Greek land hit her with stark despair.

"Cool!" Isaák danced down the stairs to the tarmac. "Another limo."

"As if we were going to met by anything else, idiot." Aarōn strolled across to stand by his brother.

A twitch of concern tightened in her neck. Tam didn't think it was good the boys were getting used to this kind of lifestyle. The nonchalant acceptance of luxury wasn't a good thing.

"Get in." Rafe's impatient voice cut through her worry.

The boys' chatter kept her from any further rumination as they drove away from the airport and into Athens. Before she could strengthen her confidence, the limo was turning into a familiar driveway.

Except it wasn't.

Ten years ago, the driveway had been gravel, the line of carob trees had been untrimmed, the gardens behind the drive had grown in glorious disarray. Now the limo's wheels drove efficiently up a concrete path. The trees were cut back in rigid formation, the gardens tamed into austere elegance.

"Wow!" Isaák hopped up and down on the seat beside her. "Look at that!"

Aarōn twisted around to stare at the villa appearing over the hill. "I didn't expect it to be so rich looking."

She hadn't either. While the Vounó villa was set in the exclusive northern suburb of Ekali, when she'd been here last, the graceful home had been slightly

shabby. Rafe had told her the house had been in his father's family for a hundred years. Clearly the Vounós
were proud of their home, but it had appeared to her
interested eyes at the time that there wasn't quite
enough money to keep everything maintained.

Not anymore.

The limo drew to a stop at a black-spiked gate. A
large medallion hung in the center with the image of a
centaur edged in gold.

"That is Chiron," Rafe said. "A figure in Greek mythology."

"I don't know much about mythology." Aarōn
frowned, obviously offended he didn't know everything
about his new home.

Another stab of guilt slashed at her heart.

"You will." His uncle waved at the attendant in the
gatehouse. "It's your family crest."

Tamsin slumped in her seat, dazed. When she'd last
been here, this particular gatehouse had been a crumbling structure. The gate before them had needed some
paint. Only the medallion had gleamed with familial
pride.

"We'll be at your new home soon." Rafe eased forward, catching the twins' interest. "I've had some major work done during the last few years."

"I can see that," she blurted.

His dark gaze ran over her and then away. "Behind the main villa," he gestured. "Is the new pool and cabana."

The limo rolled along, relentless, as the boys shot eager question after eager question at their uncle. She sunk back into the leather seat, wishing she could sink back into her old life where she'd been important.

The limo stopped. The door opened.

Out of the villa poured a swarm of laughing, crying people. Rafe hopped from the car and reached in, drawing both boys into an adoring group of Vounós.

Their family.

Tam sunk farther back, angry at her cowardice, but unable to force herself into a crowd she'd been warned was antagonistic towards her.

She spotted Rafe's mother, Nephele, her grey hair now tinted a becoming silver, her big dark eyes filled with happy tears. Rhachel stood by her mother, a small boy held in her arms, his lolling head showing the loud chatter around him wasn't disturbing his sleep. Tam recognized her best friend from long ago, Rhouth. No longer a young girl with a sweet smile on her face. Now, she was a woman fully grown, her long, black hair pulled into a fancy coil, her baby fat melted away into an elegant figure. She stood, smiling at the twins, a handsome man standing beside her, holding her hand.

A tear slipped down Tam's cheek as she stared through the limo window. Her friend. All grown up.

"*Eláte.*" A hand suddenly appeared in front of her face. A masculine hand, long-fingered, with a slight wisp of dark hair on its back.

She didn't want to grasp the hand, the strong hand before her. Grasp it and be pulled into a world she'd left so painfully. A world that would not welcome her if what he said was to be believed.

Yet, she wanted to take this hand. Touch the elegant length of the fingers. Take the warmth and love it had offered her when she'd been sixteen. Believe there was acceptance in this hand.

"Tamsin." He leaned into the limo door, Rafe's eyes meeting hers. "Take my hand."

Sliding her fingers along his, she noticed the play of her light skin on his dark. Felt the crease of his palm as he tightened his hand around hers.

And pulled.

A hush came over the happy crowd. She felt as if every eye landed on her with a potent punch.

He let go of her hand and she stood alone.

The eyes around her, the eyes ranging from deepest black to amber brown, the eyes of this family all stared at her.

With hostility.

"Tammy." Isaák bounded over and wrapped his arm around her waist. "Isn't this cool?"

Cold would be the word she'd use. Extremely cold.

Aarōn stepped in front of her and grabbed her hand. Her cold hand. "Come on, Tam. Let's go inside."

"Together," Isaák chimed in.

She forced herself to smile. The boys loved her. That was the only thing that mattered. Without thinking, she glanced over and met another set of eyes. Black eyes filled with turbulence. Filled with mistrust.

Filled with male need.

And Tam knew deep inside, like a shot of pure pain, that the boys' love was not enough.

Not any longer. Not anymore.

CHAPTER TEN

"They are precisely like Ben." His mother wiped joyful tears from her cheeks.

Hopefully not. The betraying thought shot into his mind before he could quash it.

Rafe strode to the antique oak desk his father had once presided behind and leaned on the edge. The sounds of the rest of the family rang from across the hall, their excited voices a restless backdrop to the comparatively quiet library he'd brought his mother to so she could recover her composure.

"I can't wait to hold them again." She beamed.

"Soon, *Mitéra*," he said. "They needed to wash after the traveling."

"*Nai.*" She straightened on the plush velvet sofa. "They appear healthy. Well cared for."

"*Nai.*" He echoed her one word, the truth of it sticking in his throat.

"I highly doubt Haimon Drakos or his wife had much to do with that." His mother's voice went dry.

He crossed his arms, tapping one finger on the linen of his sport coat. He couldn't force another confirmation out because it would lead to yet another conclusion he didn't want to agree to also.

Her mouth firmed. "We can't say Ben had anything to do with it either."

The ache in her voice brought an ache to his throat. "*Mitéra—*"

"No, no, Raphael." She closed her eyes, suddenly looking all of her fifty-eight years. "We must face the fact your brother abandoned his responsibilities."

He could think this, but he didn't want his mother to. The acknowledgement of her oldest son's lack of conscience would only cause her unnecessary pain. "Who knows what really went on? This is all in the past."

Her eyes snapped open to alight on him. "So. You don't wish to share what else you found in Ben's papers."

He straightened his stance; his jaw tightened. "There wasn't much."

Her gaze narrowed.

"What is important is I found the boys." He shifted his weight. "That's what we need to focus on."

"You know more." His mother never yelled. Never screeched. Instead, she used her indomitable will in a relentlessly mild way. The method could be just as effective in handling her children as any loud fight.

Still, this time he would not budge. She didn't need to see the damning letters, the filth his brother had rolled in, the ugliness he'd uncovered. "I don't know everything. I can't be sure of what Ben was thinking when he kept the knowledge of the boys from us."

Maybe Ben knew the man you'd become—angry, hateful, ruthless—and didn't want his sons anywhere near you.

The memory of the accusation, and what he'd done when it had been thrown at him, made him suck in his breath.

"What?" His *mitéra* swiveled on the sofa, her expression alert and focused.

"Nothing." Rafe tried to thrust the accusation and the memory of what had happened after away. Far away. Yet the memory curled back around. Swished past his intention to forget. The argument and the kiss swamped his brain before he could push the thoughts back once again.

The way her mouth wrapped around each painful word, slurring them into his heated blood.

The flash of her green eyes as she hurled another insult at him, making him burn with anger and lust.

The taste of Tamsin. *Theé mou.* The taste of her.

"Raphael?" His mother's gaze pierced him. "There is clearly more going on here."

He wrenched himself upright. "I'm sorry. I am a bit tired from traveling. There's nothing else wrong with me."

A frown creased her brow. "We were talking about your brother's papers."

"*Nai, nai.*" He cursed himself under his breath. The last thing he wanted his mother to scent was his turmoil about Tamsin.

"Is there something wrong with you?" Concern flashed across her face.

"I just told you exactly the opposite."

His *mitéra* cocked her head. "There is something more here." As usual, her voice was calm and cool and hard as marble. "Tell me."

"No." He held himself still. "There is nothing more than two boys who are now welcomed back into the family."

A chilly silence fell and for a moment, Rafe felt all of eight-years-old. The force of his mother's wishes pushed against his rigid determination.

Then she sighed. "All right. We will visit these topics at another time."

Topics. Plural. God help him. There would be no re-
visiting. But he didn't want to pollute this important
moment with an argument. "Let's focus on the boys."

She turned to gaze at the open doorway, a pensive
look filling her expression. "I don't have to know everything you do to know who I can thank for the boys' obvious health and well-being."

The conclusion he had not wanted her to jump to
rolled right toward him. Why did he even hold out a
hope for any other outcome?

This was his mother.

The mother who had instantly known who had broken the dining room window when he'd been seven.
The mother who'd known he'd needed a special place to
keep his collection of wounded birds and rodents. The
mother who could read minds and hearts and souls
even when a man attempted to keep all of it hidden.

Naturally, his mother would have taken one glance at
the boys and known.

"Tamsin," she said softly.

He stiffened, but was able to mask the reaction by
prowling across the room to the marble fireplace. "I
had to bring her."

"Of course you did." He felt her gaze, her strong,
knowing gaze burrowing into his back. "She's grown
into a beautiful woman."

Beautiful would not be the word he'd choose.

Stubborn. Sly. Seductive. Those were more appropriate words for her.

"As a girl, she was very pretty." His mother continued to muse in a low, thoughtful tone. "Now, though—"

"What does it matter?" He jerked himself around to meet her gaze. "She'll be gone before too long."

A dark brow, much like his, rose. "Is that so?"

She didn't sound approving. How could this be? More than anyone else, his mother should hold a grudge against any person with the last name of Drakos. She gazed at him now, her eyes opaque, her face no longer filled with emotion.

His temper, his frustration stoked. "The twins won't need her after they've adjusted. A few weeks at the most."

"Hmm." She brushed her hands down her silk dress, a slight frown furrowing her brows. "We'll see."

He'd thought his entire family would agree. No Drakos should be around the boys. Yet he read his mother well. She wasn't on board. She didn't agree. "Why can't you see—?"

"*Mana.*" His sister, Rhachel, burst into the room, her face flushed with excitement. "The food is ready."

"I'm also sure your uncles are hungry." Nephele laughed as she rose. "I will go—"

"Wait." He needed to make this clear, didn't he? He needed to make sure his *mitéra* wanted Tamsin gone from here as soon as possible.

His mother swung around to stare at him, her dark gaze keen and wise. The look shook him deep inside, where he never ventured to go.

Not anymore.

Not since he'd managed to patch his family together in the best way he could.

Immediately after his father's death, his *mitéra's* eyes had grown dim and distant. For a long time. He'd worried for endless hours. He'd worked hard to pay the bills and to give her luxury and stability, if not the love of her husband. Over time, her dark eyes had cleared, the pain and sorrow washed away by the life he managed to give her.

His sisters had done their part during the years, too. Marrying good men, having babies, staying with his mother as she nursed her grief. Even now, ten years later, none of them had left Nephele. The villa had become a compound: Rhachel and her family on one side of the vast garden, in a home he'd built for them, Rhouth on the other side of the pool cabana, settled nicely in another house.

And Rafe himself. Never straying far. Always coming home to make sure his mother's eyes were no longer dead. *Nai,* he had his house in Sparti, yet he never spent more than a long weekend there.

"Raphael?" The dark eyes of his mother never left his face. "Did you have something to say?"

The bitter words clutched in his throat.

We need Tamsin to feel unwanted, unneeded here.

We need her to leave.

I need her gone before...

He opened his mouth—

"Raphael." His youngest sister barreled into the room and ran over, throwing her arms around him in a tight hug. "How wonderful you are."

He didn't feel wonderful. He felt tortured and angry and frustrated. He'd thought this would be easy. He'd thought his family would drive Tamsin out of the boys' life. Out of his life. However, if his mother wasn't in agreement, then what the hell was he going to do?

Rhouth lifted her head and gave him a wide smile. Her amber eyes twinkled with happiness. "Isaák and Aarōn are a gift to us. A gift from Ben."

Not Ben. Ben hadn't raised them to be the boys they were: smart, well-behaved, stable. The person who'd done this, given this gift was—

"Tamsin." His youngest sister spat the word out, her face turning dark with disgust. "Tamsin is the only problem."

The bitter words clutching in his throat sank into the pit of his stomach, making him sick. Not because he hadn't said them but because he knew, suddenly, he didn't believe them. God help him, he didn't want her to leave, he wanted her—

"We'll get rid of her." Rhouth hugged him once more, a tight strangle of raging emotion. "Don't worry."

"Rhouth." His mother sighed.

"You know I'm right, *Mana*." She dropped her arms and turned to meet Nephele and Rhachel's skeptical gazes. "We've talked about this since we knew they were coming."

"You talked," Rhachel inserted. "We listened."

Tension vibrated from his youngest sister's thin body. "I thought you agreed."

"I think the boys need their sister. There's obviously a bond there." His mother's quiet voice slid above the simmering conflict.

Her words sank into him, the truth in them too clear and pointed to ignore. When he'd decided to take Tamsin with them to Greece, he'd convinced himself it was only because his solicitors had counseled him to do this. They'd advised it would be extremely difficult to radically change the boys' guardianship so quickly. Better to pretend to work with her, cajole her with the perks money could buy, lull her into a false sense of security. Then, when the timing was right, only then would he drive her away.

But now?

Now he knew better. What he'd tried to push back before, hit him with stark clarity. Pulling her apart from the boys now or for the near future would damage them.

And he wasn't going to do it.

"Tell me you have a plan to get rid of her." Rhouth rounded on him, her expression intense. "Tell me, Rafe, you'll get rid of her."

Her passionate fervor struck him. "Why do you care so much? She's merely the boys' sister. So what if she stays for a while?"

His mother let out a soft breath.

"Why do I care?" His sister's spine went rigid. "After what she did to you?"

"Ten years ago." The realization hit him that the fierce anger he'd held so tightly to when he'd first confronted Tamsin at the rundown hotel and morphed into...into... "A long time to hold a grudge."

His *mitéra* made a low sound in her throat, and he pivoted to stare at her. Her face was devoid of emotion, yet something in her eyes moved. Something that tweaked him inside.

"What she did changed you, Raphael." His youngest sister continued, relentless. "Not for the better either—"

"Now, now." Nephele's quiet voice was implacable. "Enough."

"I won't forgive her." Rhouth marched to the fireplace and stared at the cold logs waiting for a match. "I don't care how many letters I got from her."

He jerked his gaze from his mother and stared at his sister. "Letters?"

The sleek twirl of her dark hair bobbed as she shook her head. "Never mind."

He shouldn't mind or care. "She sent you letters?"

"Not many." She turned to face his disbelief. "She stopped sending them after a few months."

"When you didn't respond," he guessed.

"Of course I didn't respond." Her mouth moued with remembered anger. "She'd broken your heart."

No man wanted to hear those words spoken about him, even if they were true. Which, in this case, they were not. "Stop with the girlish imaginations," he scoffed. "I barely remember Tamsin."

"That's not true—"

"Then there should be no problem in welcoming her to the family for an extended stay." Nephele walked over and slipped her hand under his arm. "It's time we go and greet the family and begin the meal."

"The first meal with Isaák and Aarōn." Rhachel's face creased with a wide smile.

"And Tamsin," his mother added.

Rafe frowned at her, knowing she'd detected what he'd tried so hard to conceal. Her dark eyes didn't tell him what she thought about the turmoil roiling inside his gut. But he knew enough to know his *mitéra* wasn't going to allow anyone in this family to drive Tamsin away.

Other than himself.

The bedroom had new wallpaper.

The change didn't do much to stop the slide into ten-year-old memories.

Tamsin plopped onto the bed. She smoothed her hand across the misty-blue coverlet. The same. She scowled at the cream bedding with the golden-filigree edge. The same. She tried to focus on the blue-sprigged wallpaper that had replaced the plain, painted walls she remembered. There wasn't enough difference to stop the painful recollections.

She forced herself to look.

Look over at the far end of the bedroom. Past the antique chestnut armoire and dresser. Past the pretty vanity table and the pillowed stool where she'd perched as a sixteen-year-old gazing at her flushed cheeks in the mirror. Past all of it to the window.

The same misty-blue cushion on the window seat she remembered.

The same window seat she'd sat on when she'd stared at the stars and dreamed her silly, girlish dreams. The same seat where she'd peered down right into a pair of dark eyes laughing up at her.

The same window seat where she'd lost her heart once and for all.

Restless, she surged off the bed and walked to the low oak table where the servant had put her suitcase. After the chilly reception on the front steps, Tam had expected to be led to the farthest, tiniest bedroom. Instead, the servant had graciously ushered her into this beautiful bedroom filled with painful memories.

She flipped open the lid and inspected her pile of cheap clothing. If she wasn't mistaken, Nephele and her daughters had all been wearing couture. They were supposed to wash and dress for dinner, but she knew nothing in this suitcase was going to compete with anything worn by the other women downstairs.

She slammed the suitcase shut. So what? So they'd just have to deal with Tamsin Drakos as she was. Simple green cotton dress and plain leather sandals.

"Tam!" Isaák threw open the bedroom door, a big grin on his face.

"You're supposed to knock—"

"You won't believe how big our bedroom is." He stuttered to a stop and took a look around. "Wow! Yours is even bigger."

"Surprise, surprise." She was suddenly tired of trying to keep it together. Tired of trying to keep a stiff upper lip. Tired of always being a Goody Two-shoes painted as some kind of villain.

Aarōn popped his head around his twin. "What's wrong, Tammy?"

I don't want to be here where I'm not wanted.

I don't want to know Rafe as he is now.

I want to go back to our old life.

"Nothing." She paced to the vanity and bent down to look in the mirror. Her hair had fallen out of the twist she'd stuck it in earlier this morning in oh-so-distant London.

So what? She didn't care.

"There's something wrong." Isaák edged into the room as if tiptoeing toward an explosive. "I can tell."

She rounded on her brothers, ignoring their wide, surprised eyes. True, she rarely lost her cool...actually, she never lost her cool with the boys, but at this moment? She didn't care. "Did you wash?"

"Yeeesss." Aarōn stood in the doorway, a frown on his face.

"Then let's go." She marched past Isaák and nearly stomped on his brother before he quickly stepped aside. "Your family is waiting for us."

The twins silently walked behind her as she stalked along the carpeted hallway. She ignored the new paintings on the walls. She ignored the gleam of satiny wood on the antique tables lining the hallway. And she absolutely ignored the rich scent of the white lilies blossoming in ivory bowls on the glossy tops.

She turned the corner and glared at the wide carpeted stairs. The sound of laughter echoed up from the downstairs like a taunt.

"They are your family now, too, Tam," Isaák said softly.

No. They aren't.

The words trembled on her tongue, yet a last vestige of protectiveness stopped her from saying them. The boys couldn't do anything about what the Vounós thought of Tamsin Drakos. Plus, she'd promised Rafe she wouldn't interfere with their connection to this family.

She was stuck. And flying apart.

Aarōn came to stand right beside her. "Tam." His expression shone with resolve, as if he had heard the words she couldn't force out. "Don't worry. We're always going to be your family."

She fought back the tears. She knew she had the boys' loyalty, but if she insisted on keeping it, she very much feared she'd tear them in two. "Come on." Her voice wavered and to cover it, she coughed. "Let's go and eat."

Both boys frowned as if they were about to object or argue or press the point, still, she couldn't do this right now. She had to have a moment to figure out what she was going to do, how she was going to hang on to the twins without hurting them. She turned away and started down the steps.

"Finally." The one word, spoken in an accented, male voice made her head pop up from the contemplation of the carpet. Rafe stood at the bottom of the stairs. He'd changed into a white cotton shirt and tan chinos. The shirt clung to his broad shoulders and he'd rolled the sleeves up to show muscled forearms.

A frizz of unwanted lust stripped any words from her mouth.

"Rafe!" Isaák bounded down the stairs, all thoughts of grumpy sisters clearly left behind. "Our room is brilliant."

"Good." A long-fingered hand landed on the boy's shoulder in a firm grip. "I'm glad you're happy."

"I'd be happier if I didn't have to share it with the idiot." Aarōn stayed by her side.

"Here we go again," Rafe said, but his eyes lit with humor.

From the corner of her eye, Tam saw the twitch of Aarōn's mouth. Before she could say or do anything to stop this growing connection or even figure out if she wanted to, he'd bounced down the stairs to stand by his uncle too.

"I guess it's okay," Aarōn admitted with a shrug.

"I'm hungry," his brother announced.

"Then it's a good thing your *giagiá* has produced quite a spread." Rafe patted his other nephew on the shoulder. "The tables have been set outside. Why don't you go out and see."

Her brothers dashed through the open terrace doors, leaving a cool silence behind.

He glanced up, his gaze giving nothing away. "Do you like your room?"

Did he know what room his mother had put her? Did he remember or care?

"It's fine."

"Fine." He rolled the word around his mouth, sarcasm edging it.

Anger surged once more. "I said it was fine and it is."

"I'm glad we could accommodate you to your liking." The sarcasm was now ladled onto his sentence.

"But not for long, right?" she spat out, her anger boiling inside.

His eyes widened. Yet before he could tell her what she already knew, his mother smoothly interjected. "Is there a problem?"

Her son swung around. "Not with me. However, Tam—"

"Ah." Nephele raised her head to meet Tamsin's glower. "Please. Come and eat with the family."

This woman was nothing other than kind and genteel. There wasn't an ounce of anger or distrust in her dark eyes. But everything in her rebelled. She wanted to strike out. She wanted to hurt someone like she hurt. She wanted to hit.

Him.

"Come, Tamsin," the woman's calm voice continued. "Come join the family."

CHAPTER ELEVEN

*S*he had to get a job.

Tamsin rolled off the bed. The last two days searching for a job had been fruitless, but she couldn't back down. Sitting in the middle of the entire Vounó clan the night of their arrival, it had become very clear.

She wasn't wanted.

A quiet puff of air escaped her lips. Okay, that wasn't entirely true. Nephele had been everything gracious. Rhachel had greeted her warmly. A smattering of aunts had chatted to her about the boys.

But Rhouth, her old best friend, had pointedly ignored her, even in the face of a whispered rebuke from her mother.

Rafe had ignored her, too.

Even when his mother and Rhachel had given him hard stares.

Her laughter huffed out of her mouth, a faint sound in the cool bedroom. Not only did she have to worry about forcing the boys to choose between this family and her somewhere down the line, she also was in danger of tearing the Vounó family apart.

Spending another night staring at another ceiling, she'd tried. Tried to figure out how she could possibly make this work. One overriding conclusion had sat right in the middle of her brain.

She needed a job.

A job would get her out of the family's hair. She could find a place to live. A place somewhere near for her and the twins. Aarōn and Isaák could come over anytime they wanted and she wouldn't have to darken the Vounó door ever again, forcing various family members to take a side.

A job would also give her some standing with Rafe.

She hated, just hated, being beholden to him.

So. A job.

Walking to the armoire, she pulled out the simply cut white dress with laced edges she'd worn the last two days. This wasn't the kind of dress you'd normally wear to interviews, yet it was the only thing she had that projected an air of professionalism.

Slipping the dress over her head, she tugged it in place while sliding on her sandals. The past two days had been depressing. No one seemed to be hiring and her rusty Greek hadn't helped her objective. Still, she'd find something. She had no choice.

She turned to look in the vanity mirror.

Two worried eyes stared back.

"Don't worry," she whispered to herself.

She'd find a job soon. That would give her some sense of security. She'd applied to several hotels hoping for a management job of some sort. However, if she had to, she'd take a waitressing job. Or one as a maid. Anything that gave her a toehold in Greece.

Anything that gave her some power.

Brushing her long hair back into a bun, she slapped on some mascara. She'd do. Grabbing her purse, she opened her bedroom door and slipped into the hall.

"There you are."

The woman's voice was kind and warm, but Tam stiffened in shock. She'd been sure to give everyone time to leave. Weren't they all going to tour Rafe's office before having lunch near the Acropolis?

She glanced over. "Mrs. Vounó."

"Please." The older woman gave her a gentle smile. "Call me Nephele."

Tamsin straightened. The friendly gesture offered only a checkmate in the future. If she responded in kind, at least two-thirds of this woman's children would howl a rebuke and leave this nice lady in a fix. "Um..."

"I thought we might have missed you today."

"Missed me?"

"These last two days you've disappeared right after breakfast." Nephele's steady gaze never left her own. "We haven't had a chance to reacquaint ourselves."

"Reacquaint ourselves?" Although Nephele and Rhachel had been gracious, she had assumed it was merely to preserve the peace—not any real interest in her.

"But I'm sure we'll have plenty of time on the drive in to see the office this morning." The woman walked over and patted Tamsin on the arm. "During lunch, too."

"No." She stepped back. "I can't."

"Really?" A fine brow rose and the dark eyes grew distant. "You have more old friends to visit today?"

She'd used it as an excuse. She was wary of letting any of the Vounós know what her real agenda was. Better to get a job, find a place to stay, and then make a stand for a part of the boys' life. "Yes," she muttered. "More old friends."

"Hmm." Nephele looked behind her and smiled. "Ah, here are your boys."

Your boys.

She stared at the woman. Did Nephele mean her words? Did she understand the bond? Or was the older woman merely biding her time while she drew the twins into the Vounó clan, before cutting her out once and for all?

"Tam!" Isaák hooted while he ran down the lengthy hall.

"You're coming with us today for sure." Aarōn smiled at her as he dashed behind his twin.

A great well of love washed through her at the sight of her boys. She'd missed them these past two days. Yet, beyond the fact she needed to find a job to establish some control over this situation, she'd also realized hovering around them as they got to know their new family wasn't wise. Plus, she'd promised Rafe not to do so.

"And my boy," the older woman said, a warmth, much like the warmth inside of Tam's heart, filled the words.

Rafe sauntered behind Aarōn and Isaák, his gaze pinned on his mother, ignoring Tamsin.

"Raphael." His mother greeted him with a smile as she wrapped her arms around the twins.

A wrench of bittersweet grief threatened to close Tam's throat at the sight. She'd been the only one to ever touch the twins like that. Only her. She gazed at her boys' faces. They were smiling. They were happy. They were safe with Nephele.

She should be grateful and happy for her boys. She should. She knew she should.

But she wasn't.

"Are you ready to go?" Rafe's dark gaze finally landed on her in an opaque stare.

"She says she's made plans again." His mother's voice was soft, disappoint in each word.

Real disappointment? Or fake? Tam couldn't tell.

"Come on, Tammy." Isaák pouted. "You've said the same thing for two days now."

"You can't have that many old friends," Aarōn chimed in.

Their uncle's stare turned steely and his words shot out like a command. "I believe you can forgo your friends for one day."

This arrogance was why she needed a job. "I'm afraid not."

The twins moaned. Nephele's quiet gaze never left her face.

Rafe's expression turned stony. "*Mitéra*. Could you take the boys downstairs? I would like to discuss something with Tamsin."

She curbed the impulse to run down the stairs after the departing group. Instead, she straightened and stared at the man standing before her. He wore a crisp white shirt under his dark blue suit. A red power tie cut a line down his broad chest.

"You're not visiting friends." His accusation came, tough and sure.

"No?" Her hand grasped the leather of her purse. "How do you know?"

"I had you followed."

"What?" Outrage blended with her now familiar anger at him. "You have no right."

He stuck his hands in his pockets in a sharp jerk. "For all I knew, you could have been meeting with Haimon."

"Haimon?" Gaping at him, she waved the accusation away with a snap. "He's sick. He's surely still in London."

"Who knows?" He shrugged, the linen cloth of his suit clinging to the broad length of his shoulders. "What's important was I had to find out what you were doing."

"It's none of your business."

"Why are you searching for a job?" He stared at her, the edges of his mouth grim.

Her hand tightened on the purse's leather handle. "How do you know that's what I've been doing?"

"Don't try and lie." His black eyes went flat. "You visited a total of ten hotels in the past two days."

"You really have been watching me." She should have thought about this. She should have realized Raphael Vounó would think nothing of invading her privacy.

For years, she'd never been questioned about what she was doing or where she was going. Sometimes she'd wondered what it would be like to have someone lovingly care about her daily agenda. Yet this, this wasn't loving. This was all about control.

"Answer the question, Tamsin."

"I don't have to." She made to walk past him, but he caught her arm at the elbow. The contact sizzled across her skin and flushed her cheeks.

He stilled. Then dropped his hand. "Don't be a child," he growled.

"That's precisely why I'm searching for a job." Why not tell him? He'd figured it out anyway. "Because I'm an adult."

A frustrated frown crossed his brow. "You don't need a job."

"Yes, I do."

"You've got everything you could want here." His hand lifted, waving at the riches surrounding them.

"I don't belong here." Swiveling away from him, she started walking down the hallway. "I need some independence."

She felt him behind her, a looming, disgruntled presence.

Worry, mixed with anger, zigzagged inside her.

Rafe was rich and clearly powerful. She didn't think he had any connections with the hotel industry. Still, if he didn't want her to get a job, was it possible he could get her blackballed?

Stopping at the top of the stairs, she turned to confront him. "Don't you dare stand in my way."

"What?" Pure puzzlement crossed his features.

"Don't go throwing your weight around with friends so no one will hire me."

Puzzlement turned to shock. "I wouldn't do that."

"You would." She took a first step down. "I'm sure you would."

"Are you also sure, *kardiá mou*," his voice lilted with sudden amusement, "that I know every hotelier in Athens?"

Ignoring him and his humor, she stomped down the last of the stairs. The hallway was filled with a bevy of laughing children, scolding mamas and aunts, and Nephele and the twins. All of them turned quiet as they watched her and Rafe approach.

"*Mitéra.*" His voice came from behind her, the amusement still curling on the edges of the words. "I find myself unable to convince Tamsin to join us today."

At the look of disappointment on Nephele's face, Tam rushed in. "I'm very sorry—"

"She's insisting on getting a job," he continued.

"A job?" His mother's expression filled with astonishment. "Why would she need a job?"

"Apparently, she doesn't like our hospitality." The words came off as teasing, yet this couldn't be true, could it? The Rafe she knew now didn't have a teasing bone in his rigid body. There had to be an ugly intent. She became sure of it when she watched the effect his statement had on his family. They didn't see the joke at all.

The silence after his words went hostile immediately.

"No, that's not exactly..." She stumbled to a halt.

Rafe walked to her side. She felt his heat along her body and took in a deep breath. Which made it all worse when the smell of him—heated chocolate, sweet and spice—filled her lungs.

"Come on, Tam." Aarōn gave her a worried frown. "You don't need a job."

"I do," she said. "I really do."

The silence deepened. She glanced around and met a fleet of flinty glares.

Her gaze stopped at Nephele, who was staring at her son. A smile flashed across her face. "Stop your teasing, *gios mou.*"

The silence changed in an instant from hostile to confused.

And then amused.

"What would a girl want with a job when she has all this?" One of the aunts tutted. "Foolishness."

"Raphael is always teasing." Another aunt smiled at him and wagged her finger.

Always teasing? This man who'd been filled with barely contained rage from the moment she'd seen him again—this man teased? Tam looked over and met two dancing black eyes.

A sudden shot of memory tore through her. These same eyes years ago, looking up at her from the garden. His teasing words that made her laugh as he laughed with her.

"Come on, Tamsin." His voice was low and quiet, but the slightest whiff of long ago tease clung to his plea. "Come with us."

Eláte.

The oh-so-familiar entreaty echoed from her past, pulling her into a present she knew she should fight. Fight for her independence. Fight any lingering hope there was any of the old Rafe in this new one standing before her.

Straightening, she pushed herself to fight.

Something moved in his eyes, something alive with memories and yet also full of new promise. The something clutched in her throat and made every promise she'd made to herself inconsequential.

"Okay." The word pushed through her turmoil.

His eyes blazed.

With what? Triumph at the fact he'd stopped her from establishing her independence? Or happiness she was coming with him?

He turned before she could figure it out. "She's coming with us after all."

Rhachel laughed. "Not only is Rafe the ultimate tease, he's able to charm anyone into doing what he wants them to do."

A flush of mortification heated her skin. Charm? It hadn't been charm choking her throat. It had been old stupid memories and wishes. Ones she should have ignored. "Wait. I think—"

"That's great." Isaák bounced around her, a big grin on his face. "Rafe says his office is ultra cool."

"We've missed you." Aarōn mouth twisted, the admission clearly disturbing to his teenage masculinity.

The words stopped her from fighting any further. What did it matter if she took this one day off from hunting for the elusive job? The boys were still in a new world and needed her.

"I've missed you guys too." She patted Aarōn's shoulder. Isaák threw his arm around her waist as his twin leaned in to give her a quick kiss on her cheek. For a moment, she basked in their certain love, a smile coming to her face.

She dared a peek above their heads and met two dark eyes that no longer danced or blazed. That something moved again in the black. The something she couldn't put a name to and yet it touched her just as powerfully as the love for her boys did.

"This is so cool." Isaák's excited voice echoed in the long, brightly lit hallway.

The office *was* cool. The air-conditioning wafted across Tamsin's skin, making her shiver.

"We need to keep this area chilly," Rafe had said moments ago as he'd ushered the twins, his mother and sister and Tam into the medical section. "This is where we run various experiments that react poorly to heat."

She peered into one room, stunned again at the high-tech machinery and white coated scientists peering into microscopes and busily typing into wide-screened computers. Everything gleamed with icy superiority. Whitewashed walls curved above them as they kept walking up and up the slanted walkway. She felt as if she were hiking into a space tube.

"So what are they doing here?" Aarōn stared into a particularly large room staffed with a dozen people.

Rafe stopped his march with an abrupt jerk. He'd wanted to show all of them his work. He'd been clear about that and almost seemed excited about the outing. His mother and sister had admitted they hadn't been to his new facility and were glad to take the time to go on the tour with the boys and herself. But ever since they'd tumbled into the limo—the twins, his mother, Rhachel, and Tamsin herself—he'd grown quiet.

Why?

Tam watched as he turned and moved slowly to Aarōn's side. Now that she had a second to analyze this outing so far, it had seemed as if he marched through his building like he wanted to finish the tour in less than five minutes.

Why?

"They are testing a new product I'm thinking of investing in." Rafe's voice was as cool as the air around them.

"What's the product?" Isaák piped in.

"A microscopic enzyme that can be injected into cancer patients." Finally, for the first time since they'd left his home, the edge of Rafe's mouth lifted in a smile. "It's used with a neuron-electronic device that we're also testing."

Aarōn cocked his head, disbelief crossing his face. "An injection? Like a shot?"

"I hate shots." His brother frowned.

"You'd want this shot if you had cancer." Their uncle's smile turned into a grimace. "At least, I believe you would. We still have to run more tests."

"I don't get it."

Rafe stared at his eldest nephew. "If the tests come back the way I hope, it will show these microscopic enzymes will kill the cancer. No need for surgery or radiation or chemotherapy."

"Wow!"

The man kept his eyes on Aarōn even though Isaák had started dancing around his uncle in excitement. "We're not sure it works, but if it does, we'll buy the patent."

Aarōn nodded. "And make a ton of money."

"Also help many, many people." Nephele's quiet voice insinuated into the conversation.

A look of frustration shot across her son's face. "*Nai, Mitéra.*"

Yet the undercurrent beneath his short agreement was rejection. This was an old disagreement, Tamsin could tell. Not by anything Nephele did. The woman gazed at her son with a faint smile, her eyes mild, her stance soft and accepting. However, Rafe's whole attitude screamed dismissal and repudiation.

Why? Why would he object to helping people when his entire being had been about helping anything and anyone years ago?

"It must take a bunch of money to run this place." Aarōn tapped his fingers on the glass separating them from the medical scientists. "Tons."

"*Nai.*" Rafe crossed his arms and tapped a finger on his dark suit.

"Where'd you get it?"

His uncle's mouth tightened. "When my father died—"

Nephele took a quick breath and her daughter stepped close to her side, slipping a hand into hers.

Her son stopped and frowned, but when his mother nodded her head, he kept talking. "There wasn't much left."

"Yeah?" Aarōn, with typical teenage obliviousness, only wanted the story.

Tam felt the vibrations of pain coming from Nephele and Rhachel. "Aarōn, it's not our business—"

"Actually, it is." Rafe cut through her words, his dark scowl stopping any further protest bubbling in her throat. "The boys need to know the past so they can prepare for the future."

"A future here?" Isaák's black eyes widened.

"If you wish." Leaning on the glass wall, the uncle gazed at his two instantly amazed nephews.

"Like..." Aarōn glanced back at the scientists. "Like we could run this place?"

"Raphael." Nephele stepped in. "Tell them the past before talking about the future."

Her son stared at her. "You are sure you can take this, *Mitéra*?"

"I'm sure."

Rhachel tightened her grasp on her mother's hand and nodded.

Rafe straightened, his gaze flashing back to Aarōn and Isaák. "After my father died, there wasn't much left."

The grief edging his words filled Tam's throat with tears. The boys looked at each other before focusing again on their uncle.

"But I found a small fund apart from the family's finances." His mouth twisted. "The finances that had crumbled into dust."

"A fund?" Aarōn's question was quiet but insistent.

"Money in only my name." Rafe ran a hand across his mouth before palming the glass wall, a slight tap of one finger plunking a soft sound into the hushed silence.

My money. My gift to my love.

She let out a short, harsh gasp.

Everyone turned to stare at her.

"Are you alright, Tamsin?" Nephele inquired, a worried expression replacing the stoic one she'd held as her son had told his tale.

"Tammy?" Isaák moved to her side and took her hand.

"I'm fine," she managed to choke out.

Rafe gave her one of his opaque glances before continuing. "No one knew where it came from, but it couldn't be confiscated by my father's creditors."

"The money was yours," Tam whispered before she could help herself.

"*Nai.*" He leaned on the wall again; his body relaxed, his eyes hard and sharp. "I used it to start this company."

"And saved the family home," his sister stated with pride.

"And saved us." Resolve shone in his mother's eyes. "Yet, did it save you, Raphael?"

The query shot out, soft and deadly at the same time. Her son shot back a frown of more than frustration. A look of anger and annoyance. A look of simmering resentment.

"A question," he said, a hard layer of wrath in his tone, "that is meaningless."

A sudden rush of tears threatened to wash Tam away. Before she could betray her emotions, she jerked around and walked down the hallway.

"Tam?" Isaák's voice followed her.

"Bathroom." She flung over her shoulder.

Conveniently, she saw one a dozen steps later. She pushed the door open and sighed with relief when she found it empty. Swiping some tissues off the sink stand, she stared into the mirror.

This place was amazing. A sleek, well-organized machine whirring in ideal order, in impeccable synchronization. The business was a testament to the tenacious will and steely determination of its owner. Yet in the last few minutes, she'd seen so clearly, knew so surely, this wasn't what he should be doing. The owner didn't belong here.

Her money was the foundation for this fabulously wealthy company.

And it appeared her money had trapped Rafe into a life he wasn't meant to live.

CHAPTER TWELVE

"*Y*ou won't have to worry about school clothes." His sister's voice was filled with sugary spite. Rhouth was at it again. "We'll take care of that for the boys."

Rafe sliced into the leg of lamb, breathing in the familiar spices of garlic and rosemary. He ignored the hush spreading across the family dinner table. It wasn't his job to protect Tamsin.

"Rhouth," his *mitéra's* voice came, cool and calm. "Please pass the *patates*."

He knew if he glanced over he would see only serenity on his mother's face. She would ignore his sister's attacks until she didn't. During the last week and a half, ever since they'd arrived at the family villa, he'd

seen it time after time. Nephele always came to the rescue and somehow kept smoothing over any potential
minefields his sister tried to plant.

He merely had to wait.

He sliced another piece of meat.

"After all, you won't be here when the time comes."
Rhouth had always been a child who could do more
than one thing at a time. Now as a full-grown woman,
the challenge of handing a plate across the table while
continuing the attack was not a problem for her in the
least.

"What do you mean?" Aarōn's sharp tone cut
through the last murmur of conversation coming from
the end of the table. His two aunts and three uncles,
Rhachel and her husband, all the children scattered
along the long wooden table, everyone stopped. The
hush went to silence. "Tamsin's not going anywhere."

He stared at his nephew. Since arriving in Greece,
this was the first time either of the twins had lifted the
gallant sword to defend their sister. He was quite sure
this was because she'd warned them. He had caught
several frowns and heard various quiet whispers from
her to confirm his suspicions. But it appeared as if this
time, her warnings were going to go unheeded.

Tamsin had plenty of protectors. Even if she didn't
want them.

"Aarōn." Her face carried a slight flush, making her
porcelain skin glow in the flame of the sturdy candles

lining the middle of the table like a spine. "There's nothing to worry about."

Frowning at his meal, Rafe had to give her credit. Not that he wanted to, yet he had to. She'd done precisely what she'd promised. She could have easily used Rhouth's continued attacks to sow resentment into the boys. Easing the twins into this family, into a new way of life, could have been a golden opportunity to not only alienate them, but cause friction and tear the Vounó family apart. Instead, she'd smoothed the way, made sure Aarōn and Isaák had plenty of time with their grandmother and cousins. Made sure they found their new life full of hope and happiness.

"So true," Rhouth said. "There's absolutely nothing to worry about for you boys..."

Her voice trailed off, leaving a very big *but* lingering unsaid at the end.

His mother didn't step in with a cool command or a change of subject. Instead, for some irritating reason, she said nothing.

Rafe looked down the table again.

Aarōn and Isaák were both glaring at him.

He slanted a look at his mother. She and Rhachel were staring at their meals as if their food had suddenly turned to gold.

"Rafe." His other sister, the one who would not let things be, his other sister demanded his attention.

"*Nai*, Rhouth?" He finally glanced her way.

Her amber eyes were alive with fevered hate. It was as if the presence of her ex-best friend during the last eleven days had steadily stoked the fire of her antagonism instead of dousing it.

And it should have been doused. Tamsin willingly shared the boys. She'd gone out of her way to be friendly with the rest of the family. True, she'd spent most of her days away, searching for a damned job. But when she was around, she was always charming and cordial.

Exactly as she'd been as a young girl.

The memories threatened to swamp him, just as they'd done for days on end. Watching Tamsin interact with his family had brought back the good memories he'd determinedly buried so long ago.

"Tell them, Rafe." Rhouth's expression beamed with heated delight. "It's really time to tell them, isn't it?"

No, it was not time to tell the boys their beloved half-sister was going to take a flight back to London in the near future. True, this had been his original plan. A plan he hadn't shared with Rhouth. Still, his sister was...his sister. She'd always been able to read his mind.

Yet it was a plan he'd discarded.

"Tell us what?" Aarōn's voice was no longer sharp, it was angry.

Rafe scowled at his mother. She gazed back. Her face smooth and sedate, her countenance placid, but also pointed.

She wasn't going to step in this time.

"Aarōn. This isn't the time to have this discussion." Tam's voice was insistent.

"What discussion?" Isaák frowned. "I don't understand what this is all about."

"Rhachel." Rafe spooned the last of the garbanzo bean and chard salad onto his knife. "Why don't you tell the family about Filip's recent triumph in football."

His sister's oldest child, even at eight, was a rising athletic star, and his mother was his most enthusiastic fan. After shooting him a quick look, Rhachel launched into a recital of the last game.

He leaned back in the padded oak chair. Pretending to listen to his sister, he watched Tamsin as she whispered into Isaák's ear. The boy's frown eased off his face and he chuckled at something she said.

A peacemaker. Just like his mother.

Yet not like his mother at all.

From beneath his lashes, he let his gaze slip down. Tamsin wore a simple white cotton blouse of a dress. Classic, crisply contained. The night air had blown the edge open, though, leaving behind a glimpse of delicate collarbone and pearly skin.

The beginning of cleavage.

The lust flamed, unwanted. He'd managed to contain any thoughts of her kiss or her scent or her touch by focusing on the boys and his relatives during the last eleven days. The most important thing was to bind this family together. Still, the lust for her was always there, lurking inside, clutching at his groin when he least expected it.

The time when he'd literally run into her as she came out of her bedroom and felt the plush weight of her breast on his arm.

The time when he'd caught her laughing with the boys as they ran across the green lawn, her face alive with love.

The time he'd heard her slurred, lilting voice while she talked with his mother about the twins.

"There's no doubt," Rhouth's excited voice cut through his thoughts. "Filip will be a superstar."

His other sister laughed as she leaned over to cover her son's red ears. "Not in front of him, please. He already has a big enough ego."

"Not as big as his uncle's, so there's still room to grow." Fydor, Rhachel's husband, shot him a quick grin. An aunt twittered while an uncle guffawed. The last lingering tension eased out of the gathering.

He loved his family. Every one of them. Even Rhouth at her most irritating. Even Fydor at his most obnoxious. Yet, all at once, he wanted to leave, run from the expectations surrounding him. The assumptions laid upon him during the past ten years. He wanted to leap from his chair at the head of the table and escape to his home in Sparti.

Taking only the boys.

And Tamsin.

The knowledge sifted inside. The spike of yearning was so sharp, he took in a deep breath, almost a gasp.

An echoed breath reached him. He turned to find Tamsin staring at him. Her green eyes were dark, mysterious pools in the candlelight. Behind the mystery he thought he saw concern and compassion.

He didn't need her concern or compassion.

He only needed her under him. For one time. To stop this need building inside him for something more than sex. Something beyond the joining of his body with hers.

"Rafe." Rhouth's voice grated on his hyper-sensitive nerves.

"*Nai?*" He forced himself to glance away from the woman he lusted for and into amber eyes blazing with anger.

Rhouth had seen. Seen him gazing at Tamsin. Seen something he refused to define.

"You're going to work tomorrow, right?"

He scowled. What was this? This almost *demand* from his sister? True, he'd spent less time at work than usual. Other than the one day he'd taken the boys and

Tamsin to see his office, he'd only spent one other day there. But he was always in contact with his staff. "Why do you ask?"

His youngest sister flashed a glare at her ex-best friend. As if Tamsin had anything to do with his work.

A clutch of remembered emotion coiled in his stomach. The memory of her curious questions, the way she'd taken in his business, his creation. How she'd examined each room and examined him as he talked. The way she'd looked at him before she'd walked away toward the bathroom.

As if...as if...he'd failed.

Anger surged and behind it, much to Rafe's disgust, swelled bewilderment and hurt.

"Because it's clear the boys have settled in here." Rhouth kept glaring. "They don't need you around all the time. They have us."

A howl of denial swelled in his throat. With one swift slice, his plan to leave the twins in his mother's and sisters' care while he went back to the business collapsed. "No."

Rhouth jerked back in her chair. "What do you mean? You said yourself this was the plan."

"Not anymore." He looked at the boys and their sister. "We're going to Sparti."

An aunt murmured into her napkin. An uncle coughed.

"What do you mean, Raphael?" His mother smoothed a hand along the table edge, the flash of her marriage diamond sparkling in the light.

"We?" Rhachel bent forward, her expression filled with curiosity. "Are we finally getting an invitation to this place of yours?"

"I'm sorry, Rhach. Not this time." He took another deep breath and plunged. "I want Aarōn and Isaák to come. And Tamsin."

"No." The heated word shot from Rhouth's mouth.

"No." At the exact same time, the same word came from his green-eyed tormentor sitting across the table from him.

The hot pain of rejection jerked him upright. Not his sister's.

Tamsin's.

"The boys are going to Sparti with me," he said to her, the words cold and clipped. "You can come or not."

"But...but..." She grimaced. "I accepted a job today."

"Woot!" Aarōn leapt from his chair and hugged her. "I knew you could do it."

Rafe didn't want her to have a job. He wanted her to depend on him. He wanted her to have no way to be independent. He wanted her—

"Well, this is wonderful news." Nephele beamed her smile across the table. "Tell us, what is the job?"

"An assistant manager. He said, the manager, he said I have possibilities." She stuttered to a stop when she met Rafe's glare. "So I'll start as an assistant manager of a hotel for now."

Possibilities. He'd lay a bet on what kind of possibilities the man was talking about. He'd continued to have her followed. The fear of her meeting Haimon had subsided, yet she was still under his protection and Athens was not a particularly safe city. However, somehow, his security had not heard about this job offer.

"That's fantastic, Tammy." Isaák gave her a grin. "I know how much you wanted this."

"Fantastic," Rafe inserted. "But fruitless."

She gazed at him, her eyes troubled.

"The boys and I are going to Sparti," he continued. "Are you?"

Tamsin wrapped a hand around her wrist and squeezed. The dull pain did nothing to alleviate the sharp pain in her heart.

The house stood right where they had planned.

"This place isn't as big as your other house," Aarōn said as he rolled down the limo window to get a better look.

"I like it more." Isaák leaned forward, his head tilted in contemplation. "It's got a nicer atmosphere."

"Idiot." His brother snorted. "What do you know about atmosphere?"

The crunch of wheels on gravel echoed in Tam's head as the car turned into the short driveway leading to the limestone house. Well, actually it was a castle. A miniature castle with a tower at one end.

Exactly like she'd described to her love years ago.

"What I mean," Isaák grumbled. "Is that it's way cooler."

"It's not hot?" His twin grinned at him.

His brother responded with a punch.

"Boys." Tam turned away from the house of her dreams to focus on her brothers. This was why she was here. Isaák and Aarōn. She was not here to moon about a house she had nothing to do with or obsess over why he built this house, this house they'd dreamed of together.

The limo stopped at the simple stone steps leading up to the wooden door, painted a burnt red color.

Exactly as she'd described.

The vehicle's door opened and the twins tumbled out, as if they'd been released from a cage. They scrambled down the graveled lane running around to the back of the house, whooping and hollering.

"Hey, you guys," she called.

"Let them be." Rafe eased back in the leathered seat. "They need to let off some steam after the two-hour drive. They're completely safe here."

The driver looked in and saw something. Maybe he noticed the tense *atmosphere* the boys had missed as they drove toward Sparti. Or perhaps he saw the way her hands were twisting in her lap. Or it could have been he caught the shine of tears in her eyes. Whatever the reason, the driver abruptly turned and walked away, leaving only the quiet sound of the wind filling the silence.

She breathed in, trying to stuff every one of her emotions and questions down. The scent of oranges filled her nostrils and it hit her—he must have planted an orange grove somewhere near.

Precisely as they'd planned.

"Why?" she blurted before she could stop herself.

His long finger tapped once on his jeans-clad knee. His dark gaze was trained on her face, but gave her nothing. "Why?"

"This." She gestured toward the house. "This house is exactly—"

"Exactly." Before she could respond, he got out of the car and stood. "Why don't you come in and see."

He acted so blasé. He acted as if the fact he'd replicated her every word about her dream house was only a coincidence, nothing to comment on. Yet it couldn't be so, could it?

Tam squeezed her eyes shut, trying to understand.

He'd taken her here once, mere weeks before she'd split with him. To the land of his ancestors, he'd told her. The land where his grandfather had once grown olives and grapes. They'd hiked Mount Taygetus, up past the tree line. She needed to see everything, he'd told her as she strode beside him.

Coming to the crest, they'd gazed down at the valley. Down at the entire town of Sparti. That's when he'd laid out the blanket and they'd eaten their picnic. And he'd told her all of his plans. All of his hopes and dreams and passions. All of it wrapped around her.

"*Eláte.*" His voice came through her memories, from the past into the present.

She'd come with him through all of it, he'd stated. She'd be with him as he trained to be a doctor. She'd move with him to this town to start a practice. He wanted the small-town life, he'd said. He wanted her by his side. He wanted her to have his children.

"Tamsin?" A hint of impatience was now in his voice.

Tam opened her eyes to find, once again, a long-fingered hand in front of her. Just as before, she reached out and slipped her hand into his.

He pulled her into the Greek sunshine. Up here, in the foothills of the mountain, the air was cooler than down in the valley. However, it had been even hotter

when they'd left Athens. When they'd left the rest of
the Vounó clan. Well, almost every one of them.

Nephele had smiled and hugged each one of them including Tamsin. Rhachel had laughed as she ruffled the
twins' hair. The aunts and uncles and cousins had tutted and chuckled around them.

Rhouth had been absent. Along with her husband
and children.

That had hurt. Not for the rejection of her, she'd
come to expect this, but that it had hurt Rafe and so, it
had hurt her. Tam had noticed his frequent glances
toward Rhouth's house and how he'd grimaced at the
end of the farewell. Without meaning to, her arrival
had caused a rift in the family. Even when this was the
last thing she wanted to do.

"Come on." He tugged at her hand now, his mouth
no longer firm and tight. She wouldn't say he smiled,
but there was an ease about him. Almost an eagerness.

To show her this dream house? Why?

She followed him to the simple stairs. Dropping her
hand, he slid a key out of his pocket. An old-fashioned
iron key some long ago prince would have used to open
a fairy-tale castle.

"No security?"

He glanced at her as he slid the key into the door.
"On the perimeters. Not here."

Gazing back down the lane, she didn't notice any guards or elaborate fencing. Who knew though? She was certainly not an expert on security.

The bright-red door opened and he stepped back. "Welcome." He waved her in, his eyes still opaque and telling her nothing.

Tam tiptoed into the foyer. The open floor plan was precisely as she'd described to him that long ago day on the top of the mountain. An arch of cypress wood led into the family room. Floor to ceiling doors with white cotton drapes framed a terrace leading to the pool. Wicker chairs with cream padding mixed in with antique wooden tables laden with candles and books.

Her throat filled with tears.

Rafe sauntered into the main room, as if nothing monumental was happening. As if there was no significance in the fact that this house was her house. "The kitchen is to the left. The bedrooms are to the right."

"I know," she said to his back.

The muscles on his shoulders went taut. Why? He had to know. He had to remember.

"Aarōn will be glad to know he doesn't have to share a room with his brother." Padding to the first terrace door, he opened it. The floor-length, wispy curtains lifted in the slight breeze.

Tam forced herself to walk across to the fireplace. The red-brick hearth glowed rich in contrast to the background of whitewashed limestone. On the mantel were a smattering of pictures—Nephele holding a baby in her grasp, laughing at the camera; Rhachel and Rhouth standing by a pool, arms around each other; a picture of the entire family, sitting at the long wooden table they'd eaten at many times during the last ten days.

"Does your family come here often?"

"No." The stark word cut through the room, his voice crisp and curt. "Never."

Remembering Rhachel's comment at dinner last night, she turned to look at him. He still had that damned opaque stare. "Why not?"

He shrugged. "I like it quiet here."

Isaák popped his head around the open terrace door. "The pool is cool."

Rafe smiled, a tight smile. "Glad you like it."

"Tam, let's swim." Aarōn bumped against his brother.

She didn't want to swim in the cool pool. What she wanted to do was swim in a sea of her tears. Because she didn't understand what this meant. Confusion mixed with sorrow threatened to overwhelm her. Was he baiting her by showing her this house? Was he pressing her nose into the fact she'd walked away from her dream? Or was there something more here? Something she couldn't quite grasp? Because he wasn't gloating or sneering.

He stared at her suddenly, the opaque now gone from his eyes.

Still, she couldn't understand what replaced it. Fear? Hope?

"Your sister might be tired."

"Come on," Aarōn scoffed. "It's not even noon."

"I am tired." Exhausted. Fatigued to the bone trying to figure out this man and his mixed messages. Drained by the effort to keep these boys well, keep herself together, keep everything and everyone happy and safe.

"Then let me show you to your bedroom."

"How long are we going to be here?" Isaák's demand stopped his uncle from moving down the long hallway leading off from the family room.

Turning, he looked at the boys. "All summer."

"Woot!" Aarōn crowed.

"Wow!" Isaák jumped up and down.

"What?" She froze. "But I told my new boss I'd be able to start later this month."

"Too bad." Rafe's gaze frosted. "Call him and tell him you'll have to decline the opportunity altogether."

"Now wait a min—"

"I thought we were going to summer school," Aarōn cut in on the beginning of her tirade. "I thought we needed to learn Greek before starting school."

"You'll learn Greek from me." Propping himself on the wall, he appeared casual and nonchalant. "Much more fun."

Isaák grinned. "Do I have to call you Teach?"

His uncle chuckled. "Rafe will do."

"I can't stay here all summer." Her nails cut into her palms. "I need to work."

"Fine." He didn't even look her way. Instead, he stared out at the pool, his whole demeanor one of complete disinterest. "There will be plenty of work to do around here."

"What do you mean?"

"There is no great army of servants here." His gaze still didn't meet hers. "I only have one woman, Aspasia, who comes in once a week to clean."

"Totally diff compared to your other place," Isaák chirped.

"Correct." His uncle finally glanced at her, but gave nothing away in his expression. "So there will be plenty of work to do. Cleaning. Cooking."

A fire of anger leapt into her blood. "So you want me to be your unpaid housekeeper?"

Rafe's mouth curved into a sardonic smile. "You said you wanted—"

"It's no different than what you did before with us, Tam." Aarōn frowned in confusion. "Except there's a big pool and other stuff to enjoy."

Tam scowled at her brothers and then at the man who had the gall to smile even wider. She was outflanked and overruled. Anger bit into her and she wanted to scream. Again, she was asked to take it, to make it work. "I don't have much choice, do I?"

"Sure you have a choice." He kept his negligent pose on the whitewashed wall as if oblivious to her bitterness and frustration. Yet there was something in his black eyes that told her different. "You could do nothing. We'd have to fend for ourselves in the kitchen, keep the place clean, and do our own laundry."

Both Aarōn and Isaák appeared horrified.

Reality hit her. She'd babied them. Rafe was right. She'd done everything for them throughout their lives because she wanted to be needed and loved. She was sorely tempted to tell them that for once, she wasn't going to come to the rescue, that yes, this time she was going to go on strike—

"Of course," he mulled. "It's not as if I haven't done this before. I spend quite a bit of time here and manage not to starve and also have clean clothes when I need them."

His nephews gazed at him, horror still covering their faces. "Really?" Isaák peeped.

"Sure. We could actually have fun."

"Fun?" Aarōn murmured.

"I think your sister might need a break." Rafe glanced at her, his eyes once again opaque. "She's been doing quite a lot for you guys for years."

A silence fell as the twins both turned to gape at her as if she were an entirely different person than they'd ever seen before. Abruptly, Tam felt nude, uncovered, unsure. This might be his way of making sure she wasn't needed in the boys' life. She wanted to plunge in immediately, say she'd take care of it, make sure everything was fine.

Except something held her back. Perhaps it was the thick curl of anger still lodged in her gut. Or the coat of despair lining her throat. Or maybe it was the look of challenge shining in Rafe's eyes.

So he thought she couldn't laze around for days and do nothing? He thought she'd fold and do what everyone expected her to do? He really believed he and the boys would be able to keep this house clean and cook food which was edible without her help?

"Fantastic." She forced a smile. "I guess I'm on vacation."

CHAPTER THIRTEEN

*T*he rustle of the eucalyptus leaves above her head woke Tamsin from her nap. The sun still lay warm on her skin, yet she could tell it was late afternoon. The heat was no longer blistering.

She stretched.

Glancing over, she slid her hand around the glass of iced frappe someone had brought out for her while she slept and put on the small table beside her lounge chair. She avoided thinking it could have been Rafe. The thought of him staring at her in her swimsuit while she slept made her...oh, well. More likely it was Aspasia, the housekeeper. Who rarely did anything she wasn't told to do.

Come on, Tam. Get real.

She sipped on the cold drink, enjoying the sugared coffee as it rolled down her throat. It was exactly as she liked it. Exactly. How Aspasia knew this information, she had no idea.

Whatever, Tam.

Ignoring her inner irritating voice, she put the glass on the cypress side table and eased back on the lounge chair. The pool water beckoned, but she didn't want to move.

A week had gone by.

A solid week of doing absolutely nothing. Every time she was tempted to pitch in and help—whether it was sorting the boys' clothes for laundry or opening the refrigerator to search for something to make for dinner—she got a cool, dark stare.

A challenging stare.

Did he think she was incapable of relaxing? Or did he think she thought he was incapable of taking care of the house and the twins?

Either way, it was a challenge. A challenge that made her angry enough to accept.

So she'd done nothing.

Well, she'd slept. A lot. She'd done some reading. She'd lazed around the pool. She'd played some games with the boys. One day, she'd gone on a hike, but she'd been too tired to go very far. It was as if the years of working hard had all slammed into her body at the same time and she realized she was tired. Really, really tired.

So she slept.

A frustrated grunt came from her throat as she straightened on the chair. Grabbing a magazine she'd found in the study, she started to flip the pages.

Time to get busy.

Time to remember her reluctance about living off Rafe's money.

Time to get some direction in her life.

There were small hotels in Sparti. She could bike down there every day and work at something. Although she couldn't promise a prospective employer she'd be around for much longer than the end of summer.

Frustration bubbled. She flipped another page and paused.

The ad proudly proclaimed the delights of getting an online degree from anywhere in the world. Her finger slid along the list of degrees offered.

Accounting

Computer Science

Human Resources

Psychology

Business

Her finger stopped at the last entry. For years, she'd never thought of anything except getting the boys and her through the next day. Sure, she'd run the hotel, but again, it had been with a survivor's mindset, not a firm plan of where she wanted to go in her life.

Student loans available.

Something inside her trembled.

"What are you looking at so intently?" His deep voice, the voice she listened for every day, came from behind her.

She slapped the magazine shut. "Nothing."

Rafe walked into her sight and sat on the lounge chair next to her. He was dressed as he'd been every day here. Gone were the red power ties and icy blue suits. In their place, he wore cargo shorts and plain T-shirts.

He appeared even more delectable in casual clothes than he did all decked out.

"Nothing, huh?" His mouth quirked.

"No, nothing." Before she could drop her gaze, she caught his as he looked down.

At her body. In her bikini.

A blaze flushed across her skin.

"You've gotten too much sun," he said, his accent rolling the words.

"Yes, that's probably true." She grabbed her coverlet and yanked it on. Was there something more than an accent rolling in his voice? Something hot? Sexy?

She didn't know and for the millionth time, she cursed at herself because she didn't know men better.

Didn't have any practical knowledge about what went on between a man and a woman.

Not that she wanted to do anything with Rafe.

Come on, Tam.

There was a stillness between them, something hazy and blazing and snappy. She stared at her toes and wondered if she should do anything, say anything.

"Tam!" Isaák's excited voice shot through the stillness like an arrow.

"Look what we found!" Aarōn's voice, for once, was just as excited as his twin.

"*Kaló Theó.*" Rafe's rough curse brought her head up.

She swung around to see her boys running down the hill behind the house carrying a...

Big. Black. Hairy. Thing.

Scrambling off the lounge chair, she lunged toward them. "What is it? Drop it."

"Calm down, *kardiá mou.*" Rafe's voice came from behind her. "It's only a dog."

"A...dog?"

Isaák roared into the conversation, the big, black, hairy thing bouncing in his arms. "Isn't he great?"

"He's hurt though." Aarōn jogged to his brother's side. "Something's wrong with his paw."

Tam frowned into two bright, brown eyes encircled with springy black hair sticking out all over. A long pink tongue lolled from its mouth and the front paws were as big as dinner plates.

"He's big," she managed. Living in a London hotel, they hadn't had the time or space for any pets. Although the boys had begged for one many times.

"He's a puppy." Rafe's voice came from right behind her shoulder.

She jumped. Not only because his voice was so close, but because the puppy had eased forward to lap at her hand.

"How do you know?" Aarōn demanded. "He looks awfully big to me."

Biting her tongue before she blurted out one of Rafe's past hobbies, she made herself keep quiet. It wasn't her information to share and she highly doubted he'd want to claim a skill he'd clearly rejected.

"I used to take care of animals. All the time."

Surprise rippled through her. She chanced a glance over her shoulder, but he wasn't looking at her. He was staring at the puppy with eyes gleaming with interest.

"Honest?" Isaák's face beamed. "That's brilliant. Then you can help us figure out what's wrong with his paw."

"He limps," his twin contributed.

The keen interest in Rafe's black gaze dimmed. "I'll call a vet."

The memories inside her twisted into a knot.

"No way." Isaák stared at the dog with determination and what she feared was the beginning of a lifelong love. "I'm not letting him go into some hospital."

"He's only got something in his paw," Aarōn exclaimed. "I'm sure you can fix it."

The hero worship running through his words would have made her scream a few weeks ago. Watching the boys with Rafe during the last week, though, had convinced her of the true attachment coursing between them. Rafe was going to be the father the twins never had. He might not realize it yet, but the boys did.

She looked at him as he stood there, all tense, all rejection. All confusion.

"Rafe," she murmured, trying to find the words to reach him and pull him into his new reality. "Why don't you—"

"I have to cook dinner."

Both of the teenagers gaped at their uncle in shock.

"This is way more important than cooking," Aarōn finally stated.

"Way more." Isaák nodded his head.

"I can cook dinner while you take care of the puppy." She was ready when the challenging scowl came and met it with one of her own. She admitted it was time to examine her life and make some changes. Would he have the courage to do the same?

He glared at them. Then glared at the puppy. Then swung around and glared at the pool.

"Come on," Isaák said. "This can't be that hard."

Apparently, it was that hard. Inside, she wept for the young man who'd lost so much of himself when he'd lost his father. "Rafe—"

"All right." The man turned back to stare at them. "Bring the dog into the mudroom and I'll go get the first aid kit."

He walked away at a brisk pace as if running from the hounds of hell.

"What's wrong with him?" Aarōn stared after his uncle in bemusement. "*Giagiá* told me he liked animals."

"She told you that, huh?" She swept a hand across his dark curls. "Maybe he's out of practice and is worried he'll hurt the puppy."

"He wouldn't hurt a dog." Isaák shook his head in instant rejection. "He couldn't."

The absolute trust in her brother's voice reaffirmed her belief in this growing relationship between her twins and Rafe. This was right, she felt it to the center of her soul. She didn't know where she fit into the puzzle, but there was no way she was ever again going to think about breaking the three of them apart.

The puppy woofed, a sharp, excited call. She looked at the animal. His eyes shone like shiny, brown pennies.

"He's amazing, isn't he?" Isaák grinned.

"He's going to be an excellent hunting dog," Aarōn added.

Her boys were becoming too attached too quickly. She couldn't imagine Nephele wanting this big dog in her elegant villa and her plan to find a small apartment in Athens didn't include housing an animal. They were going to be disappointed if she didn't nip this in the bud. She suddenly wished she'd agreed with Rafe's suggestion about bringing the puppy to a vet.

"What do you need with a hunting dog?" She forced a chuckle. "You don't hunt."

"Rafe said he'd take us someday." Aarōn's face turned mulish. "So we'll need a good hunting dog."

"Come on, A. We can talk about this later." His twin clutched the panting animal closer to his chest. "We need to get the puppy to Rafe so he can fix him."

Tam followed the boys into the back of the house. She heard Rafe's voice greet them as they walked through the side door of the laundry. Continuing down the hallway, she entered the spacious kitchen and immediately smiled. Okay, she'd needed this past week. Needed the sleep and the time to relax. However, now, her hands itched to use the shiny steel pots and pans hanging from the walls.

Cooking in this beautiful kitchen would be pure pleasure.

She strode over and opened the gleaming fridge. There was about an hour before they traditionally sat down to eat. Consequently, it would have to be fairly simple and light.

Within a minute, she'd decided to do a *meze*. Putting together a dozen small plates of a variety of foods would be easier and faster. Plus the boys loved the meal since their sometimes finicky tastes could always find something to eat.

Tam was surprised to find herself humming as she sliced the cucumbers and tomatoes. Despite all the indecision and uncertainty in her life, there was still much to be thankful for. After a week of freedom, she felt refreshed. Even invigorated. The boys were happy. There was a bit of peace between her and Rafe.

Yes, there was much to be thankful for.

Glancing through the kitchen window, she watched as the huge golden sun slid down past the edge of the mountain, gilding the pool with sparkles of sunlight. The boys' lighter tones mixed with Rafe's deeper voice.

A burst of happiness deep inside blinded her, flooding into her heart. She wanted to stay here, right here, slicing vegetables, admiring nature, and listening to the voices of the men she loved.

Loved.

Loved.

"Oh, no." She stared at her trembling hands. "No, you don't. No."

"No what?" Rafe's presence filled the kitchen.

And her heart.

Titus snored. Loudly.

Bending down, Rafe patted the puppy's head. The twins had agreed the best name for such a beast was the Greek translation *of the giants*. The naming had occurred when his checking around Sparti had delivered no owner and no trace of Titus's roots.

"He's ours," one of them had stated emphatically.

"It's meant to be," his twin chimed in.

Somehow, neither he nor their sister had been able to refute the argument, much to Aarōn and Isaák's delight.

The dog snuffled into his makeshift bed of old blankets and sank into his dreams once more. The bed seemed to be permanently occupying his study, although he'd initially decreed the puppy should be limited to the mudroom and kitchen.

Titus, with the twins' help, had decided otherwise.

Rafe eased back in his office chair. Perhaps it had been because he'd foolishly done the boys' bidding and found the burr in the dog's paw. This could be the reason why Titus had latched on to him with a tenacious intensity. Or perhaps it was because he'd been the first to feed the damn dog, dropping pieces of Tamsin's *me-*

ze feast onto the floor the first night, much to the twins' amusement.

Or maybe, it's because you have an affinity for healing creatures' pain. Always have, always will.

Restless, he leaned forward and tapped on the next email. These last two weeks had been a great time with the boys. He'd bonded with them, definitely. In fact, he couldn't imagine life without Aarōn and Isaák. Something he was going to have to figure out come fall. There was no way he was going to allow the twins to go off to boarding school, leaving him behind.

Leaving Tamsin behind.

His finger clicked through the emails, impatience and frustration making him hit the computer keys with a sharp snap.

Tamsin. Who'd arrived here, in the house she surely recognized as the one she'd burbled about so long ago, and promptly turned into a couch potato. At his insistence, of course, yet the first week, she'd been almost comatose in her behavior. Enough to get him agitated about her health. He'd been ready to call the doctor and get her checked.

Then Titus arrived, and she had shrugged off her lethargy.

In fact, she'd turned into a dynamo.

She swam every morning, in the damn green bikini which left little to his imagination. She supervised the twins like an army sergeant. She'd cornered his house-keeper and dictated terms.

Sliding back in his chair, he sighed.

He hadn't wanted the comatose Tamsin to return, but by the end of this last week, he was even more worried about this dynamo. She was going to wear herself out. This was clearly some kind of personal quest to make everything happen at once.

Then there was the whole issue with his laptop.

Thinking they'd only be in Sparti for a few days, she'd left her own laptop at his mother's. When it had become clear that wasn't his plan, she'd stated it was only fair he let her use his. At first, he'd said no. The mistrust of any Drakos had bubbled inside. He had his work projects on the computer. His professional and private email. Still, she'd been strikingly determined.

They'd finally come to an agreement. She could use it under his supervision.

She'd been annoyed, but she'd agreed.

He'd been stunned at what she focused on when she went online. No shopping or peeking at gossip or checking her email and Facebook.

No, she'd started paging through online university classes.

"Why are you doing this?" he'd muttered. She had her brothers. She had everything she needed around here.

"It's time I think about my future." A frown of concentration creased her brows. "It's time I make some plans."

Making plans that didn't involve him or the twins, it appeared. Somehow, this didn't sit well. In fact, it irritated. "You've got the boys."

"The boys are thirteen." Her mouth firmed as if she were talking to herself as well as him. "They won't be around forever."

He'd slanted closer to stare at the course she was reviewing. "Business?"

"Yes." She shot a glare his way. "I ran our hotel, don't you remember?"

He slid back, hitting the soft padding of the armchair he'd pulled over when she'd plunked herself on *his* chair, behind *his* desk. "I remember."

"Then remember it takes some business skill to make that work." Typing impatiently on the computer keys, she pulled up another website. "I think getting a business degree would be a good idea."

Ever since she'd emerged from her semi-coma of sleeping and taken over as much command as she could, his home had been completely different. She'd come to some kind of an accord with Aspasia because the woman now reported to Tam, instead of himself. There were no longer streaks of soap on the foyer's tiled floor. No dishes were to be left sitting in the sink.

Bedtimes for the twins were strictly enforced. Everything in his house ran like clockwork. Tamsin's clock.

The clock ran very well.

For the first time in his memory, there were always fresh flowers in the foyer. Never before had he feasted on better, healthier food. He'd never realized the house had been cleaned haphazardly. Yet now, with renewed vigor and explicit instructions from Tam, his housekeeper had every inch of the place gleaming.

Tamsin was right.

She would do well in business. She had an organizer's mind, the ability to set clear goals for employees, and an iron will. The entire train of thought had kept him awake throughout the following night.

Titus groaned as he rolled over in his bed, his sturdy legs kicking out as if he were running after a hare.

Forcing himself, Rafe focused on his emails. He was falling behind, much to his staff's disgust. He just couldn't seem to gin up any enthusiasm for the work. Somewhere, he'd lost his drive and he needed to get it back.

The company needed him. His family needed the company.

There wasn't any other choice.

For the next hour, he plowed through the remaining email and read several reports from his staff on the neuro-electronic nanodevice his team had been testing.

The results were good. Really good. Obviously, the company should place a bid on the patent.

He couldn't care less.

Rafe leaned his head against the top of the chair. Where was the excitement he used to feel when studying new medical research? When he'd first started the company, he'd dismissed his old dreams and boldly embraced his new future.

He'd built at a frantic speed.

He'd planned with ferocious intent.

He'd worked with fierce eagerness.

Now with the most amazing patent ever put in front of him, he couldn't seem to summon an ounce of excitement. This couldn't continue. Jerking himself straight, he focused once more on the laptop, forcing himself to do the calculations on what kind of bid they'd need to produce.

"Rafe?" Aarōn's voice startled him into glancing at the doorway. The teenager was dressed in his pjs and for a moment, he could imagine what the kid looked like when he'd been little.

A tender smile edged his mouth. "What's going on?"

"Um." The boy shuffled in, one hand scratching at his arm. "We need to talk."

Titus rolled out of his bed, plodding over to rub his big head on the boy's leg.

"Then you better take a seat."

There was a slight frown on Aarōn's face as he slumped into the brown leather chair facing the desk. He absently scratched the puppy behind his ears.

"So..." Rafe waved a hand in the air after a few seconds of silence.

The boy glanced away, his brows furrowing. "It's about Tam."

"*Nai?*" He kept his gaze steady, yet the inner muscles of his abdomen tightened. He knew instinctively; he wasn't going to like this conversation.

"Tamsin isn't happy."

The muscles along his back knotted. "She's fine."

"No." The boy's frown deepened. "I know her better than you and she's not happy."

"Okay. But it can't be anything too problematic." Shrugging in a nonchalant way, he tried to quiet the teenager's fears and at the same time dislodge the feeling of guilt seeping inside. "And I don't know what you want me to do about it."

"I want you to fix it." Aarōn suddenly stared at him, his dark eyes determined. "You can fix it."

The total trust in the statement wrapped around Rafe's heart and squeezed. Along with the warmth, came a shot of terror. Because making Tamsin happy was an impossible task for him.

"You can, you know." The boy nodded his head decisively.

He noticed with faint despair that sweat dampened his back. "Since I didn't even know she was unhappy, I'm not sure how I can fix what's wrong."

"You can marry her."

The stark statement rang in the room and the teenager flushed when Rafe gaped at him.

Still, he didn't stop. "The idiot and I have talked it over. Many times."

The image of the two boys huddling together plotting this impossible proposition should have made him laugh. Yet this was no laughing matter. This was absurd. "I don't think—"

"The whole thing's perfect." Aarōn's mouth firmed. "She can stay with us, you can stay with us. We'd be a family."

"I'm not—"

"She doesn't feel like she belongs. That's why she's talking about going to school and getting a job."

Crossing his arms in front of his chest, he let the boy keep going. He would have to stop eventually. Wouldn't he?

"Isaák and I don't want her to go to school or get a job." Aarōn mimicked his uncle, his bony arms showing white in contrast to his dark pjs. "We want her to always be around."

"You're growing up." The irony of this conversation was profound. He'd imagined saying this exact statement but with a totally different intent. Before he would have been protecting the boys' interest. Now he was protecting Tam's. "She has a right to have her own life."

The teenager scowled. "She would have her own life if you married her."

"Marrying Tamsin," the words scratched on the scar in his heart, "wouldn't keep her from searching for a job or going to school."

"You would keep her busy."

Rafe's fervent imagination roared to immediate life at the thought of what he could do to keep her busy. "Not enough—"

"And if she got bored." Aarōn cocked his head. Evidently, there were more outrageous ideas floating through his mind. "She could help you with your business."

Before any more crazy ideas were dreamt and expressed, he needed to put a stop to this once and for all. The thought of Tamsin strolling the halls of his company's building, making him even more unfocused was insane. "I'm not marrying your sister."

"Why not?" The boy's face flashed with indignation. "She's pretty—"

"That's not the point—"

"You watch her. I know you do. You think she's pretty, Isaák and I can tell."

If he didn't stop this conversation soon, he'd find himself blushing over this kid's accusations. "Your sister is not going to be interested in marrying me. I can assure you of that fact."

Worry crossed the boy's face. "That's what Isaák said when I told him about my plan."

"You might call your brother an idiot, but he clearly isn't."

"It doesn't matter, though." Aarōn rushed forward. "Because I know if you put your mind to it, you can make her fall in love with you."

"Your sister doesn't like me."

"She would if you'd be nice to her."

He couldn't be nice to Tamsin Drakos. Nice inferred a level of passive liking or mild attraction. His relationship with her was never going to be anything except black and white. Black-filled hate and the white intensity of lust. He didn't think the teenager in front of him would like either of those feelings being expressed about his sister. "This conversation is going nowhere. It's time for you to be in bed."

"Promise me you'll think about it." A mulish glare was the boy's response.

The expression on Aarōn's face was enough to tell him he might as well take the easy way out. Although he had no intention of following through. "I'll think about it."

"Good." The boy jerked from his chair, gave Titus a pat, and shuffled out of the room.

Rafe stared after him. What a bizarre conversation. He'd had no idea the boys were hatching such a crazy scheme.

Tamsin isn't happy.

Lurching from his chair, he paced to the window. The moonlight poured over the shadows of the garden and laced the mountain top with silver. He yanked the window open fully and took in a deep breath of cool air.

A sound, a rustling sound, caught his attention. He peered into the gloom at the side of the house. After a second or so, a shadow separated itself from the others and walked into a shimmer of moonlight by the end of the pool.

A person. A woman.

Tamsin.

Had she glanced his way? Seen something of his turmoil? Yet his fears disappeared like soft swirls of air as she turned from him and started walking past the pool, through the garden and onto the path leading to the ridge of mountain behind his house.

Tamsin isn't happy.

afe found her standing on the ridge directly above the house. Moonlight silhouetted her figure against the backdrop of the dark crevasses of the mountain behind her. The small grassy patch of land where she stood lay just beyond the rough rocks and dirt of the pathway.

The place she'd chosen to stand held more than memories. This patch of land had once held his heart and his dreams.

Something alerted her although he hadn't moved, hadn't spoken.

She turned.

He couldn't see her eyes, yet the moonlight was strong enough to show how she tensed, the line of her shoulders tightening, the hands at her side clenching.

Rafe shifted the blanket lying on his shoulder. The rough weave of the basket rasped in his hand.

She kept staring at him, but said nothing. The light wind sifted through her long blonde hair, making it dance in a bright halo around her head. The moonlight concealed her face, only highlighting the edge of her cheekbone and the tilt of her chin.

The night surrounded them, the hush of silent thoughts mixed in with dark dreams.

He broke it. He had to. "A midnight walk?"

"Sure. Why not?" She shrugged her stiff shoulders.

"To here?"

Her hands unclasped into a jerky wave making it clear to him she'd recognized the place, the patch she stood on. "To wherever."

An owl hooted in the distance accenting the still, silent something running between them.

Stepping off the path, he yanked the blanket off his shoulder. "I thought we could sit here and talk."

"Here?" Her voice went wispy and she took a step back.

"Here." He had to be firm. Had to figure out what to do. What to do to make Tamsin happy. The impulse was too strong to deny; it overwhelmed the pain of the past and the puzzle of the present.

"I don't want to talk right now." She took a deep breath in and as always, he noticed the lift of her breasts under the simple white T-shirt she wore. "I need to be alone."

She turned and took a step. Away.

Another step. Away.

"Wait." Frustration beat in his head. He needed to figure her out, make this odd relationship between them work, make everything right. The instinctive need rose inside, filling him with determination. Aarōn's suggestion of marriage wasn't even imaginable. Tamsin despised him and although he'd admit to softening towards her, he couldn't trust her. Still, this didn't mean he wanted her upset. Not anymore, not any longer.

The realization stunned him. And yet, he knew it to be true.

She glanced over her shoulder at him. The light slanted along her mouth, her lush mouth. "What?"

Another frustration beat in his blood. A lust-filled frustration he'd been denying and delaying for too long. She must have seen something in his face, something she didn't like or want. Her lips pursed in displeasure and she took another step. Away.

He lifted the basket. "I brought food." His voice sounded too strained and abrupt. Another layer of frustration ladled onto the others. "I noticed you didn't eat much tonight at supper."

"I wasn't hungry." She stopped walking, though, and turned back to gaze at him.

He stood on the grass.

She stood on the rocky path.

The moonlight lit full on her face now. The shadow of long lashes shielding her eyes, the stark beauty of her cheekbones, the point of her piquant chin.

For a moment, he recalled the past. The softness of her cheeks, still with a lingering plush of baby fat. The blaze of love in the leaf-green gaze looking at him with everything clear and true. The smile of acceptance making his young heart beat hard.

This was not that girl. This was a goddess.

Horrible beauty tempting him. Feminine power threatening his soul. Sexual secrets she would never reveal. Not unless he gave everything.

Cold sweat broke on his neck.

"What did you bring?" she said, as if questioning whether the offering was good enough.

He should be angry. He should walk away.

He should stop thinking she was powerful and he was not.

Rafe knew he wasn't making an offering to a goddess. All he was doing was trying to get this frustrating woman figured out so he could make her happy and he could get on with his life. And yet, it felt nothing like that. Rather, it felt as if he'd stepped into another world. A world where goddesses ruled and men...offered.

"Um." He suddenly felt foolish. "Fruit."

Tamsin tilted her head as if sensing his weakness. A smile slid onto her lips. "Fruit?"

"You like fruit."

The night's silence hummed now, as if it was alive, another personality in the drama unfolding.

Drama.

He was becoming deranged.

"*Eláte.*" Dropping the basket, he shifted the blanket off his shoulder and spread it out on the patch of grass. "Sit."

The edge of his voice took the wry smile from her face. But she didn't turn away.

Not yet.

Rafe tried to ignore the anxiety pulsing through him. Yanking the basket cover open, he looked in. "Grapes. Cherries."

She didn't move from her stance on the rocky path.

"Oranges."

She took a step closer. She'd always liked oranges. Kneeling, he dipped his hand into the basket and produced one of his own, grown in his orchard. The one she'd predicted he'd have.

She reached out and plucked it from his fingers. Peeling the fruit open, her nostrils flared at the juicy smell and she made a sound deep in her throat.

He sat down to cover his sudden erection.

Dropping a section of orange into her mouth, she made the sound again.

Rafe tried to focus on anything else. The cool mountain air. The half-moon above. The uneven ground beneath him. Yet all he could see was Tamsin in front of him, her mouth sucking on the fruit, her eyes closed in pleasure, her skin alabaster in the moonlight.

"Why don't you sit down." Maybe if she were at his level, her power wouldn't be as strong.

Her eyes opened and she swallowed the last of the orange.

"*Eláte.*"

The word wasn't a command this time. It was his entreaty to the goddess.

He held his breath as she stepped off the path and onto the blanket. She sat down, a millimeter away from him. Her fresh scent washed over him, carried by the soft wind. With it came the inevitable memories, the dreams.

Ripping off another section, she popped it into her mouth, seeming to ignore him. The movement of her mouth, the way her lips parted then closed, the way her cheeks sucked in, then out; it tore something inside him open.

Lust poured through his veins.

Neither of them spoke as she ate the rest of the fruit and he watched. It was like being frozen in time, a time when he'd given her fruit before and watched her eat. Right here. In this place.

But then she'd been his love. Now she was his enemy. Wasn't she?

She glanced at him. Her hands lay quiet on her crossed legs now, the last of the orange consumed. Her eyes were dark pools of mystery. She gave nothing away. She gave him nothing to work with, go with.

"You have more?" Her lips formed into a provocative moue, driving him into desperation. "All of a sudden, I'm hungry."

Her last words crashed through his thoughts and emotions, crushing any conscience.

Lunging at her, he grasped the back of her head and used her gasp to plunge his tongue deep inside her. The tang of orange still filled her mouth, but it didn't obscure the essence of her.

Clean and sweet and pure.

To his utter surprise and blinding delight, she didn't reject him. She didn't throw down a goddess lightning bolt or curse his human need. Instead, one tender hand smoothed across his cheek and into his hair.

"Tamsin," his whispered on her lips.

Her eyes opened, but unlike before, years ago, when her baby fat still clung and her gaze was wide with wonder, now there were only shadows. Nothing he could discern. Nothing he could figure out and fix.

So he kissed her again and again. She took him in, took his tongue deep into her throat. Took his hand on her breast. Took his body next to hers on the blanket.

He kept giving. His body and his need and his want. He was a man and didn't know the words. Words to make this right. Words to make her happy. He knew in his heart, there was no right for them, no way to happiness.

So he kept kissing.

Until she pushed him away.

She was a fool.

Tam knew it, yet she was going to do this anyway. She was going to offer her body as a gift to this man who'd hurt her over and over. Who'd never forgiven her for the damage that had been done. Who would never believe her or love her or honor her.

Still, she was going to do this anyway.

"Hey," Rafe protested. He loomed above her, his hands splayed on the blanket near her shoulders, his arms tense and taut, keeping him from laying on top of her.

She gave him another push, her hands hard on his chest. She might be a fool, but she wanted to be strong when she did this. She wanted to be all woman. She wanted this to be everything she'd dreamed of.

His mouth tightened as he obeyed her unspoken command and rolled to the side.

She rolled with him.

His eyes widened as she spread her legs and landed on top of his outstretched body. "Tamsin?"

She answered by leaning down, sliding her body across him until her lips met his.

This time she kissed. She took. She won.

Rafe was the only man she'd ever kissed in her entire life. This might mean she was inexperienced, but it also meant she knew exactly how this man wanted to be kissed.

He'd taught her to kiss.

So she did. Taking him by surprise helped her in the quest to lead. She lingered on his open mouth, sucking on his lower lip until he gasped. She nipped his upper and then slipped her tongue in, dancing along the ridge of his teeth, tasting the lingering bitterness of coffee, the potent salt of male underneath.

Groaning, his hands grabbed her arms and pulled her closer, tighter. The heat of his body blasted through his T-shirt, making her stomach *flip, flop, flip, flop*. She straddled him, kissed him, led him, but she knew the power of this man beneath her. Knew she rode a wild male intent on having her.

As she was intent on having him.

Long fingers slid under her shirt, pushing the cotton off her back. Tam shivered as the edge of his nails skimmed along the length of her spine.

"Take this off." His voice was blurred with lust, sending her heart racing.

She pushed herself up to look at his face. His dark gaze met hers, a challenge in the depths.

Will you do this? Will you be with me?

Will you be mine?

She didn't want to think. She didn't want to answer questions. She didn't want to confront the fact she was acting the fool.

All she wanted to do was feel.

Placing her hands on his flat stomach, she rolled her hips on the hard length beneath. She tipped her head back and closed her eyes, blocking out the moonlight, blocking everything except feeling.

Felt the heat and virility of the male. Her male.

For now.

Strong hands grasped her, guiding her movements. She heard his breath quicken and reveled in her power.

"Take your shirt off." He paused and she wondered if he were thinking or only feeling like her. "Please."

She opened her eyes at the word, uttered with a husky plea. The tone shot through her like a long-lost dream. His voice had been like this before, before when they'd loved and he'd been unafraid to be vulnerable.

His face gave her nothing as she stared at him.

Yet his voice, the tone, had given her what she needed.

Grasping the edge of her T-shirt before she let doubt cloud her determination, she slipped it over her head. For a stark moment, she wished she had put on her one pretty bra instead of the old cotton one she wore.

Then, a sound came from his throat. A growl, a rough, urgent call, wiping the wish from her mind in one instant. Rafe skated his hands from her hips onto the naked skin of her waist and she was dazed with sudden heat.

Tam shivered, keeping still.

His fingers slid slowly across her stomach, brushing, drifting as if he had all the time in the world to take her.

She shivered again.

"Cold?" he murmured.

"A little." The confession wasn't true. She burned with need. Still, there was something deep inside that continued to quiver.

"Don't worry, *kardiá mou.*" The sudden flash of his smile hurt her heart. "I will keep you warm."

Two hands slipped under her bra as the words were spoken. A hot well of heat flushed her skin and she whimpered.

"You like this." His fingers plucked at her stiff nipples. "I like it, too."

Before she could gather herself, her bra was off and his hands were everywhere: lifting her breasts and rolling them in his hot hands, skimming over her shoulders and down her sides, sliding the tips of his fingers into the edge of her shorts.

"I have to taste you." His head reared up and his mouth latched onto one of her nipples, sending a shot of sparks into her bloodstream.

She'd dreamed. Many dreams. Every one of them starring this man. But she'd never dreamed of the heat and the hot and the heedless need enveloping her. She dimly noted her hands grasping his head and her body bending into his mouth. She wondered if she should do something, say something, yet nothing came into her head.

She was body. She was female.

She was his.

"*Écho na káno tin agápi se sas,*" he muttered. "*Prépei na káno tin agápi se sas.*"

I have to make love to you. I must make love to you.

The words were tortured, like he had no control over what was happening. Just as she had none herself.

They were in this together.

"Rafe," she breathed on the skin of his brow. A trickle of his salty sweat touched her lips. "I want you."

A sharp crack of laughter ruffled against her breast before he leaned back and ripped his shirt over his head. "You have me, Tam," he said, a wry twist on his mouth. "As always."

Before she had time to think of what this meant, her attention was caught by the breadth of his shoulders and the gleam of his skin. She'd seen him swimming many times during the last few weeks. This was different, though. His nakedness was hers now, hers to touch and stroke and inflame.

When she touched him, he took in a deep breath, but remained silent.

She took this as encouragement to keep going. His skin was hot, almost steamy. The pads of her fingers slid down, across his biceps to his elbows. Before she let herself stop in shivery fear, she drifted her hands across his pectorals to his tight nipples.

He sucked in a quick breath, then went still once more.

The tuft of hair between his nipples was glossy, soft. She followed the line of hair down his stomach, watching her fingers with fascination as they explored her lover's body for the first time. Exactly as he had, she let one finger slid under his shorts, reveling in the next quick breath he sucked in. Enjoying the heat of his slick skin.

"We have too many clothes on."

Glancing up at his rough statement, she met eyes black as midnight and yet lit with a fiery glow.

"Take all your clothes off, Tammy," he demanded.

Another shiver quivered in her heart. Not only at the demand, one she'd never heard from any man, but also because he'd finally, finally said the nickname she'd never thought to hear from his lips again.

"I'll do it if you do." She pushed away the yearning in her heart with her quip.

His mouth quirked. "*Eláte.*"

Come with me.

Come by me.

Come to me.

She wanted to blurt, *come into me*, but she didn't have the guts. Instead, she stood in a rush. Wobbling on shaky legs for a minute, Tamsin rocked at the blast of awareness shooting through her as Rafe rose to stand beside her.

She was going to have sex with a man for the first time.

Should she tell him?

"What is it?" His voice came low and insistent. "Are you having second thoughts?"

Tam looked at him. Standing still and tense, his hand stopped at the button of his shorts. He towered above her, the tops of his shoulders gilded with the white light of the moon, his face shadowed, only the line of his tight jaw showing his emotions.

"No." Her own hand went to her shorts. "Not at all."

She wasn't having sex. She was making love to this wounded man. This was her gift to give and she couldn't imagine giving it to anyone except him.

Not that he would ever know.

She would never tell him of her love, of her gift. And she knew enough about virginity and sex to know the likelihood of him figuring anything out was slim. Taking her courage in hand, she unbuttoned her shorts and pushed them down, along with her panties. She let them drop to her feet, and stepped out of them.

And stood before him.

She was proud of herself at this moment. She wanted to present herself as a woman, fully grown, ready to be his mate.

"Tam," he inhaled. "Tammy."

Forcing herself, she looked into his eyes, except his gaze didn't meet hers. It flitted over her naked body, seeming to drink in her entire being.

"*Eísai ómorfi,*" he breathed.

He thought she was beautiful. Tears filled her throat, but she managed to husk out, "I want to see you, too."

A sudden grin lit his face, as he pulled a condom from his pocket.

The action stopped her cold. "You planned this?"

"No, I..." He dropped his head, shielding his expression. "I've been walking around with a condom in my pocket from the moment we got here."

His husky confession should have made her angry. Instead, she found a strange sort of amusement running through her. "You were so sure of me?"

A crack of laughter came from him. "Hardly."

"Then..."

"I dreamed." He lifted his head and met her gaze.

Everything inside her melted. "Okay."

He puffed out a relieved breath.

Chuckling, she ventured a tease. "You can't put it on unless you take everything off."

He gave her another grin. "Whatever you want, *kardiá mou.*"

His hand flicked and his shorts dropped.

Now it was her turn to breathe in deeply. She knew what naked males looked like. She'd seen pictures in school, she'd changed enough of the twins' diapers, and she hadn't been clueless about the Web.

Still, nothing prepared her for having a fully grown, naked man in front of her.

A man with an erect penis. A very big erect penis.

Were they all this big?

A shiver went through her once more and this time she could safely say there was a bit of fear running in it.

"Hey." His smile faded as he reached for her and brought her against the length of his body. "What's wrong?"

"Nothing," she whispered on the hot skin of his chest.

"Don't lie, Tam. Not now."

An echo of old pain made her tense, but he began stroking his hand along her back, soothing away the ugly memories.

"Tell me what's wrong."

His command rang through her. Should she confess her virginity now? Would he think the less of her and maybe even laugh at her naïveté? She didn't want to be laughed at, she wanted to win this, rule this. She wanted to be his equal.

She grasped at the first thing that popped into her mind. "You're really big."

His cock bobbed against her stomach as if agreeing with her words. Tam had a sudden urge to giggle which would have made her appear to be about sixteen.

His hushed laugh came from above her head. "Don't worry. We'll be perfect together."

They'd been perfect together from the start. She'd fit perfectly in his arms. Their mouths had touched and created perfection. Even the words they shared had communicated in a perfect way.

Their hearts had once been perfectly matched, too.

All that was gone and she grieved deep inside. Yet she had this moment, this perfect moment with Rafe. In this one area, she wanted to still be perfect with him.

Lifting her head, she kissed his collarbone, then his jaw. "Lie down."

He met her gaze, his black eyes like shiny stones glittering in the moonlight. She thought he might disagree or take command. Instead, he kneeled in front of her and stretched out.

Male beauty at her feet.

They stared at each other; a silence filled with memories and dreams and reality blurring together. As she watched, he ripped the silver package open and slipped the condom on.

Slowly, carefully, she came down on him, relishing the warmth of his body, the silk of his skin, the hardness of his muscles. Lying on top of him, she kissed his cheek, his nose, finally his mouth.

The movement of their bodies started like a soft wind that soon turned into a raging storm. Tam's thoughts and emotions were swept away, leaving only her aching body and heated blood. She'd thought having sex would be about doing it right, and making it happen, but the only thing she could hold on to was her lover and her heart.

"Tammy," he panted in her ear, his hand tight on her hips. "It's time."

Deep inside, she shook. This was Rafe, though; this was her love. Planting her hands on his shoulders, she raised herself up to stare into his face. His jaw was tense, his cheekbones stark. His mouth was taut with need. A shimmer of sweat lay on his brow.

"Take me," he cajoled. "You know what to do."

No, she didn't.

Yet somehow, she did.

Deep inside her, the womanly core blossomed. Her hand reached back and took him.

Hot. Hard. Male.

"*Nai,*" he groaned as his head went back.

Tamsin placed him at her entrance.

And took him.

CHAPTER FIFTEEN

*O*ne more acceptance.

A bright blast of happiness exploded inside Tamsin as she stared at the computer screen. Or perhaps happiness wasn't the word.

Perhaps the word was astonishment.

One month ago, when her determination to make her own way had been all-consuming, she'd doggedly sent in over twenty applications to every Greek university and several online colleges. She'd figured if she could be accepted into only one, she'd be satisfied and on her way.

Of the twenty, nine had responded so far and every one of them had sent her an acceptance. Of course, it was too late to start this fall, but all of the entrance departments wanted her to start after the New Year, and four of them had even offered her help with covering the costs.

She was smart.

She could get a degree.

She could be something more than the boys' sister.

More than Rafe's lover.

"Tam." Isaák's excited voice forced her to jerk her gaze away from the newest acceptance letter. "Look at me!"

Closing the laptop, she smiled as her brother galloped down the diving board and splashed into the pool. The early-afternoon sun shone bright, hazing the yellow-and-blue tiles with a golden glow.

"I can do better than that," Aarōn scoffed as he lurched out of the water. "Watch me."

Another gallop. Another splash. Titus barked at the side of the pool, his yips of joy echoing in the air.

A tear of regret and fear and anticipation ripped at her heart. Her boys were growing so fast and she loved them so much. For a moment, she wanted to stop time, tell it to come to a standstill so she could relish the love binding her to her brothers.

Not only this love, Tam. Be honest.

Sucking in a breath, she threw another cheerful smile at Aarōn as he ran by, water dripping from his red swimsuit. His skin, like his brother's, was deeply tan from the month of Greek sun. When he smiled back, his dark eyes danced with happiness and complete fulfillment.

To the boys, everything was settled.

They loved Tam. They loved Rafe.

Therefore, Tam should love Rafe.

Which she did.

Her heart tore straight through, but the knowledge wasn't new, wasn't surprising. What was new and surprising was that maybe, just maybe, Rafe loved Tam.

Maybe.

"Hey." A deep voice startled her out of her reverie and she turned to find her other love leaning on the arch separating the patio from the family room.

"Hey, yourself." She was glad for the sunglasses shielding her eyes from his because she didn't want him to see her torn heart. This past month had been an endless dream of sunny, happy days with the boys laughing and playing, and dark, delicious nights filled with this man's heat and desire. And all the time, she'd hid some part of herself from the twins, another from Rafe, and much from herself.

She only wanted to love. She didn't want to think.

He wore a plain white T-shirt and his usual tan cargo pants. Barefoot, he padded to her side and without a glance at the boys, dipped in to nip at her neck.

"Stop." Leaning away, she shot a frown toward the pool. "Aarōn and Isaák."

"They aren't stupid." He nuzzled along the side of her throat. "They know what's going on."

She'd made it clear to Rafe she wanted to keep their lovemaking between themselves. He'd agreed at first, completely. The fact had ironically hurt her. But during the last two weeks, he'd started to touch her at the dinner table, or bring her to his side with a strong hand, or sneak a tug at her nipples when they swam in the pool.

The boys were smart. She'd caught their sideway squints and the quirky smiles. She hadn't known what to say or do. So she'd said and did nothing.

"We decided—"

"Decisions can change, Tam." Straightening, he sat in a chair beside her. "You know that."

"Sure." She gazed into his dark eyes trying to figure out what decisions he was talking about. She hoped, dreamed that perhaps it was more than merely a decision about PDA. "But—"

"No buts." He flicked a finger at a buzzing bug, his mouth turning down. "The boys know and I'm tired of pretending it's not going on."

She almost blurted out—what is *IT*?—then the ding of the laptop receiving an email interrupted her thoughts.

"For you or me?"

Tam flipped open his laptop. "For me."

Along with their lovemaking, there'd been an ease in his restrictions and a building trust. She no longer had him staring over her shoulder as she used his computer to check her own email and send out her applications.

The implied trust sat like a small seed of hope in her heart.

A seed that had steadily grown during these last days and weeks.

His chuckle weaved through her hope. "I'm beginning to think my staff has forgotten about me."

"Right," she tsked. "Not if the hundred-plus emails you get a day has anything to say."

"That's about half the emails I usually get." He eased back in his chair and clasped his hands on his stomach.

She eyed him and took a chance. "You don't appear to be too upset about it."

"I'm not." Abrupt surprise clouded his eyes.

The air stilled around them and Tam forced herself not to smooth it over. More than anything else—the boys' future, her future, their future—she wanted Rafe's future to be what it should be.

He didn't want to be a mover and shaker.

She'd seen it in every glower he gave to his business email, every time his mouth tightened when he went into his office here at the house. She'd seen it in the tenseness of his body the two times he'd left to drive back to Athens to take care of critical business.

He was supposed to be a doctor.

He was supposed to heal people.

He was supposed to be happy at work.

Still, she couldn't fix this for him. He had to find this knowledge in himself. To her grief, during the last month, she hadn't seen him move toward this realization.

Until now.

His eyes slashed closed, dark lashes masking the clouds of indecision. When he reopened them to stare at her, the black was impenetrable. As if the cloud of doubt had never been.

To mask her frustration, she clicked on the email. A yelp she couldn't stop burst from her mouth.

"What?" His voice held a tinge of amusement.

"I...I..."

"Got another acceptance."

Jerking her head around, she stared at him. "How did you know?"

"Oh, I don't know." His broad shoulders shrugged, but his dark eyes danced. "Maybe by checking my own laptop every once in a while."

"You looked at my email?" Outrage mingled with annoyed affection as she watched his mouth quirk into a grin.

"Just like you check mine?"

"I don't open—"

"Tam." One long finger tapped on his forehead. "It doesn't take a sneaky jerk to open an email when he can easily read the *You have been accepted* in the subject line."

"Okay." She slumped out of her outrage back against the rattan chair.

Keeping his hand up, his fingers straightened one by one as he talked. "I have counted not one, not two—"

"Rafe." A flush of amusement and embarrassment heated her skin.

"Not three. Not four."

A laugh escaped her and she threw her head back, her hair falling across her shoulders. When she lifted her head to meet his gaze, she caught the sizzle of sex in his slanted eyes. The ever-present lust between them rose like a phoenix reawakened.

This was all so new—the sex, the lust. She relished every second of kissing, every moment of touching. To her great relief, he'd never questioned her on her virginity the first night, nor her inexperience in the following encounters. She'd been secretly pleased at how he responded to her touch, how he appeared to revel in every move she made toward him in the bedroom. She was his equal, at least in the bedroom.

"How many?" His question shot across the space between them with quiet intensity.

She shifted her fingers on the keys of the computer. "This one would make it ten."

"Ten."

"Yes." She couldn't make sense of what was on his face or in his eyes. Was he happy for her? Was he proud? Impressed? Or perhaps he didn't think it was a big deal. Or didn't want to think of her going off and doing something more than what she did here for the boys and him. "But I'll go to the one who offers the most financial help."

"There's no need for that." A frown furrowed his brows. "You should choose the best and go there."

The confused blur inside her ratcheted up. "Of course I need to think of finances."

"No, you don't."

His empathic statement slammed into her and she suddenly turned angry. What was he saying? That he'd pay this bill like every one of the others? Or that because she was sleeping with him, he'd do this for her?

"I'll hire you."

"What?" Shock ricocheted inside.

"I'm always in need of smart, organized people." His finger drummed with impatience on his other hand. "You're not starting this fall, right?"

"Um. Right."

"Then you'll have the fall to save and once you begin your studies, we can work around your schedule."

He thought she was smart. Organized. He thought she should go to the best school. A wash of joy so intense it caught in her throat welled up. This had to mean something, right? This had to mean he'd put their past behind and looked at her as who she really was.

Someone a person could trust.

Someone worth loving.

The words of love bubbled underneath her tongue.

He gazed at her, his expression bland. "You agree?"

"What would I be doing?"

"I'd have you start in human resources so you could get a sense of the entire company." His black gaze held nothing but polite interest and her love snuck back down her throat.

"I see." She wanted to know about his company. Unwillingly, she'd been intrigued when they'd visited and although she knew he didn't belong there, it was a part of him. A big part. "I guess that sounds fine."

"Good." He glanced away, watched as the boys tussled in the water.

Good? All he could say was good?

"Hey, Rafe." Aarōn lunged to the side of the pool, a big grin of welcome on his face. "Come in and swim with us."

With a matching grin, his uncle stood, whipping his T-shirt over his head and shoving down his shorts.

"Ha!" Isaák laughed beside his twin. "You already have your swimsuit on. You were planning on joining us, weren't you?"

Rafe's dive into the deep end of the pool answered the question. The boys whooped and hollered as they plunged to meet him in the water. He rose, the water glistening on his shoulders. Throwing his head back, he laughed as the twins pounced on him.

Good. He said everything was good.

She had to believe it. Wanted to believe it.

Her mobile buzzed in her pocket. Tam jumped. She hadn't received a phone call since they left London. Out of habit, she kept the phone near to keep track of the boys' events on her calendar and to make notes about what they needed for the kitchen.

The phone buzzed again.

She slid it open. The number wasn't one she knew. It could be a college calling instead of emailing.

"Hello?"

Aarōn's scream of delight echoed in the background and Tam absently watched as Rafe threw her brother over his shoulder.

"Tamsin."

She froze at the familiar voice. The insides of her heart shrank into a pit of horror.

"Tamsin?"

"Yes," she whispered.

"It's Haimon." The oil in the voice threatened to choke her throat. "We need to talk."

If it was possible, he appeared even worse than the last time she'd seen him in the hospital.

Sallow skin enveloped the dark patches under his eyes. Haimon's hand shook as he grasped the water glass in front of him. A black button-down shirt did nothing to disguise his weight loss. But most troubling to Tamsin was the feral look in his eyes.

"You appear well." He coughed into a napkin before smiling, his teeth as yellow as his skin.

She stifled the impulsive reply that he didn't.

Then, the awful smog of guilt overtook her. She and the boys *were* well: happy, fed, content. This man, who'd been part of their family for so many years, was clearly not. Forcing a smile, she reminded herself she'd given him everything they had and even more importantly, this man had damaged Rafe and his family irreparably.

She shouldn't feel guilty. She should feel angry.

Instead, panic slid along her skin, making her shiver.

"How are the boys?"

She jerked herself straight and kept the smile on her face. "They're good. They like Greece."

"Of course they like Greece," the old man huffed. "They are Greek."

An unsettled hush fell over the wooden table. The lone waiter in the Sparti taverna Haimon had told her to meet him at, lurked behind the shabby red curtain separating the dining area from the kitchen. The smell of grease wafted through the smoke coming from the one other patron's cigarette.

"For whatever reason," she stated. "They like it here."

His eyes narrowed and something fevered flashed across them. "Happy with all of Vounó's money, eh?"

"Money has nothing to do with their happiness." Anger surged, wrapping around her panic. "They were happy before Rafe came into their life."

"Rafe, is it?" he scoffed. "You've fallen under his spell again. Stupid girl."

The comment would have hurt her once. Not now. Tamsin absorbed the knowledge with relief. She didn't care about this man's opinion anymore. This should make it easier to deal with whatever Haimon demanded. And she knew there would be demands. "When we met last, you knew I was going to let the boys be with him. It's why I gave you the money."

"Speaking of money."

Tam kept her gaze steady. She'd known, deep within, what this was about. She was just glad this was all it was about. "I gave you everything we had."

The man across from her snorted. "Don't take me for a fool. You are living in the million-dollar home of a billionaire."

"The home isn't mine—"

"You and the boys have everything you could possibly need."

Her dread billowed. Haimon knew their circumstances. Knew where they lived. This crazy old man could do anything to them.

She should tell Rafe. She should make sure the security was on alert. After all, she'd found it easy to escape their scrutiny to get here. Suggesting Rafe take the boys for an afternoon hike had been a snap. After that, the only thing she'd had to do was walk up the mountain and around to the road to catch the bus. There'd been no security patrolling her route.

So security was fairly lax. Which meant this man could cause trouble.

Her nails cut into the skin of her palm. If she told Rafe, he'd find her stepfather and arrest him. Throw him in jail where he'd probably die. Could she live with that?

No, she couldn't.

She didn't want anyone to know about Haimon. She could handle this herself.

"Living with a Vounó. The man who destroyed everything we had."

She wanted to blurt out—*precisely as you destroyed everything the Vounós had*—but she didn't. Because the wild glare he threw at her told her she must tread carefully. "I had no choice. You got all the money we had."

"You had a choice, Tammy. You always have a choice. And you chose the wealthy man instead of loyalty to your family."

They weren't a family with him any longer. Yet, his words still burned.

She was beholden to Rafe. She lived off his money.

Giving him her body only made it worse.

"Nothing to say?" Haimon leaned in, the smell of his bad breath hitting her like a blast of poison.

"We are staying with him for now," she started.

"For as long as he'll have you in his bed."

She kept going, ignoring his slur, intent on getting this over with. "But we don't have anything of our own."

"You don't need anything of your own. Everything's provided for you."

"I have nothing to give you."

"Does Vounó know you're meeting me?"

"No." The switch of topics shot her heart right into her stomach. "He doesn't need to know."

"Or you don't want him to, right, Tammy?"

"Don't call me that." She didn't want to be reminded she once tried to see this man as a father figure.

"Does he whisper your name in your ear as you sleep with him?"

"Stop." She forced herself to meet his gaze. "This is getting us nowhere."

He relaxed on the wooden bars of the taverna chair. "I need money."

His bald statement shook her resolve, not because of the actual words, but because of the fevered determination behind them. "I told you. I don't have any."

"Come on." The old man gave her a sly smile. "I know you do the grocery order every week."

He knew this? Such a small, intimate detail? If he knew this, he'd been doing a lot of digging. Horror crisscrossed her brain. "I charge the groceries on his debit—"

"I also know you and the twins came into town recently." He paused, then smiled again. "To do some clothes shopping for school this fall, perhaps?"

A chill of dread swept through her. He had followed them. He'd been close to the boys without her even noticing.

"Nothing to say?"

She did have some money. Rafe had started giving her a weekly amount to cover anything his nephews needed beyond groceries. She even had the job of paying the housekeeper now.

She had a little. Not much, but a little.

A little of Rafe's money. Not hers.

The thought of giving Haimon any of Rafe's money poured a deep pile of guilt inside her. Rafe would see this as a betrayal. Even more then sneaking away when the twins and he had taken a hike this morning. Even more than meeting with this man.

Giving Haimon money.

Rafe would never forgive her.

"Tamsin." Her stepfather shifted closer, the chair creaking under him. "Give me the money you have or I make trouble for the boys."

"You can't mean this." Instant loathing writhed in her gut. "Don't threaten them."

"They aren't mine, are they?"

"You raised them."

"So. You didn't answer the question." The old man eased away, the ugly smile back on his face. "Yet, you did, didn't you? You let Vounó do a DNA test."

"Haimon—"

"The boys aren't mine so I have no more interest in them."

The loathing rose in her throat and turned to pure hatred. "I can't believe—"

"No interest in them other than using them to get what I want." He sighed, his eyes closed as if he were in pain. "What I need."

Reluctant worry mixed with anger, a sick brew in her heart. What choice did she have? She could confess to Rafe—he would find a way to get rid of Haimon. But that way likely involved jail and the way this man in front of her appeared, he wouldn't survive.

She didn't want to be responsible for his death.

If she didn't give him money, he'd find a way to hurt her brothers. She knew it deep in her soul. Maybe she could keep them safe while they stayed in Sparti. Still, eventually, they'd go back to Athens and the boys would go off to school. If Haimon could follow them here and find out their routine, he could definitely do the same in Athens. Aarōn and Isaák knew him and wouldn't run away until it was too late.

She couldn't risk it.

"All right." She snatched her wallet out of her purse. She wanted to finish this, now. "I only have a little."

"This is it?" He frowned in disgust at the bills she'd slapped onto the table.

"That's it." Tamsin managed a glare. "That's it for-ever."

"Mmm." He stuffed the bills in his shirt pocket and rose. "We'll see, Tammy. We'll see."

She watched as he plodded out the door, dread leaching into every cell of her body.

CHAPTER SIXTEEN

*S*omething was wrong.

Rafe slid his hand up and down Tamsin's arm. At his touch, she murmured in her sleep and curled closer to his side.

Her scent, clean and pure, mixed with the smell of their sex. Although they'd made love only an hour ago, her scent still made his cock twitch with need. But he couldn't mask his worries with sex. Not anymore. He'd tried to ignore all of it for the past two weeks, yet there was no getting away from his conclusion.

The right conclusion.

Something was definitely wrong with Tamsin.

He gazed at her sleeping face. The room was dark, but his memories provided everything he needed. The golden arch of her brow, the way her mouth pouted as she slept, the smooth purity of her skin.

She murmured again and this time it was coupled with a frown.

A frown he'd seen quite a few times in the last couple of weeks.

The boys had immediately detected the tension emanating from their sister. Aarōn had been at his office doorstep more than once demanding to know what was going on. He'd been a hero to the twins for a month while they'd watched their sister turn into his lover. Now, though, it appeared he had work to do.

He usually attacked problems head-on, yet something niggling in the back of his brain had made him reluctant to tackle whatever was going on with her.

However, it was time to stop being indecisive.

"Tam." His hand tightened on her shoulder.

"Hmm." Her frown grew more fierce as if she was now not only battling her nightmares, she meant to battle him.

"Tam, wake up."

"I'm sleepy," she muttered.

Even in the midst of his distress, he almost chuckled at her surly tone. "We've got to talk."

She opened one eye. "I must be dreaming."

"What?" He tucked his chin into his chest and met her gaze.

"A man wants to talk?"

His chuckle escaped. As they'd grown closer, he found to his delight that Tam still possessed her sense of humor, more refined and tart than when she'd been a young girl, and more likely to make him laugh. Her humor had been one of the things he'd loved about her.

Loved.

He paused for a moment, his body going taut.

She noticed. She noticed everything. Pushing herself onto her elbow, she stared at him, her eyes clear even in the shadows. "What's wrong?"

Shaking off his thoughts, he zeroed in on her worries. "I could ask you the same thing."

Her body didn't move. He felt her withdrawal, though, saw it in the downward brush of her lashes, shielding her eyes.

Silence whispered around them.

"Tam?" The niggle in his brain turned into a twisting menace.

"I asked you first."

The childish response intensified his frustration. "Come on. You've been weird for two weeks."

"Weird." Finally meeting his gaze, the edge of her mouth tried for a smile. "What does that mean?"

"The twins have noticed, too." He sat up and leaned against the carved cypress headboard. "You've been too quiet. Short with Aspasia. You even forgot to put the roast in the oven last night."

She smiled, but it was forced. He could tell by the way she gritted her teeth. "You and the boys didn't go hungry. I managed to find something for you to eat."

"That's not the point." He folded his arms on his chest. "The point is there's something wrong."

They stared at each other for a moment, a silent battle of wills. But he wasn't going to let her wave away his concern this time. He'd tried a couple of times in the last few days. Tried to crack through to what was going on with her. Yet she always succeeded in changing the subject and he hadn't pushed.

Tonight he was going to push.

"There's nothing wrong." Her gaze fell from his face down across his shoulders, to his chest.

She made a sound deep in her throat. The sound was pure sex and, as usual, his body responded. She noticed that too, the observant female. Her focus went right to the burgeoning tent in the sheet.

She laughed, a husky call.

Her hand reached out—

He caught it in one of his own.

"Tamsin." He glared at her. "I asked you a question."

"And I answered." Tugging her hand from his, she splayed it on his chest, making his heart pick up a beat.

She leaned in and kissed him.

And like all the other times, he wondered who else she'd kissed. Who else she'd been with.

The first time, the very first time he'd entered her, he'd known it couldn't be many. Not by the tight squeeze of her muscles when she'd settled onto his body. Not by the way her face had pinched in the moonlight as if it had been a long time. The satisfaction he'd felt at that moment had been medieval, primitive, and foolish. Still, the realization hadn't stopped the satisfaction flowing through his veins along with the lust.

Now, though, was not the time to be thinking of that. He wanted to get this, whatever *this* was, out in the open and done with.

"Tam—"

She cut him off with her tongue. Her talented, tempting tongue. It twined around his own, then slid across the ridge of his teeth. "Touch me, Rafe," she whispered on his lips.

His name, said with her familiar, sensual slurring, finally broke through his mind's determination.

His desperate body took over.

He clasped her arms and tugged her onto his body. The silky sweetness of her skin moving along his made him sweat. The musk of her excitement, mixed with his, swirled around them, making him heady with need.

Leaning in, she nipped at his lower lip.

He growled.

She laughed.

Her green eyes met his, brimming with heat and mirth and triumph. For a moment, his brain yelled at him for losing track of the conversation, letting her win using her feminine wiles.

Then, a softness came over her—her mouth tipped into a gentle smile, the muscles along her jaw relaxed, her leafy eyes went dreamy with something. Something he'd seen long ago in these same green eyes.

Something he needed even more than her body.

Her body slid across his, a sensual challenge he couldn't ignore. Every thought whipped away as she moved her lower body on his. The thin sheet between them did nothing to diminish the electric zap of connection.

His cock went completely erect.

She laughed once more, a taunting call to his masculinity.

With a surge, he reached for the bedside table and jerked at the drawer.

"Let me." Her hand grabbed the condom from his grasp and ripped the packet open.

Rafe pushed the sheet away, exposing everything to her.

His lover smiled, a loving movement of her lips.

Lover. Loving.

The chug of what he felt, yet didn't want to acknowledge, pumped through his blood. Before he forced himself to confront his new reality, her hand moved to his cock and he lost all focus.

"*O Theós,*" he groaned as he arched into her grip.

Laughing again, she swung her leg over him, preparing to take him.

Something inside him rebelled. The something tied to the love he didn't want to look at or take in. The something tied to the deep, dark fear that she'd done it again, made him love and lust and lose himself in her to the point of madness.

Grabbing her hips, he swung her beneath him and slid between her legs. A thrust, harsh and needy, wanting and desperate and hoping, one thrust and he was inside her.

She locked her intent gaze with his as she wrapped her smooth legs around his waist.

"Tammy," he whispered as he drew himself out and then back into her core.

Her hand smoothed along his shoulder to his jaw. As if to comfort him or calm him. Comfort wasn't what he wanted from this woman. A man didn't need to be comforted by his lover.

Did he?

A smile crossed her face, a wistful, bittersweet smile that clenched his heart.

He wasn't calm. Far from it.

And yet, the only thing he could think to do was use his body. To answer her comforting touch, to turn her smile into something more. To calm them both, God help them. His body quickened its pace while inside, something frantic and broken turned, pushing on the barriers against the hurt he'd built so long ago.

"Rafe." Her voice came to him, delicate, feathering along those barriers, sending shivers down his spine. "Rafe."

She lifted her hips into his rhythm, matching his pace, giving him what he needed. What his body needed. He needed something else, *O Theós na ton voithísei.* Something just out of reach.

"Raphael," she gasped, rearing up, her face contorting in ecstasy.

He needed something God couldn't give him. His body pounded while his heart raced. He needed something from her, this female gazing at him as her orgasm faded, her body relaxing beneath him, her hot core still warm and willing and wet as he moved in her.

His pleasure surged, tightening his muscles, making his blood roar in his veins. His brain whirled with physical need, twining around the something deep inside he still needed to find before he could be full and whole.

Her hand swept across his mouth, then to his shoulder. A simple gesture that left him gasping for breath. The leafy-green eyes grew dark, drawing him in, farther and farther. Into her, into this something he searched for.

His hips beat faster and faster.

He felt his balls tighten, his leg muscles contract.

His jaw clenched as he came to his peak.

"I love you." Her words filtered through him, pouring over his sexual excitement like a potent alchemy.

Finally, he'd received the something he searched for. He spilled himself inside her.

Complete.

She had to put a stop to this.

She had to.

Tamsin stared at her phone as if it could answer her one big problem.

A problem who kept calling her on this phone.

Haimon had insisted on two more meetings during the last two weeks. Two more times she'd slid around security and given him every penny she had. Not much, and he stated his dissatisfaction in a way that scared her. But she'd at least managed to keep his threats at bay.

For now.

She lifted her head and gazed out the kitchen window. Her guys were in the pool, as usual. Aarōn laughed at something Rafe said and Isaák jumped on his uncle's back with a wide grin on his face.

A tight wrench in her gut made Tam suck in her breath. She felt as if she were walking on a very thin line in the sand. One step wrong and she'd land in a quagmire on one side or quicksand on the other. If she didn't meet Haimon this afternoon like he'd demanded, he'd hurt her boys. If she decided to put an end to this and told Rafe what was going on, he might strike back at not only the old man, but her.

Could she trust Rafe to believe her story? Could she trust him to listen to her before acting against his enemy and maybe even herself?

A sick feeling in her gut told her no.

She hated that. Hated that she didn't trust.

Even though she loved.

Yet the fact Rafe hadn't acknowledged her admission last night lay like a fog of indecision and fear over her.

I love you.

He hadn't said it back.

Swinging away from her laughing guys, she wandered down the hallway and into her bedroom. The bedroom she no longer slept in. Closing the door behind her, she bent over and pulled out her battered suitcase from under the bed.

The green velvet bag was old, threadbare in places, the silk ribbon fraying at the edge.

Tears built behind her eyes, but Tam pushed herself to open it.

The bracelet was a child's. The freshwater pearls were laced with blue stone beads and sterling silver tubes. The silver twinkled in the shaft of Greek sun slanting through the blinds. The bracelet her real father had given her when she'd been too young to even know who he was. She slumped on the floor, leaning her back on the side of the bed. She hadn't taken the jewelry out in years.

Too busy. Too painful.

A huff of aching regret escaped her and one tear dripped onto the edge of her sleeve. Before she lost all control, she stuffed the bracelet back into the bag and stood.

She didn't know of any pawn shops in Sparti or Athens. Still, she'd bet her last euro, or in this case, her last possession, that Haimon did. Value was in the eyes of the beholder, but her mom had always had an eye for any piece of jewelry. Skylla had been clear: the small bracelet had been worth a significant amount of money.

Thank goodness Tam had been smart enough to hide it away as soon as they'd landed in London. She had no doubt her mother would have taken it without a second thought.

This was all she had. All she had left of her real father, and it was the last thing she was going to give the man who had never been her father. Once she let him know—there was no more—he'd walk away.

He had to walk away.

CHAPTER SEVENTEEN

"Here." Tamsin shoved the velvet bag across the wine-stained table. She ignored the lurch in her heart as her fingers slid along the plush fabric for the last time.

Haimon eyed the bag with disdain. "What is it?"

"It's the last thing I have to give you."

He glanced at her, his wily grey eyes narrowing. She'd worried he might reject her offering outright, but to her surprise, he gingerly opened it and shook the jewelry into his hand. The silver caught the light of the bulb hanging above their table, making it sparkle.

"Hmm." He lifted the bracelet closer. "A nice piece."

A nice piece? The only piece she had of her real father was merely nice? A scream of anger and pain nearly escaped her, yet she had other goals.

More important goals.

If she had to give the last piece of her father away in order to drive this one-time father figure away, then she would. Gladly. "Take it and leave me alone."

Haimon jiggled the bracelet in his hand, as if weighing its worth. "I could get a few euros selling this."

"Go ahead and—"

"A few."

The two words spiked into her heart like two jagged cuts. "I've given you all the money I have and this is the only thing left to give you."

"Like I've mentioned before, you live with a billionaire."

"His money is not my money."

"In a way, though—" He eased back in his chair, rubbing his hand over his bald head. "—it is. Isn't it, Tamsin?"

"I don't know what you mean."

"What I mean is I don't forget where any of my money goes. Ever."

She met his challenging look with a blank stare. What was the man talking about?

"Ten years ago, you forced me to give you quite a large sum of money."

His meaning became clear and with it, came a great gush of fury. "We made a deal."

"Deals. Blackmail. However it happened, it was my seed money Vounó used to start his precious company." His contorted logic was so ridiculous, she should walk away. But she needed his assurance he'd leave them alone forever and until she got it, she had to stick with this absurd conversation. "What happened years ago has no relevance now."

"Really?" His mouth tightened. "I think it does."

"I've just given you a piece of valuable jewelry. That should be enough to sustain you for several months."

"I appreciate the gift." He slipped the bag, and her bracelet, into the pocket of the drab cotton shirt he wore.

Tamsin stood. "Now what I want from you is your promise—"

"Gifts. Promises." The old man chuckled. "We are a happy family, aren't we?"

Her hands tightened on the handle of her leather purse. "No. We aren't."

"No?" He gestured at her, a sharp slash. "Sit down, Tammy."

"I've got to go—"

"We're not done." His tone went flat.

Every atom of her demanded she leave except one, her instinct. Because the look in Haimon's eyes told her the truth.

They weren't done. Not at all.

"What?" She eased down on the hard wooden chair.

"I've decided I'm no longer interested in the paltry amount of money you've given me."

"I don't have access to any more."

"I've also decided it's time I get a dividend from the investment I put into Viper Enterprises so long ago."

She leaned across the table, anger surging in her blood, swamping her fear of this man. "You had nothing to do with it. Rafe did it on his own."

Haimon snorted. "Without the money he was given when we left for London, he would never have got his company off the ground."

Even though she believed Rafe shouldn't be running his company, Tam was still so proud of what he'd accomplished. The gall of this man sitting in front of her, to claim any part of Rafe's success, made the anger inside swell until it burst. "He wouldn't have had to launch the company at all if you hadn't stolen from his father and driven him to his death."

The accusation shot through the air. The old man lurched back, his eyes going blank, his mouth slackening.

That hadn't been smart, but Tam didn't care. The words had spilled out of her like a poison she needed to expunge before it destroyed her.

"So." Her stepfather recovered quickly. "He's been spewing lies and you believe him."

"Rafe doesn't lie."

You do.

The unsaid accusation lay between them.

He finally chuckled, a soft, chilling sound. "I guess what you said is true. We aren't a family anymore."

"After what you've threatened to do to the boys—"

"This makes it easier in many ways." His grey eyes grew cold and hard. "I no longer have to worry about your too-tender heart."

Long ago, she had thought he cared; had hoped. But the ugliness she saw in front of her drove the last of her hope into death's maw. "I have no heart for you, Haimon. I have nothing."

"Except access to my money."

It was her turn to snort. "None of Rafe's money is yours. Or mine."

"I provided the seed money." His gnarled hand rose to brush across his mouth.

"No, it was mine. Bought and paid for when I made the deal with you."

"The deal that, in a way, Tam, you've broken."

The fading blare of a car horn echoed in the silence that fell.

"What are you talking about?" She'd begun to think this man might be deranged. Which only heightened her fear of him. Mixed with her growing anger, the combination made her feel like her insides were going to break apart.

"Our deal was you were to split with Vounó for good. Then you got the money."

"I did exactly that."

"Yet, here we are, many years later, true. But still, you are back in his arms, in his life." He tutted under his breath as if she were a child needing to be chastised.

The fear and anger broke free once more and flooded her caution, drowning it in a sea of frustration and wrath. "What do you want?"

"A portion." He slid his hand over his head again. "A minor portion of what your lover has."

"How am I supposed to get this for you? I don't have access to his bank account."

"You do have access, though, don't you?" The old man hummed under his breath. "Don't you, Tammy?"

An aching dread threatened to leave her limp. "Spit it out."

"So impatient." Waving at the waiter, he ordered more coffee for both of them. After the waiter had finished filling their cups and shuffled away, he turned his focus on her again. "I have had a conversation or two with Tobba Laboratories."

"Who?"

"Vounó's biggest competitor."

"So?"

"They are extremely interested in the neuron-electronic device your lover is testing at this moment."

A flash of memory swept through her. The visit to Rafe's work. The cancer shot that her brothers had been so interested in.

It's used with a neuron-electronic device that we're also testing.

She sucked in a breath.

"Ah," Haimon murmured. "You know of it."

"I know nothing." She kept her composure. "Nothing that would help your friends at Tobba Laboratories."

He ignored her claim. "Vounó is about to bid on the device. Tobba wants to know what that bid is going to be."

A sick brew of fear and dread swirled in her stomach. "I have no idea what that bid would be."

"Once I deliver this information to them, they'll pay me a substantial fee."

"I can't help you."

"Then, Tammy, then you'll have what you want."

Another silence fell. She felt the threat, the demand running through her, a wash of ugliness she couldn't escape.

"I'll be gone for good." He smiled, a sinister, slick move of his lips. "That's what you want, don't you?"

"Yes," she said. "That's what I want."

"I suppose I should be hurt." He mournfully shook his head. "After all the years we were a family."

Should she shriek at him? Should she strangle him?

"However, business is business and I understand why you want to latch onto your rich lover while you can."

To say her relationship with Rafe was business made her want to retch. "I won't do it. I can't find out what you want."

"But you do have a way to find out, don't you?"

"No, I don't."

"Then you'll find one." His gaze grew hard, like steel planks pinning her down. "Or there are going to be problems."

Problems for the boys.

The threat wasn't stated, but it hovered between them as clear as if the words had actually been spoken.

"How could you?" Leaning forward to stare into his eyes, she tried to find a piece of decency in this man she'd lived with almost her entire life. "Even if you aren't their father, they were still once a part of your family, a part of your life."

"All of us do what we have to, to survive." He met her ferocious gaze with a mild one, like he were discussing the weather. "I get what I want, you get what you want."

Desperate, she used her last card. "I'll tell Rafe. He'll keep the boys safe. He'll come after you."

"Will he?" A chuckle. "Will he believe you?"

Her greatest fear swung into the forefront. "He'll believe me."

He took a sip of his coffee, the chipped side glinting in the dull light. "Will he believe in your word when I show him how you signed over the money from our hotel account so I could escape?"

"You'll be in jail before you can show him anything."

The old man seemed unfazed by the challenge. "Will he believe you when he sees the photos of us meeting many times without his knowledge?"

Horror clutched at her throat. "What do you mean?"

He waved a hand to the one other patron in the taverna. The man smiled and waved back, a fancy mobile phone in hand. A phone that took photos, surely.

Horror turned to frozen panic.

"He won't, will he, Tammy?"

No. He wouldn't. Their relationship was too fragile, too precarious and he was too wounded. If she had a few more weeks or months, maybe she could overcome this, but now?

"Get me the bid amount." Haimon rose and shrugged into his coat. "Send it to me by text within twenty-four hours."

She stared at him, too afraid to say anything.

"I'll want proof, also." He hiked up his trousers, his expression turning to calculation. "Best to take a mobile phone photo of the bid letter so I know it's real."

"How am I going to get that?" A sick brew of hopelessness swirled in her stomach. "Maybe I just get the number."

"Ah." He smiled again. "So you will get this for me. Good."

"I haven't agreed."

"You are negotiating terms." His grim smile never wavered. "That means you've agreed."

"I might be able to get you the number—"

"I want proof. Something on Viper's letterhead. Something I can depend on."

"You don't trust me?" The question was childish, a stupid thing to say, yet some remnant of her childhood with this man reared its head.

"That was always your problem, Tammy." Haimon shook his head in disgust. "You always believed in trust."

A well of tears threatened to burst. "There has to be—"

"Don't trust anyone. Ever." He brushed his hand over his head, his gaze never leaving hers. "How many times have I told you that?"

"Then why should I trust your word that once I do this, you'll leave us alone?"

"A very good question. Perhaps you are learning at last." Putting his hands on the back of the chair, he leaned in. "The boys aren't mine. We aren't a family."

She kept her gaze pinned to his narrowed eyes.

"I have no ties to any of you." His stare was hard as stone. "Once you get me this money, I'm leaving Greece."

"Where will you go?" Some last, lingering tug of emotion slipped from her heart.

"Don't pretend to care." He gave her an indifferent shrug. "Only know I'll be gone for good."

"There's got to be another way."

"No. There isn't." He didn't even glance behind him as he walked away. "Do it. Or you'll lose everything you love."

Finally. Rafe slept.

Tamsin edged her way out of his warm embrace and stepped onto the cool stone floor. Grabbing her night-gown from the end of the bed, she slipped it over her head before turning around to look at him.

His face, shadowed by night, still held an aura of
power and strength. The tough edge of his jaw, the
strong arch of his brows, the black hair contrasting
with the white silk sheets—all of it, him, warned her
who she was dealing with.

A powerful man.

A man she had to betray.

Her gut lurched and writhed.

If only she had a bit more time. Just a few more precious weeks, even days, to nurture what she was sure
was blooming between them.

She knew he cared. She knew it.

Rafe had watched her through the entire evening
meal with the boys. He'd known something was troubling her. But his eyes didn't hold anger or distrust.
No, they'd been filled with puzzlement, worry, concern.
Yet she knew in her heart if she blurted out that
Haimon was around, that she'd met him many times,
that she'd given him money...

She knew those dark, black eyes would fill with rage.

Not only rage at an old man.

Rage at her.

Trying to punch her anguish back, she swung away
from him. Tam tiptoed through the door and closed it
behind her with a soft thump. The shadows followed
and swallowed her as she crept down the hallway and
into the kitchen. Needing some consolation, she opened

the refrigerator and poured herself a small glass of *vinsanto*.

She couldn't avoid it any longer.

She had to make a choice. Her boys. Or her love.

The irony slammed into her. Ten years ago, almost to the day, she'd had to make the same choice. And exactly as before, she had to make the only one she could.

Forcing herself to focus, she plodded into Rafe's office.

Titus rolled from his bed and padded across to where she stood. When he rubbed his big head on her leg, she absently smoothed her hand through his rough hair. A small fizz of comfort shot through her for a moment.

Only a moment.

The laptop sat on the desk. Closed. Yet open to her. No locks anymore. No password needed. No lack of trust. So easy to betray someone who trusted you.

Tam clenched her jaw. What other choice did she have?

The question had been whirling in her mind for the past fourteen hours. Ever since Haimon had left her with the warning.

Do it. Or you'll lose everything you love.

If she didn't send him something tonight, she put her boys at risk. If she didn't send him a quote, he'd expose her dealings with him to Rafe.

She couldn't chance it. She had to text Haimon something. She had to betray her lover to protect her brothers.

And the fragile love fighting for life.

Because texting him what he wanted bought her some time. Bought her boys their health. Bought the concealment of her dealing with her stepfather. Bought her time to build on the love she hoped grew between Rafe and her.

The ugliness of her choice ran like poison through her veins. She shouldn't do this. She should confront Rafe and let things fall where they may. But then she'd lose. Lose him and lose the boys. Lose herself.

Lost. She'd be lost without her loves.

Maybe Haimon would keep his promise and leave Greece. Rafe might never figure out why he'd lost this one contract. She'd be able to live with the secret knowledge she'd given his enemy a way to steal from him, couldn't she?

A sick slide of self-loathing coated her throat.

Yet what else could she do? She only had maybes and desperate hopes to cling to in order to keep everything she so desperately wanted.

She took a sip of the wine, trying to wipe away the taste of what she had to do.

Betraying her love. Again.

Clamping down on the thought, Tam slipped into Rafe's leather chair and lifted the laptop's cover. The computer whirred; the screen lit up. With a grumble, Titus walked back to his bed and sank down, laying his head on his paws, his dark gaze pinned on her.

Perhaps she wouldn't find anything. A surge of powerful hope swept through her. Still, this wouldn't let her off the hook. She had to find something for Haimon or he'd come after everyone she loved. The realization crushed all hope until the only thing she had to hold onto was despair.

She had no choice.

She tapped into Rafe's email and started to scan the hundreds of emails. The antique grandfather clock tick-tocked in the background.

Staff meeting Thursday noon

P&L report – June

Final proposal - Nanodevice patent #122

Her finger stopped. This couldn't be that easy, could it? She'd half-hoped, half-dreaded she'd find it. Was this it? The dynamite email that might destroy her life?

She tapped open the email. Clicked on the attachment.

Final bid proposal

This had to be it. Peering at the clock, she noted the time of the email. Less than four hours ago.

Please confirm, Mr. Vounó, that this is the final number you wish to go with.

The email was signed by someone with a long string of degrees. The main scientist? Another name. Rafe's VP of acquisitions was listed below.

Had Rafe seen this? Scrolling through his send box, she found his confirmation.

This was it. The final bid. The bid amount stunned her. If Hamion were only getting a tiny portion of this, she could understand why his wheeling-and-dealing impulses were on high-alert.

Understand. However, she'd never forgive.

Tam leaned back in the chair. She could be over-blowing this situation—misreading the feral emotion in her stepfather's eyes. Maybe she should cling to the belief that this would all go away.

A flash of memory ran through her brain.

The way Haimon's grey eyes had glittered. With madness, certainly. Yet also with some sort of strange drive for revenge. As if it had become his life's calling to steal something from Rafe.

Like he thought Rafe had stolen the twins from him?

Her mouth twisted. Haimon hadn't seemed upset about not being the boys' father, but there'd been that something. That something more that told her this was personal to the old man. He wasn't going to let this go. He wasn't going to walk away.

She knew it in her gut.

The clock ticked. Tocked. Titus rolled over on his bed, his eyes blurry with sleep, yet still watching, waiting.

A sudden crazy idea smashed into her mind like a comet.

Crazy. Foolhardy. Risky.

But the idea offered her something she needed right now. More than anything.

She wouldn't have to betray her lover.

Also, the idea gave her another thing she needed right now—more time. This crazy, fool-hardy, risky idea gave her that. If she did it right. With nervous, fearful concentration, she clicked onto the internet. How long did a medical bid process take? The whole deal couldn't happen overnight, could it?

The deep, low chime of the clock tolled out the late hour. Tamsin frantically scanned dozens of internet pages. Typing in a variety of words, she finally sighed and leaned back in Rafe's chair once more. It could be months before the final decision was made. Still, given Haimon's confidence, and his circumstances, she probably had mere weeks.

Weeks. Time. Hope.

Weeks she could use to solidify her relationship with Rafe. Time to ease into telling him what was going on without setting him off. Hope that somehow, together, they could evaluate how to protect the boys from Haimon's inevitable wrath.

She clicked on the bid letter. Printing it, she placed it aside and then on an empty email she typed the new numbers, matching the font to the letter.

Within a few minutes, she'd altered the letter to her satisfaction. Running into the kitchen, she found her phone. The photo came out perfectly. The Viper logo prominent, the language the same. Only the final bid different.

Lower by several hundred thousand dollars.

Tam stared down at her mobile phone. She didn't know how many companies were bidding on the device. Possibly dozens. However, by the way Rafe had talked about it and the way Haimon had discussed it, it seemed likely there was only Viper and this other company in a bidding war.

Haimon's cronies were going to lose.

Yet not for several weeks and that bought her time. And hope.

Click.

The bid letter disappeared.

With it, the last loyalty to an old man who'd never been her father dissolved.

CHAPTER EIGHTEEN

"The deal looks good, really good, Rafe."

Rafe gazed across his desk to his CFO. Savas Pagonis had been with him since the early days. One of the first men he'd hired—not for his resume, but for his instincts. He'd never regretted it. "You're sure?"

"I'm sure." Savas leaned forward, his elbows on his knees. "You should know, there've been some whispers about Tobba having an inside edge. Still, I'm inclined to discount those."

Rafe frowned and rubbed his hand across his forehead. He should be excited about obtaining this patent. The product would skyrocket their profits. Yet the only thing he felt was intense irritation that one of his

309

oldest rivals was making a last minute play for a device they hadn't spent any time going after until weeks ago. "I don't understand it. Tobba specializes in pharmaceuticals, not devices."

"Who knows?" The CFO shrugged, bushy eyebrows drawing down. "Even if they do bid, they don't have enough knowledge of the product and what it's capable of doing to put in a bid that will win over ours."

Irritation mixed with sudden frustration. He didn't want to think about this. He didn't want to be here in Athens. He wanted to be home, up in the hills of Sparti, with the boys.

And Tamsin.

His lover, who he'd left this morning, the sunlight barely sliding across the foot of their bed as he dressed. Her face had been pale and drawn. Like she'd spent the entire night tossing and turning. However, she hadn't done that. In fact, he'd slept all night without even once awakening to a kick or a toss.

Last night, at dinner, he'd been ready to question her. The boys had eaten, in their usual hurried way, and then raced off to play with Titus.

He'd had a moment, a moment to find out what the hell was going on. The words were on his tongue, the demand for her to tell him so he could fix it. Defeat what was worrying her, clear away whatever mess was distressing her.

But when she'd glanced at him, her green eyes had been filled with such stark despair he'd nearly gasped, the words falling off his tongue and into his aching gut. Before he'd been able to catch his breath and drag the words back, she'd jerked to a stand. Bustling around the table, clearing the dishes, putting away the remaining food, chattering about nothing—all of it overwhelming the words he couldn't find.

She hadn't been the only one terrified.

He'd been as well.

"Don't worry." Savas stood, a flash of a smile crossing his face. "Take that frown off your face, my friend. Our bid went a little higher than I wanted it to be, but now, maybe that's for the best. There's no way Tobba has the knowledge or the money to take this patent away from us."

"I think we should take precautions."

"Good idea." The man clicked on his mobile phone. "I'll have security dig around. See if they can find out what inside information Tobba supposedly has."

"I trust you to handle that." Because he had no interest in doing so. In fact, he could hardly care less. The only thing he could focus on was what terrified Tamsin. The early morning call from his CFO demanding he had to come to Athens to go over final numbers for this project couldn't have come at a worse time.

"Done." His friend shoved his phone in his pocket and wagged a finger at him. "Now you can focus on the work you've let pile up during the last few months."

"I have everything in hand." His jaw tightened as the irritation returned, now with a sharper edge.

"Do you?" Savas was friend enough not to back down even in the face of a black scowl. "The company, your people, take a cue from you, Rafe. The summer has been rather...sleepy."

"I've had things to take care of."

His CFO stuffed his hands in his pockets, a look of puzzlement on his face. "You could have easily left the twins with your mother. Or your sisters."

The masculine bewilderment in his friend's words almost made him smile, because it mimicked exactly what he'd thought only a few months ago. Along with the amusement came the sudden realization of how far he'd traveled emotionally. The thought of leaving the boys to someone else's care was now anathema. "The boys need me."

"The company needs you, Rafe."

"The company is fine."

"You know what's going to happen once we get this patent. There will be a lot of work to do in order to roll this out successfully."

"Do you think you're telling me something I don't know?" A sliver of weariness mixed with aversion coursed through him. Savas was right. There were going to be many long nights and many missed days with the boys. He supposed it would be all right. The twins would be in school, busy with new friends, and his family would be around to fill in the gaps. And of course, their sister would be there, too.

The confident thought stopped him.

Tamsin. Here. For good.

In fact, he'd assured this by offering her a job and encouraging her to go to school. Once more, he realized with a shock how far he'd traveled from that moment where he'd stood in the cold London rain ready to confront his two enemies.

Tam was not his enemy. Not anymore.

"I know you're a hard worker." Savas drew him out of his contemplation with a jerk. "That's not my point."

His point, Rafe knew, was whether or not he still had the juice to run this company. Whether or not he had the enthusiasm and drive to keep the engine of Viper Enterprises surging forward. The subtle question angered him, but he'd hired this man to be an independent thinker. Savas's value for the company was in saying the words that needed to be said. Even if that angered the owner.

"I merely took some time off this summer, nothing more." Rafe slammed away any doubts. He'd built this company. He'd sweated and sacrificed and sealed a thousand deals to make Viper what it was.

"There's something else going on here, isn't there?"
Savas was not only observant; he was tenacious.

Glaring at his friend, his irritation turning to anger.
"There's nothing else going on."

"There's something missing. You don't seem capable—"

"Are you saying I'm not capable of running this company anymore?" He rose from his chair, instant, instinctive rage pouring through his veins.

Savas stepped back, a wary look crossing his face.
"I'm your friend. I'm saying I'm concerned."

He took his inappropriate rage in hand, trying to stuff it down into wherever it had exploded from. "I know. However, there's nothing to be concerned about."

"I only want to make sure we'll have your full attention going forward."

He tried to push out the promise, but it stuck in his throat. His friend eyed him, as silence fell between them. The muscles of his neck and back tightened, yet even then, he couldn't say the words his CFO wanted him to say.

"What's going on, Rafe?"

The quiet question sliced through his pride. His heart. What was going on inside him? During the last few months, he'd found himself incapable of coming to Athens without a crisis pulling him here. Before, he'd eagerly bounded to work, his enthusiasm pulling along his employees.

Before the boys.

Before Tamsin.

Before he knew in his gut—

"You can tell me what's going on," Savas insisted. "Whatever it is, we'll deal with it."

"There's nothing going on." Rafe sat back down and clicked on his computer.

"Nothing." His friend's voice was placid, but a strain of determination lined the word. "Nothing that has anything to do with the pretty lady who accompanied your mother and sister on the tour of this place several weeks ago?"

"She's the boys' sister."

"Come on," his CFO scoffed. "I have eyes."

"Keep your eyes off of her."

"Hmm." The sound was speculative. "Jealous."

Rafe glanced over in time to see the edge of a knowing smile disappear from the other man's face. Embarrassment turned to sarcasm. "You're married. I know what Thea's reaction would be if you ever looked at another woman. So, no. I'm not jealous."

"Hmm."

Irritation blended with the rage that still simmered. "Don't you have work to do?"

"*Nai.* As do you." Savas paced to the door. "Though remember this, my friend. A woman shouldn't distract a man to the point of hurting his business."

Rafe didn't look at him. He stared at his computer instead. Still, the words swirled around him, bringing guilt to mix into the toxic brew inside him.

"And yet." Savas stopped at the door and turned back. Rafe felt his gaze on him, but ignored him. Whatever his friend had to say, he knew he didn't want to hear it. "I do remember what it was like when I first met Thea."

"I didn't just meet Tamsin. I've known her for years."

"Her name's Tamsin, is it?" His friend leaned on the doorframe, a slight smile on his face. "Good to know."

"Tamsin Drakos. Now that I think about it, it's good for you to know about her." Rafe eased back in his black leather chair. "I'm hiring her."

"What?"

"She's organized. Efficient." He drummed his fingers on the edge of his glass desk. "I need you to find a place for her here."

"That's not a good idea."

His fingers stopped tapping. "What do you mean by that?"

"You can't be distracted during this rollout." Savas shook his head, his eyes pleading. "It's also not a great idea to hire family."

"She's not part of the family." The words clutched in his throat, yet he pushed them out. "She needs a job and she's talented. It's as simple as that."

"Why do I think this isn't simple at all?"

As usual, Savas's instincts were impeccable. Which only drove the frustration inside Rafe into a frenzy. "I don't know what the hell you mean."

"Fine." His friend sighed. "Be that way. But I don't care how long you've known her. I saw the look in your eye the day she visited here—"

"Now you're making even less sense." He turned to his computer and began to type.

"—and I can't think of anything else that would distract my good friend to the point of almost complete inattention to the company he built."

The rage billowed out from his belly, pouring through his bloodstream. "I have not been inattentive."

"You have been." Savas's tone was matter-of-fact and smooth. As if he were only discussing the weather instead of challenging Rafe's very purpose. "It needs to stop. You know that."

"Enough." He swung around in his chair and blasted him with a glare. "You're stepping beyond your position."

His CFO eyed him. "I am talking to you as your friend."

"And I am talking to you as your boss." He stood. "Enough."

A flush of red washed across Savas' face. "I'll get to work then, *sir.*" The door shut behind him with a clipped bang.

He'd angered his friend. He'd disappointed Savas too, by not promising him what he wanted. Because he couldn't. He couldn't make the commitment the man had been searching for.

What did this say about him?

Rafe slumped into his chair, his gut churning.

If he were a coward, if Tam were still his enemy, he'd blame it all on her. This confusion, this roiling, twisting feeling of being off-center, off-point.

Off.

However, it wasn't her.

Not entirely and not mostly. No, there was something deeper here, some kind of poison swimming inside him, tearing his goals and decisions apart.

Restless, he stood and walked to the full-length window looking down on the open, airy atrium placed in the middle of his office complex. The palm trees' leaves brushed the top of the windowed roof while the small pool in the center sparked as the fountain splashed. Tables were strewn around the water where his employees could take a coffee break or eat their lunches.

He had a duty to his employees and to his family. He had responsibilities.

He needed to get back into gear.

Weariness swamped him. Sapped him dry and knifed him at the same time.

What the hell was wrong with him? And what the hell was he going to do about it?

Shaken, he prowled out of his office. Telling his startled PA he'd be back, he ran down the white stone stairs, past the offices and labs, past the atrium and into the heat of midday Athens. Pulling his tie off, he took off at a brisk pace.

The heat burned on his neck and he welcomed it.

Because a cold touch of panic laced through his system.

His breath ratcheted up as his pace increased. Sweat broke out along his spine. His heart *beat, beat, beat* in his chest.

The crowds grew, tourists mingling with workers. The blare of car horns mixed with the sputter of motorcycles. An old woman tromped past loaded with bags. A child shrieked above him from a wrought iron balcony.

Rafe strode faster.

What was wrong with him? What was he searching for?

What was he running away from?

"Rafe Vounó. I can't believe I got lucky enough to spot ya out here." A male voice rang from behind, pulling him to a stop.

Turning, he gaped. "Cameron Steward? What the hell are you doing in Athens?"

The Scotsman strode up, his usual jaunty grin on his rugged face, the uniform of leather jacket and jeans the same as when they'd last met. Slung over his shoulder was a well-worn duffle bag. "A bit of a layover, before I'm headed back home to Scotland."

Rafe grabbed the offered hand and shook it. Although the stew of emotions and frustration still simmered in the back of his mind, he couldn't help the answering grin. Something about Cam made everyone around him want to smile. "Scotland? Home? Am I hearing things?"

A grimace crossed the other man's face. "My mum's dying."

The thought of losing his own mother cut straight through him like a lunging sword. It had been bad enough losing his father. He couldn't imagine... "My condolences."

"Nothing to be done about it." The shrug of broad shoulders was nonchalant, yet something in the movement signaled a tight, tense anger.

An emotion that didn't fit Cameron Steward.

"So you're hanging around on the streets of Athens just waiting for me to stroll by?" He tried to lighten the mood, amazed he had to with this man.

It was Cam who lightened moods.

When he'd first met this roving reporter, he'd been flying a donation of medical supplies into Libya. Part of being wealthy meant a man gave back to society and the world. His father had been clear about that. Rafe always felt like any charity work he did needed to be more than just handing over money. So he donated himself as well, in honor of his father. Unloading supplies, talking with the doctors and nurses offering their services, meeting various local authorities—he'd found the work surprisingly fulfilling.

More fulfilling than the work you do every day.

He batted the thought back.

"Thought I might look ya up." Cam's thick accent turned dry with humor. "Thought you might want to know about the happenings in the Philippines. They're in need of medical supplies in the hills."

The humor reassured him. The last thing he needed in his life was another change. In the half-dozen times he'd met this man, Cam had never been anything other than fearless and easy-going. "I can make some time tomorrow, if that will work."

"Naw, it won't, actually." The reporter grimaced again, shifting his bag higher on his shoulder. "Got to get myself home this evening."

"Send me the details by email, then."

"Email." A scoff came after the word. "As if."

Rafe chuckled. Within the vagabond tribe of traveling reporters, doctors, humanitarians, and photographers, he'd learned that Cam was known as a Neanderthal as far as modern items like laptops and Google.

Which made his success even more extraordinary.

Cam Steward had told him his story one night as they'd sat in front of a roaring fire on a dark beach along with an assortment of reporters, doctors, and rebel fighters.

A bon vivant of disasters.

A connoisseur of chaos.

An award-winning reporter. A best-selling author.

"Well, it was nice to see ya, at least." A paw of a hand patted Rafe's shoulder in rough affection. "Why don't I give ya a wee call when I've settled in Scotland?"

"Settled?" His brows rose in disbelief. "For good?"

Something ugly flashed in the man's eyes. "Aye. For good."

But this man lived for adventure. Rafe had heard the stories from Cam's own mouth. Although he had a myriad of his own problems to deal with, he couldn't help the questions. "Are you serious? What's going on?"

"Ach." The reporter threw him another jaunty grin. "I'm never serious, you know that. Just some things I need to deal with. Nothing for ya to worry your head over."

Before he could probe further, the man turned and strolled down the sidewalk. "I'll give ya a call soon."

He disappeared around the corner of the building, leaving Rafe with another stewing worry to add to his pile.

The turbulence he'd set aside with Cam's arrival, returned.

He took off at a fast pace once more.

A street vendor called out about the freshness of his pastry. The smell of cinnamon and citrus blended with the scent of sweat and smoke. He'd walked these streets for years while he'd planned his next business move or plotted the next bid.

Although he should return to work, although there were a thousand items on his to-do list, he kept pacing through the streets of his home.

Looking for something.

Finding nothing.

This area all seemed alien to him now. As if he'd stepped onto another planet and couldn't find even one familiar landmark.

He turned the corner, into a darker, older street. One filled with the ever-present pawn shops that now populated almost every street of Athens. He'd avoided them. He hadn't wanted to see the desperation and fear in the faces of those who walked into these shops. They reminded him of the time when he'd been desperate and willing to do anything to climb out of the hole his father had dug for him and his family.

No. Not your father.

Drakos. It was Drakos who'd dug the hole. Don't forget that.

His heart beat faster. Faster. Was he having a heart attack? Not at his age. Not possible. Even if he wasn't a doctor, he knew...

A doctor.

Rafe stopped cold. The people on this narrow street walked around him, a few giving him a puzzled glance before moving on.

You dreamed of being a doctor.

He closed his eyes as Tam's words swirled in his brain and heart.

You were going to be a doctor from the moment I met you.

He'd left this old dream behind along with memories of his father and his brother and Tamsin. He'd forged a new life, one filled with tough decisions and heady heights. He'd constantly killed any need to go back and rethink the choices he'd made years ago.

Until now.

Now, here, he felt lost.

Maybe he *was* having a heart attack. His skin was clammy, his breath erratic, his heart racing. If his father had stood before him right now, Loukas Vounó would have promptly taken him to the hospital.

Avoiding the thought of his father, and of doctors and heart attacks and old dreams and frustration, Rafe swung his gaze around until it landed on something sparkly in one of the pawn shops.

The bracelet was pretty. Nothing very special, yet pretty. He'd given his mother and sisters far prettier and more expensive trinkets over the years. He stepped closer. The silver caught the eye, but it was the luster of the pearls and the glow of the blue stones that drew a person in.

Drew him in.

Exactly as it had that long ago summer.

When this bracelet had been worn by his sixteen-year-old love.

Rafe sucked in a breath and came closer. It couldn't be. His fear and frustration—and hell, maybe his undiagnosed heart attack—must be fogging his mind.

The silver twinkled.

His memories were sharp and clear. And accurate.

"You like it, sir?" The curl of satisfaction laced the voice coming from the shop's open doorway. "It's a pretty piece."

"*Nai*, it is." Rafe straightened. "And I'm willing to pay a pretty penny."

The owner's smile grew.

He was a fool for admitting this. The man who'd negotiated million-euro deals knew that. But that man no longer existed. That man was lost in a fog of indecision and lust and fear and anger.

"How much?" He didn't care whether he was a fool or not. All he cared about was getting this bracelet and finding out one thing.

The owner named a number and Rafe obediently stepped into the smoke-filled store, his brain spinning.

What the hell was Tamsin's bracelet doing in this pawn shop?

CHAPTER NINETEEN

"**T**his is the longest he's been gone and I want to know why." Isaák's voice was determined, as well as grumpy.

"It's only been two weeks, idiot." Aarōn scowled at his twin in disgust, yet Tam knew her brother. The way he'd eyed the silent home office every day during the last few weeks. The way he'd stared at Rafe's empty chair at the dinner table every night. Aarōn was worried, too.

"I'm sure he's busy with business." Dishing out the white bean soup, she kept her focus on the serving spoon. The boys might be worried, but she was panicked.

She knew why Rafe wasn't here.

Because of the phone call. The phone call that had surprised her into lying.

And he'd known it.

"I think you should call him." Isaák stared at her with an earnest gaze. "I honestly think you should."

"Me too." His twin reluctantly agreed.

She wasn't going to call him. Not after she'd botched the one and only call two weeks ago. He probably wouldn't answer.

Yet what was she going to do? Time was ticking away. The bomb named Haimon would explode in the near future and she hadn't even begun to smooth the way into her confession.

In fact, she'd made it worse.

"Come on." Isaák swirled his spoon in the soup, a frown on his face. "He'll listen to you."

Rafe had intently listened to her that last time and read between the lines. The silence after his phone call had told her everything she needed to know.

She'd screwed up.

Swinging away from the table, she slammed the pot back onto the stove. She leaned over the sink and tried to think. What could she say to bring him back? And when he did come back, how could she ever find a way to explain what she'd done? He had withdrawn about something so trivial in the face of what else she had to confess, it was almost comical.

She didn't feel like laughing.

"Uh oh." Isaák's voice came from behind her, hushed. "You guys had a fight, didn't you?"

No, there'd been no fight. There'd been frozen rejection instead.

The morning after she'd sent the photo to Haimon, she'd awakened to find Rafe gone. Gone to work when she so desperately needed him here. Here where she could begin to build a bridge across the abyss separating her truth from her actions.

But he'd been gone.

A small emergency, he'd texted. *I'll be back tomorrow.*

Instead, there'd been a call.

The call.

"Tamsin." His voice had been tight.

"Yes?" Dread had dripped its icy tentacles into her heart. Because she'd known immediately, instinctively; something was wrong. Could he have found out about her text to her stepfather? Was his security team more thorough than she'd imagined?

"I took a walk today."

Her mind whirred to a halt. A walk had nothing to do with her text. "You did?"

"And found something interesting."

What could he possibly be talking about? Her mind raced around. Had he run into Haimon? Had he found out something about the bid? Whatever he'd found, she knew it wasn't good. Her mouth went dry. "Yes?"

"*Nai.*" She heard a rustle in the background. Then a *clink, clink* as if something was hitting glass. "I found something from our past."

Her mind spun into a frenzy. Their past was fraught with pitfalls. Apparently, he'd fallen into one. It wounded her to think they'd both forgotten how many moments in their past had been good and strong and beautiful. "What did you find?"

"Your bracelet."

She'd sucked in a breath, but still felt dizzy with disbelief. "My—"

"I'm sure of it." His voice went rough. "The pearl one. The one from your real father."

Had Haimon dared to visit Rafe? Surely, not. He would have landed in jail or been hustled off by security. "Where did you find it?" she managed to choke out.

"A pawn shop." The *clink, clink* became louder. Angrier. "Near my work."

What horrible, awful luck did she have following behind her? Her stepfather hadn't wasted any time, had he? The thought of him slinking around near Rafe's work, selling her precious bracelet, made her sick. "Um."

"Um?" Outrage filled the word. "Is that all you can say?"

Her mind scrambled for some rationale. "I sold it."

"You sold your last link to your real father."

"Yes."

"You sold the bracelet you told me long ago was your most precious possession."

A gurgle of pain slid into her throat. "Yes."

"When?"

The blunt question burned. Her mind scrambled again. "When we visited your office."

"When did you do that?" The disbelief in his voice was rampant now. "I don't remember you ever leaving the tour."

She was digging herself deeper and deeper. Yet she couldn't confess everything. Not on the phone. She hadn't had time to put her thoughts together, to consider how to build this bridge to where he'd understand her actions. "I stepped away for a minute."

Silence fell over their conversation, a heavy blanket of distrust. The gurgle in her throat expanded until she felt as if she were being strangled.

"Really?" Rafe's cold voice at last cut through the dead air like a Spartan sword.

How could she backtrack now? Her jumbled thoughts froze. She couldn't get one word out.

"You know what, Tamsin?" he finally said. "I don't believe you."

There was more to the last statement than mere words. There was more than simple disbelief. The chasm that had existed between them for ten long years had yawned open once again, sucking everything that had been built between them during the last two months down into the abyss.

He'd hung up.

She hadn't heard from him since.

How could she build a wide enough and strong enough bridge to find a way across this divide? And the bomb named Haimon still ticked, promising even further erosion, an even deeper hole swallowing their disappearing relationship.

Tamsin closed her eyes on the last rays of the sun, trying to push down the rabid panic clawing up from her heart.

"What did you fight about?" Isaák piped in from behind her. "We can help fix it."

"We didn't fight."

Somehow, she had to figure out how to get Rafe back here. She couldn't confess everything by phone. She needed to see his eyes as she talked. She needed to watch his body when he responded. She needed to be able to reach over and touch him, hold him while she made him understand.

"Tammy?" Aarōn said, soft and insistent. "Is everything okay?"

How many times had one of the boys asked this of her in one form or another? A thousand? A million? Certainly when they'd been little and just arriving in

London, their small hands wrapped around her neck, their fluff-covered heads tucked under her chin.

Tammy, are we going to be okay?

Or the time they came back from the first day of school, Aarōn's nose bloodied in a fight, Isaák's eyes wide with fear.

Tammy, are we going to be okay?

Or the dozens of times where the money had been so short she'd struggled to make sure their teenage bellies were full.

Tammy, are we going to be okay?

"Yes." She pinned a smile on her face and turned to gaze at both of them. "Everything is going to be okay."

"So, you're going to call him, right?" Isaák gave her a broad smile.

"Maybe tomorrow." She walked to the table and scooped up her uneaten bowl of soup.

Her brother's smile fell off his face. "I think you should call him right now."

"Tomorrow."

Aarōn said nothing. Merely watched her as she stood, staring blindly across the table at both her brothers. "I'll call him."

"No." The word was sharp, far sharper than she meant it to be. Still, the instinct to protect, to take care of everything was so strong, it felt like a knife in her hand. "I'll do it. Tomorrow."

Was she stabbing her boys or herself?

The boys went silent.

"Are you done?" She shot into the gulf opening between them.

"*Nai.*" Aarōn pushed back from the table, his face stony. "Come on, idiot. Titus needs a walk."

Tamsin busied herself cleaning the kitchen as the boys shuffled down the hall, calling the dog on their way.

The slam of the back door echoed in the empty house.

She had to do something. She'd spent two weeks hoping Rafe would make a move, yet clearly, he wasn't going to. Her boys were right.

She had to do something.

But what?

Forcing herself to move, she grabbed her phone, clicked on Rafe's name and before she could stop herself, she begged.

Please. Please come home.

Please. Please come home.

The text cut through his anger like a fiery knife. Rafe pushed himself out of his office chair and paced to the window. Staring down into the atrium, he leaned his forehead on the cool glass.

The anger still simmered deep inside, yet it wasn't what had kept him from Sparti and Tamsin.

No, it had been the fear.

The thought whipped him around and he found himself pacing a well-worn path on the gold-and-cream carpet once more. How many laps had he taken during the last two weeks while he wrestled with the demons of the past? The demon of fear. The demon of hurt. The demon of mistrust.

She'd lied to him. He knew it. His mind, his gut, his heart all told him.

She'd lied.

Again.

Rafe stopped and pulled out the bracelet from his suit pocket. The piece of jewelry he'd kept close to him for two weeks. He even slept with the damn thing under his pillow. Tossing it into the air, he caught it, then tossed it again, caught it again. He stared at the delicate ornament lying in his palm for the thousandth time, like it held the key to what was going on with Tamsin.

The tiny blue stones were cool on his skin, just as her touch was when they lay together in bed. The pearls glowed in the sunlight, just as her skin did as they lay together by the pool. The silver glittered in a brilliant flash, just as her green eyes did when she gazed at him.

Please. Please come home.

He needed to stop avoiding everything. He'd hid away at work, nursing his grievances, stoking his anger. He hadn't even notified his family he was in town, choosing instead to stay in the small bedroom he'd had built beside his office. Usually, he only used the cramped quarters when there'd been a late meeting or a long, overnight research push before a hard deadline. Now, it had served as his bolthole, allowing him to avoid...his life.

Time for that to stop.

Time to confront the fear inside him.

Time to go to Tamsin and find out why—

She'd lied.

Resolved, he strode to his desk and grabbed his phone.

I'm on my way.

As soon as the text was sent to her, he felt a swell of certainty. *Nai,* he'd been angry and hurt she'd lied, but he was willing to sit down and figure out whatever was wrong with her. Because she was worth it. What they'd had during the last two months was worth it. Unlike ten years ago, he wasn't going to slink away, letting go of the good they had.

A knock on his office door interrupted his thoughts.

"*Eláte.*" Whoever it was and whatever work issue it involved would have to wait. His personal life and Tamsin were more important. He'd spent two weeks here working at a punishing pace, making his CFO and everyone else happy and satisfied. However, they'd have to understand he had changed.

He was willing to say it now.

He had changed.

Savas threw open the door and walked in, the head of Viper security not far behind. "Good. You're still here."

"Past eight o'clock, which should make you happy. But not for much longer." Rafe stuck his phone into his suit pocket. "I'm on the way to Sparti."

"Are you?" His friend closed the door behind him with a decisive click. "Not until we go over some information."

"I've been here day and night for weeks." He forced his impatience down and gave his friend a fixed smile. "That will have to suffice for now."

"You'll want to know this information, Rafe."

"You will, sir." The head of security, Ammon Manikas, concurred.

"All right." Tapping his fingers on the edge of the desk, he stopped himself from walking out the door. "You have five minutes."

"I think you might want to sit down."

A shot of anxiety went through him. His CFO appeared troubled, worried. "Is there something wrong with the new project?"

"No."

Manikas shook his head also.

The head of Viper security.

He frowned and forced his mind to work. "There's been a breach in security."

"Maybe." Savas strode to one of the black leather chairs facing the desk and sat. "You need to take a seat. Really."

Anxiety tangled around the deep, dark fear he'd stuffed into the pit of his soul. Why the two would meet inside him, he had no idea. A breach of security in his business was a problem, but he'd dealt with this before. Many times. It came with the territory of being in the forefront of new medical innovation.

"I don't have to sit down." He straightened instead. "Spit it out."

Savas glanced across the width of the desk, a look of resignation on his face. "All right."

"What is it?"

His friend leaned back in the chair, his arms folded in front of him. "Do you know an individual named Haimon Drakos?"

The name shot through Rafe like a bullet. It blasted the deep fear lurking inside right to the center of his mind. "*Nai.*"

Savas stared at him, his eyes dark with worry.

Manikas stepped forward. "My team was able to track down a connection between this individual and Tobba."

"What is it?" Every muscle in his body went rigid. A trembling lined his gut, making him want to turn away. Turn away from what his gut was telling him.

"We have a contact within Tobba who has fingered Drakos as the one who provided insider information on our bid on the neuro-electronic scan."

"Interesting." The trembling turned into a shaking. Outwardly, he stood his ground. Inwardly, he felt as if he were falling apart. Because he knew.

Tamsin's odd behavior during the last few weeks.

Tamsin's use of her body to distract him.

Tamsin's lies.

Savas coughed—a nervous, hoarse sound. "As soon as Ammon told me this name, I remembered another name you talked about recently."

Rafe forced himself to stare coolly back at his colleague. "*Nai.*"

"Could there be any connection—"

"*Nai,*" he said once more. "There is a connection."

A dark silence fell in the room. Manikas shuffled in place while a pained grimace crossed Savas's face.

"There's no need to spare me the details." He felt as if his body was held up by mere mental force. "Proceed with what you have."

"Our contact states that Drakos claimed an inside connection to our company," his head of security continued.

"Go on."

"Drakos apparently provided Tobba with information on the amount of our bid on the neuro-electronic device."

"Keep going."

"Tobba believed him. They based their bid on this information."

"Could this be true, Rafe?" Savas interrupted. "Could this Drakos have knowledge of our bid?"

A flash of memory seared through him. Sitting watching Tamsin as she worked on his laptop. Then walking away to get a drink. Then telling her she could use the computer unmonitored by him.

This was his fault. His company, his people, would be damaged because again, a Vounó had trusted a Drakos.

"We will likely lose the bid." He leaned back on the glass window because he honestly didn't think he'd be able to keep upright without the help.

Savas's arms tightened around his chest. "You're sure?"

"*Nai.* I'm sure."

"This Tamsin has access to—"

"*Nai.*" He didn't want to hear the words, hear the accusation. But he deserved them and his CFO had never failed in delivering what was needed.

A hush fell in the room.

Viper would survive; it had survived far worse. Still, the knowledge that he'd been as foolish as his father made Rafe feel as if he might not survive himself.

"Don't blame yourself." For once, Savas failed to deliver the blow. His friend dropped his hands in his lap, his face grim yet determined. "It happens to the best of us."

"It happens?" His laugh filled the room, an ugly, tortured sound. He'd wanted the blow. He'd wanted the pain to come from someone else. Instead, he had to bludgeon himself with his guilt. "Because of my carelessness this company will lose hundreds of thousands—"

"She will be prosecuted." Manikas looked steely-eyed. "Along with her relative. This is corporate espionage."

"No." The word came out before he could think it through.

His chair creaked as Savas moved, an uneasy shift. "You have feelings for the woman, but we must send a signal. To others. To Tobba."

"No." Pushing himself off the window, he staggered to his desk. He stared blankly at the computer screen, only seeing the image of Tamsin being dragged away by the police. "I'll take care of this."

"You are personally involved." Savas stood, his tone resolute. "I have a duty to the company too. Both of them must be punished."

"They will be." A cold, hard shaft of resolve slit his heart in two and sealed his backbone in pure steel.

"Rafe—"

"This is personal." He met his friend's gaze with an unwavering one of his own. "This is old, my friend. Far older than Viper."

"What?" Savas froze. Behind him, Manikas frowned in confusion.

"I told you. I've known Tamsin Drakos for years."

The two men standing before him didn't move. However, determination no longer covered their faces. Instead, there was wariness.

"I've known Haimon Drakos just as long."

"Personal?" Savas shifted on his feet. "So you are saying these two plotted against you—?"

"As personal as it gets." Rafe smiled and the steel inside him closed around his heart. He could almost hear the lock when it clicked. "Haimon Drakos killed my father."

Savas' mouth dropped open in a gasp.

"So, you see." He broadened his smile. "No one is surer of delivering the proper revenge than me."

'm on my way.

The words sang in her heart all through cleaning the kitchen, nudging the boys to bed, and settling Titus in the office. The news tripped on her tongue, but she figured Aarōn and Isaák would get a bigger kick out of waking up to see their uncle at the breakfast table.

Rafe back at home. Rafe near enough to touch.

Rafe.

Her heart beat a dance inside her chest. She knew they had tons of things to discuss and maybe even argue about. She knew she had to explain many of her actions. Still, she also knew her heart was filled with hope.

Because he was coming home. Because he was on his way.

Tam smoothed her hand across the lace of her white dress. Putting on her best dress would send a signal. She wanted to give and be forgiven. He would see and understand. Wouldn't he?

Well, if he didn't catch on to the clue the dress gave him, then their bedroom would certainly do the trick. In a flurry, after the boys had drifted off to sleep, she'd changed the sheets, the fine weave of Egyptian cotton sliding through her trembling fingers. She'd lit a row of fat cream candles along the long, wide windowsill. There were plush towels waiting on the side of the bathtub accompanied by a bottle of ouzo and two delicate shot glasses.

Everything was ready. For him.

Where was he?

She walked out of the bedroom and down the hallway into the kitchen. The warmth of the light above the stove dulled the full moon's rays splashing into the room.

No sound of a limo driving up the lane. No car lights signaling his return.

Restless, she paced into the office. He'd taken his laptop with him two weeks ago, but there was still the old desktop the boys used to check on their friends' Facebook. The internet barely worked on the thing, yet it was better than pacing the floor getting more and more agitated. She could do some research on the university classes she planned on taking while waiting for Rafe to appear.

Plopping into his leather chair, she forced herself to go on the University of Athens website.

The grandfather clock ticked and tocked in the background as she scrolled through the classes. Her attention slowly centered on the research. The economics classes were the most interesting.

Technical writing

Accounting

Statistics

A different kind of excitement bubbled inside. She could do this. She'd run a business. She'd done the basics of accounting—the only thing she needed was some polish. A degree.

The possibilities rose inside her.

She had a future. A great future. The old dreams she'd stifled as a teenager swelled in her heart to swamp her in a welling tide of hope. Dreams of making a difference in a company that helped people. Dreams of being successful at her own enterprise, doing what she loved to do. Dreams she'd lost so long ago she'd forgotten they were even there.

Adding all these dreams back into her life would make her whole again. Matched with her hoped for life with Rafe and the boys, she couldn't imagine being happier and more alive than she was at this moment. She'd figure out how to handle Rafe's anger and she'd figure out how to make him believe in her confession once he got here.

The clock boomed.

Twelve times.

With a jerk, she stared at the face of the clock, noting with surprise both brass hands pointed north. The drive from Athens to Sparti should have taken a little over two hours. Yet he'd texted almost four hours ago. Had he changed his mind? Or perhaps he'd been delayed by some business crisis.

Then why hadn't he texted her to explain?

At that moment, Titus lurched from his bed and rambled out of the room. Following the dog, she smiled in relief as she saw the headlights of the limo circle in front of the villa.

Rafe. Home.

A breathless flash of excitement, happiness, and anxiety rushed through her. Sucking in her breath and her emotions, she strode to the front door, wanting to welcome him before he even got out of the car.

Titus jumped up and down, his toenails clacking on the tile, his low woofs signaling he knew who to expect.

Her hand reached for the doorknob, but before she touched it the door swung open, almost hitting her in the face. Stumbling back, Tamsin managed a smile of greeting. "You're home."

Without acknowledging her, Rafe bent down to pet Titus into happy submission. He wore his customary steel-blue suit and his red tie was tight around his neck. Why was he so buttoned-up? She wanted to reach up to tug the tie off and smooth the coat down his arms, but something about his body language stopped her.

The taut line of his shoulders.

The way he didn't meet her gaze.

The stiff bend of his back.

Sudden tension flooded inside her. "I was getting worried."

"Were you?" He straightened and finally looked at her.

The tension clogged in a tight knot in her throat. He was still mad at her about the bracelet. She saw it in the white line around his mouth and the icy glint in his eyes. "We need to talk."

"Talk." He laughed, a short burst of harsh sound. "By all means, let's talk."

The door stood open, the limo running in place instead of driving off. She noticed several long dark cars behind the gate, their lights glowing in the darkness. "What's going on?"

With a jerk, he turned and slammed the door shut. "First, Tamsin, as you requested, we will talk."

The tension no longer resided in her throat. It had slithered into her stomach and her soul like a thick smog of sickness. "I can explain."

"Can you?" Rafe's mouth quirked, and the familiar motion should have given her hope. But it increased the dread inside her because there was no humor in his reaction.

There was threat.

"Yes." She tried to pull herself together. What she said next needed to heal this breach because her heart wouldn't stand for anything else.

"Not here." He walked past, without touching her, almost as if she were contagious. "In my office."

She followed him down the hushed hall. Titus ambled to his bed in the corner; the lamp shone brightly, and her glass of wine stood half-full on the desk. All the little details that spelled home and hearth and happiness. Yet nothing could stop the frozen cold of Rafe's attitude from invading the surroundings.

She stepped into the office. Without touching her again, he shut the door behind her. Walking around the desk, he sat in his chair and stared at her from across the wide expanse of oak.

The scene froze inside her forever, like a photograph she'd carry with her into the future. A future of bleak and cold memories.

The quiet ticking of the clock.

The yawning expanse of the desk between them.

The black hate in her lover's eyes.

"This isn't about the bracelet, is it?" Her words landed in the silence like drips of toxic air.

"No," Rafe answered, his voice loud compared to hers. "No, Tamsin, it's not about your bracelet. Not now."

He knew. Somehow he knew.

Everything froze inside. Her brain, her tongue. Everything warm and willing curled up in her heart and softly screamed itself away.

She saw it in his eyes. There was no hope.

No matter what words she said, no matter how much she'd given, no matter how much her heart was his— none of it mattered.

She saw it in his eyes.

A sudden surge of acute, painful rage stormed past her dying heart and roared into her blood. "Then just spit it out."

His dark brows rose. "Do I have to? This is all so...predictable, isn't it?"

"Say it. I dare you to say it."

"Say what?" He eased back in his chair as if having a casual conversation. The entire time, his black eyes burned with hellfire. "Say I should have expected this from a Drakos? Say I was a fool for letting you near anything of mine again?"

Letting her near his home. His body. Maybe, oh maybe, even his heart. She wanted to weep but her rage overwhelmed her pain. Because if he had let her into his heart, he should know better. He should know her better. "That's it. Keep going."

Rafe's mouth tightened. "You're in no position to be flippant. I hold all the cards now."

"Do you?" He was going to do this without even giving her a chance to explain. Evidently, he'd found out at least some of what she'd done and yet he wouldn't even listen for a moment before handing down his decision.

She had done this to save the boys, damn him.

To save their boys.

It was also clear he'd jumped to the conclusions best suited to his cynical views on the past. The past he knew nothing about.

"*Nai*, I do." His careless, casual attitude was fake. She knew it in the way he held his body tight, the way his long fingers curled into a fist.

She supposed she should take heart that this was hard for him, that he was in pain. Instead, the memories of his contempt, his suspicions, his accusations poured over her building anger like kindling. Gas to a fire.

She'd had enough.

Enough of his arrogant decisions about who and what she was. No more Tamsin trying to make it work, trying to keep everyone happy. She'd held everything together for so long, and with a rush, she was done.

Done with Haimon.

Done with Rafe.

The rage inside combusted, burned, and scorched apart the last piece of her that wanted to heal this. The last piece of her that wanted to be loved. "You've never held all the cards."

"Enough." He reached into his suit pocket and pulled out an envelope. "You will sign this."

Tam glared at him, shaking with the knowledge—this was over. Every one of her hopes and dreams torn to shreds. A repeat of ten years ago. "We'll leave. If you want to think the worst, fine. We'll leave."

"We?" His head jerked up from contemplating the envelope and for the first time, a smile slid onto his face. An ugly, vicious smile. "There's no *we* anymore."

The words hit her like a stream of poison aimed straight for her heart. But she didn't have a heart for this man. Not now. All she had was her rage. "I don't need you—"

"I'm not talking about you and me." The smile deepened. "That was merely passing some time while I was here."

The air burned her throat when she forced herself to breathe.

"No, Tamsin. I'm speaking of you and the boys."

"What?" A dull horror seeped into her anger.

Rafe slipped a wad of papers from the envelope. "You're going to sign over your guardianship of the twins."

"I would never—"

"Tonight." He slapped the papers onto the table. The sound ricocheted around the room.

Now that she no longer had to deal with Haimon, now that she had lost Rafe forever, she had to have Aarōn and Isaák. If she didn't have her brothers...She wavered on her feet. "Never."

The ugly smile fell off his face. "I don't want to spend any more time with you."

She stood in front of him feeling as if she were facing a firing squad.

"So I'll be quick." His smile came back. "Just as you were so quick to get rid of me years ago."

"That wasn't—"

"I've come to appreciate your efficiency that day. So I'll do you the same favor."

Where had the anger gone? The rage had provided a shield to her heart as his ugly words were spoken, as the searing memories were exposed once more. Tam closed her eyes, blanking out Rafe's white face, his coal-black eyes.

"I get the boys without going through months of fighting you in court."

She squeezed her eyes tighter.

"You and your father escape prosecution and jail."

"No." The cry burst from her, hoarse, a frozen rejection. The rage inside turned to pure ice. "No."

"You have no choice."

Choice. Choice. Choice.

The one word echoed in her mind, and heart and past.

You have a choice, Tamsin. Walk away from him and I will make sure there is enough money left for his medical schooling.

At sixteen, she'd had to make a choice that had blunted her entire life. All her dreams and wishes had been lost to keep the ones she loved whole. The choice had saved her boys. That choice had saved this man and his family.

Tam opened her eyes and looked at him.

What would he say if she threw this knowledge at him now? That she was the one who'd given him the seed money for his company. That she was the one who'd made it possible to save his family's home.

What would he say?

The heated rage swept back in, burning her frozen fear away.

"You don't have to stand there thinking about it. Don't be a fool." His words spat from his mouth like knives. "You wouldn't survive in a prison."

No? She almost said the word, almost laughed in anguish at his absurd statement. She'd been living in a self-imposed prison for years. Yet the bars were falling in the face of her rage. The bars this man had built around her heart.

You had a choice, Tammy. You always have a choice. And you chose the wealthy man instead of loyalty to your family.

"I have a choice." She curled her fingers into a fist, wanting to hit him, scar him. "I choose to tell you to go to hell."

She whipped around. The door opened with a crash, her hand giving it an extra push for impact. She heard him swear behind her, but she didn't catch the word. She didn't care about his words anymore.

Racing to the back door, she flipped open the lock and rushed out into the cool night air. The full moon glowed, a golden orb looking down at her flight. Tam took off, letting the light guide her on the mountain trail.

She wanted to be up. Above.

She wanted to leave him behind. Far behind.

She wanted to be free. For the first time.

The spikes of her sandals caught in the weeds and the rocks of the path. Stopping for a moment, she yanked them off and threw them behind her, down the mountain.

She didn't need sexy shoes anymore. She didn't need to wear lacy dresses or brush her hair or try to be pretty for him. Or anyone.

She was free.

"Tamsin."

His rough cry didn't stop her. Nothing would stop her ever again because she was free from care. Free from love.

The thought stopped her.

Her breath was ragged, her skin tight and hot. She wasn't free really. She still had to take care of her brothers.

Something hard and cold popped inside her. Something selfish and needy and greedy. Something that told her the boys had had enough of her, had taken all she had to give right now. They'd taken more than she had to give.

The realization propelled her forward once more. The arm of a bush tore a rent in her lace dress. Her feet scraped on the rocks and bled. A trickle of sweat rolled down her spine.

She kept climbing.

The moonlight wove patterns of dark and light on the ridges of the mountains surrounding her. A slight wind brushed the tears on her cheeks, drying them. The chirping call of a nightingale was the only sound beyond her harsh breathing.

Maybe he'd given up chasing her.

"Tamsin." The hardness in his voice came from right behind her. "This is crazy."

Crazy. Yes. She'd been crazy. Crazy to believe this man could ever be the dream she'd once loved. Crazy to spend her whole life making others happy.

Crazy to give everything and receive so little back.

She stopped as the ping of this awareness ran through her. Glancing to her side, trying to avoid a conclusion she didn't want to make, she laughed under her breath.

How ironic.

Tam stepped off the path. Right into the hollow where they'd first made love.

Strike that thought. A grim smile came to her face. Where she'd mistakenly given her love and he'd carelessly taken it. Along with her virginity.

"Your feet are bleeding."

She turned to face him. "What do you care?"

The hard line of his jaw tightened. "Come back to the house. I've got bandages."

She laughed again, the sound lilting in the night air. "You'll play the doctor for me, Raphael?"

A muscle in his jaw rolled. "You're acting crazy."

"And saying crazy things, aren't I?" She folded her arms around her, the sweat cooling on her skin. "Crazy to think of you as a doctor, right?"

"Don't try and change the subject."

Once more, she laughed. Amazing how not caring anymore gave a person such freedom. Freedom from disappointment and hurt. Freedom to say whatever, even if it caused pain. "Do you recognize this place?"

"Of course, I do." He stuck his hands in his pockets, his eyes gleaming like ink in the moonlight. "Here's where I slept with my enemy."

Tam made a sound deep in her throat. Not caring. "Here's where you took my virginity."

He jerked straight, his shoulders going taut. "What?"

"You heard," she murmured. "You took."

He turned away to scowl out at the valley. The moonlight caressed his profile like she'd done when they'd come together. How stupid she'd been. To think they had been united. That they had been one.

"You're lying," he gritted.

How stupid. To think this man was worthy of her gift. Gifts. "Believe whatever you want."

Jerking around, he glared at her.

She laughed. Low and from deep within her, she laughed in the face of his anger. Because he had no hold on her anymore. Thank God. She was free.

"This." One hand came out of his pocket to slice in this air. "This is not the conversation we need to have."

"Say whatever you want to say."

His arm dropped to his side in apparent surprise.

He couldn't understand this new Tam, this Tam who didn't care. Good. "Go ahead. I'm listening."

"I've found out what you and Haimon have done." His hand fisted at his side. "The Drakos clan always sticks together."

She said nothing.

"In another circumstance, I'd applaud this. I appreciate loyalty. But not now."

The bite of his voice would have once upon a time caused her extreme pain. Now, now that she was free, she heard the words as if they were little wisps of wind.

"You have effectively ruined a year's worth of work on a patent that held great promise."

She didn't think she had. Clearly he knew about the bid, yet he didn't know everything if he thought this. At another time, she would have offered the knowledge to him as a gift. Still, look at what he'd done with all the gifts she'd given to him over the years.

So she didn't give him this last gift.

She had another one to give him instead.

"You can have the boys." Brushing her hands across the lace of her dress, she felt nothing. "I'll sign the papers you brought."

His mouth dropped open. Then closed with a click. "You don't want to go to jail," he sneered. "How quickly you let go of your precious brothers to escape the consequences of what you've done."

Ignoring his contempt, she focused on his words. She'd just escaped one jail, and no, she didn't want to enter another. However, that had nothing to do with Aarōn and Isaák. The boys belonged in Greece. They belonged with Nephele and the Vounó clan. And although she hated Rafe now with a fierce passion, they belonged with him too.

He hated her, but he did love the boys.

Her twins would be safe and cared for. Aarōn and Isaák would have everything they needed as they grew into men. Her brothers had been given the best she had and now it was time they spread their wings in a new direction.

It was also time for her to spread her own wings.

"Why should I be surprised?" Rafe's jeer drew her attention away from her decision. "A Drakos always looks out for their own skin when it comes down to it, right, Tammy?"

The nickname hurt. Stung like a prick of remembered pain. She brushed her hands across her arms. Brushed the sting away. None of this mattered anymore.

Time for Tamsin Drakos to be free. Completely free.

"I'll sign the papers, but I want a contract saying you won't go after me legally."

He eased back on his heels, his arms crossing in front of his chest. "And Haimon."

Let him think anything he wanted. "Sure. Why not?"

"Don't be flippant again." He clenched his teeth. "The attitude doesn't suit you."

As if he had any idea what suited her. "I'm not done."

One long finger tapped on his arm. "Why am I not surprised?"

"I want a plane ticket to London."

"And let me see..." The finger tapped faster. "Money. You probably want money, too."

She should. If she were smart, she should ask. Yet her pride rose like a fierce force inside her. "No, I don't."

"How could I forget?" He grimaced, his face hard with bitter anger. "You're going to get a tidy sum from Haimon when that bid comes through."

He'd eat those words. Eventually. If she had any luck and Viper won the contract. But she didn't care now and she wouldn't care then.

Rafe gazed across at her. "A ticket and a contract. Then you're gone."

"Correct." Her heart didn't flutter. It didn't burn or cry or sink. Her heart was gone now, burnt to ashes in the fire of her rage.

She was glad.

"All right, Tamsin. We have a deal."

CHAPTER TWENTY-ONE

"I wonder what Tam's doing." Isaák's plaintive voice floated over the family dinner table like a cloud of misery.

"She's at school just like she wrote in the note she left us, idiot." His brother glared from across the table. "She doesn't have time to worry about us."

The heartache in both boys' words made Rafe itch to leave the table. He was here only because of his mother's insistence. During the last month, since they'd returned to Athens, he'd been too damn busy at work to attend any family events at all. Cleaning up the mess he'd created by trusting a Drakos didn't allow for any private time.

Not that he needed or wanted any private time. Not at this point.

"Boys." Nephele's quiet voice came from the head of the table. "I'm sure your sister is busy in London and she'll call when she can."

No. She wouldn't. It had been part of the agreement she'd signed that ugly night a month ago. No contact. Ever. Or at least for the next five years the twins were in his care. She'd signed the form without even flinching. Not even one tear.

Theós. He'd been the one who'd felt as if he were being ripped apart as he watched her fingers wrap around the pen. He'd been the one who felt as if his world were ending. And it had been he who felt like howling out his pain and torment.

The fact disgusted him, then and now.

Because of the damn emotions running through him at the time, he'd allowed her to write a note to the boys. Some nonsense about getting a scholarship in London and having to leave in a hurry.

He'd read the note while she packed.

"I miss Titus." Isaák shot a glance down the table, his mournful gaze hitting Rafe right in the gut.

He'd stared through the window as she'd been escorted into the limo, the two security cars following her.

He'd been gutted then, too.

"A dog needs room to roam," his mother cut in again, a firm tone in her voice. "It's best he stay in the mountains."

Titus had been left behind as had Rafe's foolish feelings for Tamsin.

During the last month, he'd returned to his real life. A life of practical business decisions, of long meetings and hard choices. A life that didn't include fanciful ideas of love and happiness.

A life that didn't include the boys.

His mother had made the last point quite...pointedly this afternoon.

Because of that conversation, he was here.

"Tell us about your first week of school, Aarōn." Rhachel smiled at her nephew, trying to help their mother keep the peace.

Her attempt to smooth the troubled waters fell flat. "It's okay." The teenager scowled down at his soup. "For school."

This from the boy who, two months ago, had poured over the class schedule with Tam, chatting excitedly about each choice he made.

His mother's gaze landed on him like a torch. A quiet, firm, blazing torch.

All right. He could see there were problems. The boys were unhappy and something needed to be done.

By him.

His mother didn't have to say the actual words. He got it.

He shouldn't have abruptly left Aarōn and Isaák on their own so swiftly after Tamsin had exited their lives. He should have been here. Been here to help them settle into the Vounó clan, find their way at school, figure out how to live without the care of their sister.

He got that. He understood his mother's unspoken censure.

What she didn't get, or understand, was that he couldn't. He didn't have it in him to be around these boys.

He'd always noted the boys' resemblance to the Vounós, but now every time he looked at Isaák, he saw the arch of Tam's brows. When he stared at Aarōn, he only noticed the line of his jaw matched his sister's. When he spent even a moment of time with either of the teenagers, her name inevitably came into the conversation.

The pain was too great.

The memories too heated and hard.

Even now, he felt the howl building inside him, punching up his throat, strangling any words he wanted to say.

"You said you were going to go to my first football game, Rafe." Isaák peered at him, his dark eyes filled with lingering hope. "It's tomorrow."

"I can't." His raw throat made the statement too harsh. Still, he couldn't help it. The howl tied around his vocal chords like a whip. "I've got a business meeting."

Aarōn scoffed, his expression going hard. "Of course you do."

His twin's gaze went flat.

The boys hadn't been like this at first, a month ago. Not angry and resentful as they were at this point. The morning after Tam had left, they'd been startled to hear she was gone, but not overly worried. She'd call. She'd come to visit, they told each other. She'd miss them soon and return for good. Return to kiss Rafe, Isaák had snickered to Aarōn. They had their uncle until their sister came back. With him, they were safe—it was clear this is what they'd thought.

The knowledge had lain like a heavy sludge of guilt over him all month.

After one sleepless night in Sparti, he hadn't been able to help himself. Not even for the boys could he stay one more day in the house they'd shared. Yet when he'd announced they were returning to Athens, the twins hadn't complained. They were eager to see their cousins again, excited to start school.

Apparently, things had changed.

Rafe stared at Aarōn and saw the defensiveness, the anger, the fear in his gaze that had been there when he'd first walked into their lives. The look that hadn't been in the twins' eyes this summer.

His mother was right.

He'd been neglecting a duty.

For ten years, he'd met every duty, every pledge. For ten years, he'd been the rock his family needed when the storm hit. However, now, with this duty, he couldn't do it.

The heavy sludge of guilt turned to hardened cement.

Nephele coughed, bringing Rafe's gaze back to her. "Perhaps something can be arranged."

Nothing could be arranged to make this pain go away. Nothing his mother or anyone else could do or say would make it palatable for him to be anywhere near the boys.

Not right now. Maybe not ever.

The realization ran through him, bleeding his heart into his soul. Years ago, Tam's betrayal had scarred him, yet he'd gone on, made a life for himself and his family. This betrayal, this time she'd poisoned him in a way that would never heal.

And the boys were going to pay the price.

"Rafe," Rhouth laid a hand on his, her warm palm burning his skin. "I know you've been very busy, but the boys—"

"Leave it." He thrust his chair back and rose. Staring at his youngest sister, he remembered the hatred she'd had for Tamsin. Rhouth, of all of them, should be rejoicing that she was gone. Instead, he saw worry in her eyes, a look he remembered from years ago, when Tamsin Drakos had been able to gut him for the first time.

The thought tightened his every muscle and knotted every brain cell.

He'd been stupid once more. This was his fault. This time, though, it wasn't only Raphael Vounó who was going to pay the price. This time it was his family who was being torn apart. This time it was two thirteen-year-olds who were in his care and who were as lost as he was.

And he couldn't think of a thing to say or do to make it right for his family or the boys.

He turned away from them. From the worry in Rhouth's eyes, from the love on his mother's face, from the sneer on Aarōn's mouth. He had to figure out someway to make this up to the twins, but at this moment, there was nothing inside him except agony.

"Raphael. Stop."

Not even his mother's soft command could keep him from pacing down the hall and into the library. He slammed the door behind him to make sure no one misunderstood.

He wanted to be alone.

He needed to be alone.

Striding to the window, he put his sweating forehead on the chill of the glass. The cool air of the October night whispered along the edge of the palm trees, waving shadows of moonlight across the terrace. Something he didn't want to name wrapped around his heart. His broken, defeated, dead heart. He breathed in, trying to push the emotion away.

With no success.

Grief welled inside, clogging his throat and burning his eyes.

He missed her.

He missed his enemy, a woman who'd betrayed him so easily, who'd walked out of his life twice without looking back. The woman who'd torn his heart apart for the second time.

He missed her.

He missed the way her eyes lit when she saw him. The way she swung her blonde hair over her shoulders. He missed her slurred voice as she scolded the boys and the lilt of her laugh as she dipped into the pool. He missed her warmth beside him while he slept and the heat of her welcome when she wrapped her body around his.

Here's where you took my virginity.

The soft slur of her words slid into his thoughts for the thousandth time.

You took.

His fist tightened on the windowsill and just he had before, for the thousandth time, he pushed the thought away.

He missed his enemy. God damn him.

But he still didn't believe anything she'd said. Thank God.

The door creaked open.

"Go away." He didn't shout, yet his words cut through the air, a slice of threat.

"No."

Rhouth. *Skata.* He couldn't talk to her. He didn't want to hear how he was better off without Tamsin, that she wasn't good enough for him, that she couldn't be trusted.

He knew all this in his head, but not in his heart.

God damn him.

The door clicked closed.

"Raphael."

"I said—" he kept his gaze pinned on the moon "—go away."

"I have something you need to see."

Turning, he glared at his younger sister. "If it's about Tamsin being the enemy and Tamsin being a betrayer and Tamsin being—"

"It's about Tamsin." She stood her ground in the face of his rage. Her dark gaze didn't hold hate, though, it held sorrow. Something that nearly crippled him to see.

He was the strong one. He was the big brother.

He was the one who kept everyone together.

His little sister shouldn't be staring at him like this. Like there was something wrong with him, like she pitied him.

"However, it's not about anything you mentioned." Holding a packet in her hands, she lifted it as if offering a gift. "I decided you needed to see these."

"If it's about Tamsin, I don't want to know."

A frown of determination brought her dark brows together. "You must."

"Rhouth," he sighed. Exhaustion flowed through him and he leaned on the cool window, hoping he could stay standing until she left. "There's no need to talk about her. She's out of our life for good."

"What?" The frown turned from determination to puzzlement. "The boys expect her to—"

"You don't have to show me anything to convince me she was a viper in our nest." He crossed his arms across his chest, noting with disgust that his hands trembled. "She proved it again and I got rid of her."

"She proved it again?"

"*Nai.*" He glanced away, not willing to expose his self-disgust while he made his confession. Not until this moment had he ever planned on telling anyone in the family. His hope had been that Tamsin's memory would fade and eventually, everyone would forget her. Including him. But if this was the only way to silence his sister, then he would confess. "She stole some information from me and sold it to a competitor."

His sister gasped.

"A month ago I found out and told her to leave or face jail time."

A stunned silence filled the room.

Forcing himself to look at her again, he gritted his teeth and smiled. "So, you see, you got your wish. She left. For good."

He'd expected to see triumph covering Rhouth's face. To his astonishment, her expression screwed into a mask of disbelief. "That can't be."

"You of all people say that?" He laughed, a short burst of pain. "You? Who was so sure she'd betray us again."

"Betray you again."

The words hit him like pellets from a gun. "And she did. You were right. Can we leave the subject of her alone now? Forever?"

She frowned at the packet in her hands. "No, we really can't."

"We absolutely can—"

"I'm sorry." Lifting her head, she gave him a scowl. "But this is too important and I can't let you make this mistake."

"Mistake." He dropped his hands to his sides and they fisted in frustration. "Anything about Tamsin Drakos is a mistake. I don't want her name ever mentioned again."

His sister ignored his taut pronouncement and walked to the green velveteen sofa and sat.

"Rhouth, I swear—"

"Listen." She pulled a peach ribbon off the packet. "Please listen."

Rafe stamped down the urge to yell or run from the room. She pitied him enough. He wasn't going to act the fool and appear to be incapable of dealing with some insignificant detail about a female thief. Folding his arms in front of him once more, he glared at his sister. "Fine. Say what you have to say and then I never want the subject brought into a conversation."

She slipped a flowery piece of paper from an already-opened envelope. Suddenly, he realized the packet was a stack of a couple of dozen letters. Glancing at him, her eyes filled with tears. "These are from Tamsin."

Outrage yanked him upright. "She's been writing to you? She dares to write after what she did last month—"

"These were written ten years ago."

Blank astonishment stopped him from racing over and ripping the offensive papers out of his sister's hand. "What?"

"She wrote to me. I told you before, remember?" His sister stared at the letter in her hand. "All the time. For months. I kept every one of them."

Wrenching his emotions back into a hard grip, he forced himself to lean on the cool window. "Why the hell did you keep the damn letters? And what does it matter what a girl said ten years ago?"

"I kept them because I wanted to remember her and what she'd done to you." Rhouth glanced at him. "And it does matter. Especially at this point."

"These letters might matter to you, but they don't to me."

"I never opened them. Any of them." Her hand tightened on the packet. "I was so angry when she left. I was too mad at how much she'd hurt you."

"Rhouth—"

"Still, watching you during the last month, I realized something."

"What?" He wanted this to be done. He wanted to return to Sparti and hide. Yet the ghost of his enemy lingered in every room of his home, on every inch of his land. There was nowhere for him to hide.

"I realized I might have been wrong. About everything."

"You were right about everything. Everything about her." He tried not to shout, but the anger and pain were too great. "You were right to want her away from this family, out of our lives."

"Out of your life." She opened the letter. "I know that's what you think at this moment, except you're wrong."

He cursed. A harsh string of words intended to scare her off of what it was so clear she was determined to do.

Force him to hear Tamsin's own words.

Ignoring him, his sister began to read. Her voice was hushed, yet the words were stark and sharp. A sixteen-year-old's crushing pain blew off the letter's pages like ragged shards of steel. The emotions expressed were taut with frustration, fraught with despair.

"Stop."

She chose another bombshell, another piece of paper filled with a teenager's plaintive wail at fate. Every word hit him in the gut. This was the Tam he'd known before she'd rejected him. Kind and loving. Even through the agony-soaked words he heard her kindness. Her love.

"Enough." The harshness of his voice told too much, but he couldn't stand it anymore. Couldn't stand hearing one more word.

Dropping her hands in her lap, Rhouth stared at him. "I read every single one last night."

"Why?" The hoarse cry came from his dead heart. "Why did you keep the damn things anyway? Why did you read them after all this time?"

"I loved Tamsin." His sister sighed. "Not as much as you did—"

"I didn't—"

"Not as much as you love her now." Her bold claim slapped him to silence. "Before, I was so hurt by what she'd done to you, I couldn't force myself to read anything she had to say."

"You should have kept it that way."

His sister's dark eyes met his. In them, he saw the same determination she'd exhibited when she came into the room. "I've watched you, Raphael. I've watched the boys this last month."

"There isn't anything to see."

"I've watched the three of you suffer because she isn't here."

"No."

"I remembered. Finally." She took in a deep breath. "Remembered how wonderful a friend Tam was. Remembered how happy you were with her years ago."

Pivoting away, he stared through the window at the moon. "I don't want to talk about this—"

"You and the boys were happy this summer. You stayed in Sparti for months and the boys looked so happy when they returned to Athens." She kept at him with her relentless pace. "You were all happy when Tamsin was with you. It's clear."

"That's not what—"

"Because you're all so obviously miserable now."

"Not true." He swiveled to face her, making sure his face was blank. "And what this has to do with those letters, I can't understand."

Her mouth tightened. "I knew I was wrong about her. Somehow I'd gotten it wrong."

"As I said before, you were, in fact, right about her."

"So I read the letters."

"You're making no sense."

"Quite the opposite." She slipped the letter back into its envelope. "After I read them, I understood."

"Understood she could spin a good tale, even as a teenager?"

"Oh, Raphael." Her laugh was faint and sad. "After you read every one of these letters, you'll know she was spilling her heart out for you."

He laughed, the sound cold and hard. "I'm not reading any of them. You can burn them for all I care."

His sister tied the ribbon around the letters without answering him. Standing, she walked to his desk and placed the packet in the middle with crisp precision. Then she turned to face him. "I've read every one of them and I'll tell you this."

"I don't want to know."

"Someone made Tam do what she did to you ten years ago." Rhouth clasped her hands together as if praying he'd listen. "She was forced. Although she doesn't say so precisely, it's clear."

"That was ten years ago." He pressed himself on the window pane, trying to appear unmoved. "This doesn't matter anymore."

"This matters because I think the same thing must have happened now."

"Right." His hands fisted in his pockets. "I'm supposed to believe she sold company secrets for something other than money."

"Correct. But you have to know..." His sister took a step towards him, but must have seen something in his face to stop her.

"I can read a thousand letters written by her and I won't believe one word of them." He stared her down. "Not one."

"Why won't you—"

The buzz of his phone cut through the argument, much to his relief. Striding to his desk, he reached for the mobile and noted the caller. "I have to take this call. It's business."

His sister glared at him. "Of course it's business. That's all you ever do—"

"I need some privacy." He tapped his finger on the phone.

"This isn't over." She paced to the door and threw it open. "Not by a long shot."

The door slammed shut behind her.

"It's over," he muttered before clicking on the buzzing call. "Savas."

"Rafe." His friend's voice was puzzled. "Something odd has happened."

"What?"

"We won the bid."

"What bid?" They had dozens of bids going at the time. Even though Tamsin's betrayal had cost Viper Enterprises a bundle, it hadn't stopped them from continuing their work in many different areas of medical research. "Why is winning a bid odd?"

"Because we weren't supposed to win this one." Savas paused as if unable to find the words.

"What the hell are you talking about?"

His CFO's voice rushed over the phone, filled with excitement. "We won the patent on the nano-device."

"What?" Stunned shock froze every one of his muscles.

"*Nai.*" Savas stopped, then pushed forward. "I don't know what happened. But she didn't give them our bid. Tamsin didn't betray you."

The October rain was almost warm as it hit his face. The soft mist had driven most people off this narrow street leaving Rafe to himself.

He stared at the hotel. The garish yellow light flashed the hotel's name in the dusky gloom. The light also, unfortunately, highlighted the crumbling concrete and the unwashed windows.

Fitting. For his oldest enemy.

Stepping through the glass door, he found himself in a dinky foyer dominated by a front desk that had seen better times. Within a few minutes and after exchanging several euros, he had a key in hand.

The room stunk of desperation and cigar smoke.

"Hello?" The man on the bed rolled over and stared at Rafe's silhouette standing in the hotel door. "Who are you? What are you doing in my room?"

Rafe took a moment to admire his security's reach when given a few good tips. Within twenty-four hours of his conversation with Savas, they'd tracked this man down to this hovel. He stepped into the room and closed the door behind him with a decisive click.

He wanted answers. He needed them.

"Are you from the hotel?" The man pulled the covers to his chin.

Rafe snapped on the lights.

"You." Haimon Drakos jerked upright. "How did you...? How could you—?"

"Save your breath for answering my questions." Stepping across a pile of dirty laundry, he yanked an old wooden chair out from under the ancient desk and sat. He tilted the chair on its back legs, leaning on the wall.

"What do you want?" Drakos had apparently recovered his confidence because he managed to snarl.

"I want some answers."

"I don't have anything for you." The old man's expression sparked to life with anger. "You've taken everything away I had."

He'd hated this man before him for so long. Had wanted him harmed and hurt and dead. Yet at this moment, there was an eerie emptiness in his heart where this hate he'd stored for so long had burned. The hate had filled the hole his father and brother and Tamsin had left behind and now all he felt was...nothing. "I'm willing to pay for the answers, Drakos." He glanced around. "It appears you may need the help."

A war between pride and avarice flashed in the old man's eyes. Pride won. "I don't want your money."

"Really?" He eased farther back in his chair. "Then why did you try and steal it?"

The man didn't even blink at the accusation. "I tried to get what was mine to begin with. Only a small amount of it."

The claim was so outlandish, so preposterous, he wondered if perhaps the man before him had slipped into some kind of dementia. If that was true, he had to zero in on the most important question he needed answered. "Where's Tamsin?"

"How would I know?" The old man's eyes filled with sudden tears. "I can't believe she betrayed me."

"She wasn't in it with you, was she?" Rafe had known as soon as he'd heard Savas' voice, but he had to make sure. "She didn't want to do this."

Haimon smirked. "The girl has always been too prissy. Too perfect."

"You're proud you blackmailed your stepdaughter?"

"I didn't blackmail her." The man tightened his fists around the sheets. "I just made her see she needed to do something for her father."

"You were never a father to her," he gritted. "Never."

"Look what she did to me instead." The old man's wail cloaked the room with incredulity. "I can't show my face in Athens anymore. There are men searching for me."

"Good. You deserve it."

Drakos glowered at him, yet the light of battle slowly leeched from his eyes and face, and he slumped on the bed. "What does it matter?" he muttered. "I've lost everything."

"Tell me what you meant about getting what was yours."

"She didn't tell you, did she?" His mouth contorted. "So like her to be too soft in the heart to claim her rights."

"Tell me what?"

"It was my money, given to Tamsin," the old man spat, "which allowed you to start that precious company of yours."

The front legs of Rafe's chair hit the floor. "What the hell do you mean by that?"

"Didn't you ever wonder where the money came from?" Haimon sneered. "The money so conveniently left out of your father's estate?"

The breath seared his lungs. He had wondered. For ages. But the bank manager insisted he had no information to give him. Eventually, he'd figured it was one of his father's friends who'd anonymously made sure the Vounós weren't left totally destitute. He'd been grateful.

Now he felt enraged.

He jumped from his chair and lunged for the bed. Grabbing the man by his cotton T-shirt, he yanked him forward.

"Let go," Haimon gasped.

"Tell me." He shook the man, surprised at how thin and wasted his enemy had become. He'd always seen Drakos as a great monster he had to take down. At this moment, all he saw was a sniveling creature not worth his time except for answering his questions. "Tell me."

Blurry grey eyes narrowed. "When your stupid father killed himself—"

Rafe gave him another shake, but there wasn't any heat to it. Somehow, somewhere he'd forgiven his father and hateful slurs no longer mattered. "Keep going."

"Tammy and I made a deal ten years ago." The man's breath reeked of smoke and sickness. "I needed her away from you."

His hand loosened. "What?"

"I couldn't have you hanging around." Haimon sputtered, a dry, raspy noise. "You were too smart."

"You mean I'd figure it out. That you were at fault for my father's death."

The grey eyes glittered. "I couldn't let you have access to my house. To me. I couldn't have you following us to London and making accusations."

"I followed you, old man. From the moment I understood what you'd done."

"When was that, I wonder?"

Five years. Five long years of working eighteen-hour days to keep the new company afloat. Not until he'd been able to breathe financially, had he found the time and the contacts to figure out what this worthless man had done to his father. "I'm not the one answering questions here. You are."

"You haven't made it worth my while to answer your questions, Vounó."

Rafe's hand tightened on the shirt. For a moment, he wanted his hands around this man's throat. But he didn't have all the answers. Not yet. "What did you do to Tamsin?"

"She let you go. I gave her some money."

His heart thumped in his chest. A hard beat of deep understanding. "She set up the account for me."

"She was in love with you. Stupid girl." A dry, heaving cough came the man. "She's still in love with you if she could betray me like this. I never would have thought she'd be devious enough to change the amount of the bid."

Dropping the man on the bed, Rafe stood. He stared down at his enemy and felt nothing. Nothing except disgust. "You'll have your money, old man."

"What?" Haimon's startled gaze swerved to meet his.

"I'll give you back exactly what you gave to Tamsin ten years ago." Rafe walked to the door. Opening it, he turned around to stare at the man one last time. "Then I never want to see you near me or mine again."

CHAPTER TWENTY-TWO

"Are you all done then, Tamsin?"

"Yes, Molly." She pulled her wool cap over her head as she turned to smile at her new employer and friend. "The bread for tomorrow's breakfast is cooling on the counter. I'll be in by seven a.m."

The older woman tsked, her grey brows lowering. "Now I told you to take tomorrow and sleep in. You've been working like a dog since the day I hired you."

"I like to work." Keeping the smile on her face, she pulled open the back door. A brisk, Irish wind picked up the flap of her coat, whisking her chin with its itchy wool. "See you at seven."

The door slammed behind her before her friend could object once more. Tam let out a sigh of relief. She liked Molly's concern. She just didn't like Molly's recommendations. The woman didn't understand work was the only thing that stood between sanity and deep depression.

The wind turned colder as she walked out of the alley behind the B&B and onto Quay Street. When she'd arrived in Galway a month ago, she'd been overwhelmed by culture shock. Gone were the quiet, sunny days of the Greek mountains. In its place were rowdy, laughing crowds, the last of the summer's tourists walking in and out of the shops and pubs.

Thank goodness she'd stumbled upon Molly and her inn within the first day of applying for a job. She didn't know if she would have been able to handle being a barmaid, forced to laugh and talk with all these happy people. Thankfully, her job only entailed making beds and bread, silent witnesses to her pain. Little interaction with the guests right now was for the best.

Molly wanted that situation to change.

"You're a people person," the older woman had stated more than once. "Anyone can see that."

Another one of her recommendations Tamsin studiously ignored.

She needed time alone. She needed time to heal.

In typical Irish fashion, a drizzle began to fall. Tam shuddered in her coat, still not used to the cold.

But she'd get used to it. She had to. This was her new life.

"Tamsin." A deep, booming voice called from the doorway of the pub across the street. "Come on, now. You've worked hard and it's time for a pint."

A fiddle and flute, mixing together in a spirited folk song, spilled from the bar's doorway. The music and call brought a reluctant smile to her face. "No, Mick. Not tonight."

The red-haired, grizzled giant who owned the pub and knew Molly well, had become another concerned friend. She should go over and hang out with the always friendly crowd at Mick's, yet her heart wasn't in it.

She'd tried it once.

Once had been enough.

There was no happy in her right now. And being around happy people only made her sadness more acute.

"Ah, now, why am I not surprised?" He looked at the skies. "You're going to get wet on your daily walk."

Tam shrugged. "I'll be okay."

He tsked, exactly like Molly.

Ignoring the unspoken commentary on her choices, she turned and trudged down the cobbled street, past the rows of gaily painted shops with their smoking chimneys, along the lane to the old, crumbling Spanish Arch.

The wind picked up, as well as the rain. The biting cold was precisely what she needed. By the time she got back to her little flat off Salthill Road, she'd be good and tired. A bit of toast and some hot tea and it would be time for bed.

Time to climb under the covers and close her eyes.

Time to forget everything.

Lifting her head, she breathed in the salted air. The grey clouds tumbled above her, a warning the night would be stormy. Galway Bay lay before her: the waves rolling with the wind, the call of the seagulls echoing off the water, the bulky outline of the Aran Islands rising on the misty horizon.

Her new home.

Her real father's home.

When she'd stepped off the plane in London, her righteous anger—the anger that had carried her through her argument with Rafe, through her writing to the boys, through her embarrassing escort off his property—the anger slid out of her spine and onto the tarmac.

Going to Ireland hadn't been a plan.

The action had been one of impulse. An act of desperation.

Standing in the center of Heathrow, surrounded by surging crowds trailing luggage behind them, a tidal

wave of misery and exhaustion had threatened to overwhelm her. She'd slumped onto a plastic chair and
closed her eyes.

"Why not Ireland?" The piping voice of a teenager
had broken through Tam's sorrow.

With a jerk, she'd straightened and opened her eyes.
The boy had been laughing at his mum and pointing a
finger at the departure board. Following his direction,
like a clarion call, she'd seen the flight to Galway.

Galway.

The home of the Cleary clan. The last name she'd
lost when her mother had married Haimon Drakos.
Maybe she hadn't left all her family behind. Maybe
there was someone who remembered her father and
would want to know her.

Frowning at her meager belongings, she'd made a
snap decision.

She'd been smart in Athens. After being unceremo-
niously dropped off at the airport, she'd gone right to
the counter and turned in the first-class ticket for a
seat in coach. Pocketing the difference meant she'd had
enough cash to survive for a few weeks. Still, London
was a costly town to live in. She'd be better off spending a bit on a plane ticket to get somewhere cheaper.

Within a few minutes, she had another ticket. To her
past and to her future.

Her real father had died in a car crash at the age of twenty-three. Her mother had always said he was a drunk and deserved to die, but Tam noted a resigned sadness whenever Skylla talked about him. Perhaps her parents had been star-crossed lovers, just like she and Rafe.

Sucking in a deep breath of salty air, she turned away from her troubled memories and thoughts.

She wasn't going to live her life like her mother, sad and broken and damaged.

She wasn't going to allow Rafe to do that to her.

She had plans. Plans involving college and a new life, new goals. Plans to contact any remaining Cleary relatives. Plans of living a full, happy life with people who trusted and believed in her. People who didn't lash out and cause her pain.

She'd forget. At some point, she'd forget.

But never, ever would she forgive.

"Tamsin."

The voice came from behind her, as familiar as her own. Sharp and deadly.

A threat.

Her heart clattered in her chest. Rafe couldn't be here. Not here in her new home. She swung around, sure she'd imagined the voice that echoed in her head and heart every night.

He stood a few yards from her as real as the scenery surrounding him. A black trench coat hugged the broad length of his shoulders. His black hair whipped in the wind. Those black eyes of his stared. Sharp. Deadly.

A threat.

Pivoting away from him, she paced down the pavement lining the bay. Why had he invaded this place where she was trying to find some peace? The low stone wall running along the road turned into a blur of browns and grays. With an impatient sweep, she brushed the tears off her cheeks.

Raphael Vounó didn't deserve her tears.

How had he found her?

As soon as the question blew into her mind, though, Tam knew. His all-knowing security team must have tracked her here.

But why? Why would he have any interest in tracking down a lying, thieving Drakos?

Her heartbeat picked up, dread replacing disbelief. Perhaps he'd changed his mind about pressing charges. He'd signed a contract, yet she couldn't actually enforce it. She had been stupid, very stupid to trust his word on a mere signature.

Raphael Vounó didn't deserve her trust.

The seagulls called again, the waves crashed on the shore to the left of her. The wind and rain lashed the skin of her cheeks and neck. The sounds drowned out his footsteps.

But he followed. She knew it. She felt him.

The dread morphed into fear. Where were all the people who usually roamed this promenade? The mothers with their strollers and the joggers and the tourists. Every morning and night, she walked this path and never had she been alone. It was as if there was some grand conspiracy to leave her deserted with this man. This man who hated her while she struggled to kill the love for him she held deep inside.

Raphael Vounó didn't deserve her love.

"Tamsin. Stop."

She quickened her steps, fear sliding into panic. That last terrible night, the last time she'd looked into his eyes, the only thing she'd seen was hostility. Not once in this last month, had she thought Rafe would be thinking about her for a moment. Still, perhaps his company directors had convinced him he must press charges.

"Tam." A long-fingered hand grabbed her elbow.

Yanking herself out of his grasp, she began to run down the walkway. Horror rushed through her blood, pushing her to go faster and faster. The police might be right behind him. Rafe would want to tell her of the arrest, deliver the final blow, but eventually there would have to be law enforcement involved.

She had no money to fight the charges. She'd have no hope.

"Tam." His voice came from right behind her. "It's the boys."

The clattering of her heart stopped cold in her chest and her mad dash came to a stumbling halt. Any thoughts of her own horrible situation dropped out of her mind. Whirling around, she met his dark gaze with her own terrified one. She'd forgotten in the turmoil during the last month. She should have warned Rafe about Haimon. She should have made sure they were safe before she left for good. "What?" Her heart suddenly raced. "What's happened to the boys?"

He came to a halt, too, and stuck his hands in his pockets. Glancing away, his mouth tightened. "They're unhappy."

"Unhappy?" The chug of her heartbeat stilled once more. "That's all? I thought they'd been attacked. I thought they'd been hurt."

"They are hurt."

"Are they in the hospital?" A wall of guilt crashed inside her.

"No." A flash of black eyes met her gaze, and then slid away again. "It's not that kind of hurt."

"Not a physical hurt." Her hands shook, adrenaline racing through her system. "Haimon hasn't hurt them?"

"Haimon?" His surprised gaze locked on hers. "I wouldn't let him near them, you can be sure of that."

Something settled inside her. Rafe might have hurt her more than any other human on earth, but she believed him. He'd protect the boys with his life. "So they are only hurting emotionally, right?"

"Um, right." He shifted on his feet and swung his gaze to the ocean.

"You tracked me down and flew here in person to tell me this?" The anger, the rage she'd felt the last time she'd seen this man, rose inside her like a flaming volcano. Without thinking, she took a step toward him and whacked him hard on his chest. "You scared me to death merely because the boys are hurting? Because they're unhappy?"

His hands snatched her close, stopping her from whacking him again. "They're not the only ones who are unhappy back in Greece."

Did he dare to insinuate he was unhappy? After everything he'd done to her? The rage inside her made her brave enough to meet his wary gaze without flinching. "Do you think I care?"

Another flash of surprise blanked his eyes before she wrenched herself from his grip. Turning, she strode down the path once more. Confusion replaced the panic inside her. His reason for being here made less and less sense. No sense at all, really.

But there was one last gift she had for her boys. She stopped and turned to glare at him. "You need to know one thing."

"Only one?" He attempted a tentative grin, trying to lighten the mood.

Tam wasn't having any of it. She kept her words flat. "Haimon is a threat to them."

Rafe's hands fisted. "What are you talking about?"

"He threatened them. Physically." She swiveled back around, aiming for her new home. "Be aware of that."

"*Gamó*," he cursed. "That's how he got you to cooperate."

He'd finally figured one thing out, yet it was too late. Too late for him. Too late for them. Sticking her hands in her pockets, she kept walking away, shivering as cold reality seeped back in, freezing the fire of her rage into a block of ice.

"You might not care about me, but you care about the boys."

Without stopping, she scowled at him over her shoulder. "Of course I care about Aarōn and Isaák. I'll always love them."

Rafe's mouth twisted, acknowledging the unspoken hit. But he started walking toward her, following her again. "You said you'd never leave them. Not for any amount of money in the world."

The injustice of the accusation burned her blood. She whipped around to confront him. "You dare to—"

"I'm sorry." His lips tightened. "I shouldn't have thrown that at you. I was wrong."

I'm sorry and *I was wrong* were not words she heard from this man's mouth on a regular basis. Hell, she'd never heard them. She stared at him in astonishment. This clearly wasn't about getting her arrested. So what else could this be?

He grimaced. "I just needed you to stop. To listen."

The bid. Maybe the bid had come through, he'd won and he wanted to find out what had really happened. Still, it was too late, way too late. There was no more listening or explaining in her. Not after a month of spending all her minutes making sure Raphael Vounó was banished from her memory. She wanted this done. She wanted him gone.

"Tam—"

"The boys are almost fourteen." Turning back, she noted she was close to her flat and hastened her stride. Close to safety. If he tried to follow her in, she'd call the police. Let him feel the fear of being detained for once. "They're fine without me."

The drizzle turned to a soaking rain, dripping onto her eyelashes, interweaving with the stupid tears welling in her eyes once more.

"It's not only the boys who are unhappy." His dark voice came again. "It's Rhouth."

Surprise made her pause, her pace slowing. She shouldn't take the bait. Whatever Rafe was doing here, she shouldn't care. But she couldn't block the question before blurting it out. "What do you mean by that? Rhouth hates me."

"No, she doesn't." His firm grip came again on Tam's elbow and this time she allowed him to turn her to face him because she'd managed to control her emotions and tears. She didn't want to show him any weakness or fear.

His black eyes shone with purpose, a purpose she couldn't understand.

"You came here to Ireland to tell me Rhouth's unhappy?" The anger flickered and fought against her unwanted curiosity.

He ignored her question. "She read your letters."

"My...letters." She yanked her arm from his grip, not wanting his touch. She didn't leave, though. Not yet. Curiosity ate away at her resolve to get away from him once and for all. "What letters?"

"The letters you wrote ten years ago."

The memories came back with searing pain. The time and effort she'd put into each missive, hoping Rhouth would understand what she was saying between the words. That she'd done what she had to. That she'd needed to be with the boys. That she'd taken the only road she could at the time. Haimon had made her promise not to contact Rafe and not to tell anyone about their deal, but writing to Rafe's sister had been her one attempt at keeping her dreams alive.

She remembered the endless days waiting for a reply and the sorrow she'd felt when there'd never been a response.

"She just read them now?" Her laugh choked out, hoarse and mocking. "And what? I'm supposed to be grateful she's feeling a bit guilty because of them?"

"I read them, too." His skin appeared white in contrast to the grey of the clouds and sea. There was something in his eyes she couldn't define. Something wild and out-of-control. "Every single one."

"Really?" Another choked laugh escaped her. "I can't think why."

Rafe glanced away, as if unable to meet her gaze any longer. The silence between them grew, only filled with the rage of the building storm swirling around them.

She shouldn't be standing here, getting drenched, giving this man an iota of her attention. He didn't deserve anything from her, not anymore. The rage returned, storming inside her, overwhelming the unwanted curiosity. "I've got to go."

"Wait." He jerked his head around to meet her withering stare. The wild look had turned into a determined one. "I have something for you."

"An arrest warrant?" she spat.

"No." He frowned, a look of frustration crossing his face. "Of course not. Don't be crazy."

The memory of their last confrontation swept through her. He'd accused her of being crazy then too.

The rage boiled inside her. "I'm being crazy? The last time I saw you, you threatened exactly that. An arrest warrant. Now I'm being—"

"That was the past." His hand slashed in front of him as his eyes grew dark with aggravation. "Not now."

Now was even worse than the past.

Now meant she had more memories of him. More memories of how his hair curled around his ears and his mouth firmed when he was troubled and his eyes shone with—

"Tamsin." He rammed his hands back into his pockets. His gaze zeroed in on hers and what she saw...she couldn't, wouldn't define what she saw. "Listen to me."

She'd had more than a month. A month away from his heat and touch. A month where, damn him, she'd begun to heal. Now she'd have to start over.

More nights crying into her pillow before falling into an exhausted sleep.

More time staring blankly at the bread as she kneaded, remembering.

More pain and anguish.

"No." She jerked around and marched across the street and up the steps to the front door of her building.

"Please, Tammy." His voice was choked and hoarse. "Please."

CHAPTER TWENTY-THREE

The plea stopped her.

A rush of memories, ten-year-old memories, flooded her mind and heart. He'd said the exact same thing before she'd walked away the last time. He'd said the words in the exact same way too. Low and guttural and anguished. And the words made her do the exact same thing.

She burst into tears.

But this time, this time she wasn't far enough away from him.

This time he heard her.

"Tammy." Strong arms came around her to hug her, her back to his front.

She felt the rough graze of his unshaven chin by her ear and his breath, warm and moist, hit her wet cheek. His strength surrounded her; his long, masculine fingers tightening around her waist as he held her. "Let me go," she managed to gasp through her tears.

"Never." He stated the word with precision, every vowel elongated as if he needed to examine each sound to make sure it was correct.

The word shocked the tears from her eyes. She stiffened in his arms. "I don't know what game you're playing and I don't care."

"Tam—"

"Let me go."

Her landlady banged open the front door to peer into the gloom. "Is that you, Tamsin?"

"Yes, Mrs. Needham." Her elbow poked at his hard stomach, but the arrogant man didn't budge.

"Oh, you have a young man." The old lady grinned, her glasses flashing in the street's light. "How delightful."

Rafe huffed a quiet laugh behind her.

The rage threatened to contaminate her heart forever. "No, he's not—"

"Well, you'd best get out of this rain." Mrs. Needham opened the door wide and waved at them. "Best not to get any wetter than you both are now."

"Good idea," he murmured.

She could make a scene. She could call the police.

She could tell her landlady she wanted nothing to do with this man.

Turning in his arms, she pushed on his chest, placing some distance between them. Tam chanced a glance at his face. The black eyes sparkled with lingering amusement, but they also sparked with a resolute resolve.

Raphael Vounó wasn't going to leave until he'd had his say.

"Please." His one word was quiet yet insistent.

She didn't want this man in her place. However, she had a chance to grab something she'd mourned about for the last month. "All right," she said, in a low voice. "I'll give you five minutes."

A gleam of immediate joy danced in his eyes. "I'll need more—"

"Five minutes." She poked once more and got her release from his grasp. "In return—"

"Tam." Joy leeched away, turning the black into muddy despair. "You don't have to bargain with me. Ever again."

"In return, you let me keep in touch with the boys." She ignored his sad sigh. "I want it in writing in front of a notary."

"*Iēsoús.*" Once upon a time, the look he shot her would have made her crumble into a hopeless heap of compassion. Now she wouldn't be moved.

"Are you coming inside then?" Her landlady rattled the door. "It's getting awfully cold in here."

"That's the deal." Tamsin turned towards the building. "Take it or leave it."

"Okay," he muttered from behind.

Mrs. Needham flapped around them as they stepped into the foyer. The blue-padded steps led to the second floor where Tam's studio flat fronted the street.

"Have some hot tea," the old lady chimed in from the bottom of the stairs.

"Have a good night, Mrs. Needham." Tamsin unlocked the solid wooden door.

Rafe walked in, filling the small flat with his presence.

Her heart sank.

This was far worse than what she'd imagined moments ago. Now her memories would be filled with him standing here, in her new home, poisoning every attempt she'd make to forget him. This would be so hard. Still, in compensation, she'd be able to write to the boys. That was worth enduring this man's presence in her home for five minutes.

"Say what you have to say and then leave." The door slammed behind her.

He turned from his contemplation of her living quarters, his hands, again, in his pockets. "Your place is small."

"So what?" Pulling her wool hat off, she plunked it onto the heater. "I don't need a grand mansion to be happy. This works for me."

Striding to the bay window, he gazed onto the rain-drenched street. "Nice view."

"Rafe." Just saying his name hurt. The realization only fueled her temper. "You didn't come to Ireland to comment on my flat."

"No, I didn't." He glanced at her and then away. For the first time, she really noticed the action. Noted how unsure he seemed. He didn't hold himself with his usual confidence. Instead, his shoulders were hunched, his head down. Raphael Vounó had never found it difficult to look her straight in the eye before.

Curious.

And troubling at the same time.

She might hate this man, she might want him to hurt, yet she still cared, too. The mix of emotions inside nauseated her.

She wanted this over. "Your five minutes are almost done."

"How about some tea?"

She couldn't believe what she saw in front of her. Rafe didn't like tea. Rafe always got straight to the point. Rafe didn't shuffle his feet as if uncertain of where he stood.

"You hate tea." She jerked off her coat, trying to distract herself from her returning curiosity. Slinging it on the hook by the door, she stomped into the tiny kitchen.

All right. She'd make some tea. It didn't matter what he wanted; she wanted some. The pot slammed onto the stove.

"You have a right to be angry." His pensive words drifted across the room.

A quick glance told her he wasn't looking at her. Instead, he continued to gaze at the blustery sea.

"I don't need you to tell me what my rights are or not." Scowling at the teapot, waiting for it to whistle, Tam focused on getting him to spit out whatever was inside him so she could get him outside. Outside of her flat and outside of herself. "You told me you have something for me."

From the corner of her eye, she watched as he turned from the window. Opening his coat, he plucked out a small, silk bag. The silk was new and shiny, a blue-grey shimmering in the pale light of the overhead fixture.

"I forgot to give this to you." He looked at her finally, his mouth tight. "That night."

The teapot's sharp whistle broke the silence that followed.

That night. The night he'd destroyed her. She focused on getting two cups down from the upper shelf and dropping the tea bags into them. The hot water steamed over her face as she poured, making the heat of her remembered rage even hotter.

Gazing across at him, she asked, "Do you want cream or sugar?"

His eyes widened and she realized she'd said it in her usual way. Her pleasant, friendly, aiming-to-please way. Not because she felt any of those emotions toward this man, but because of her stupid habit of trying to make everyone around her happy. The realization made her angry at herself as well as him.

Grabbing her cup, she marched to her futon and sat. "The milk's in the fridge if you want it."

He ignored the curt invite and his tea. Instead, he walked over and placed the small bag on the cheap plywood coffee table she'd found in the garbage when she'd first moved in. "It's yours."

Her unwanted curiosity rose inside. Figuring if she opened the bag, he'd be one step closer to leaving, she plunked her cup onto the table and picked the bag up. The blue stones and pearls twinkled as they fell into her hand. Her father's only gift to her. An unwelcome tear slid down her cheek, so she didn't look at him. "You came all this way to deliver this?"

"I, ah..." He coughed.

"You could have just as easily mailed it to me."

Silence met her words. Since she now had her tears under control, she raised her head and frowned at him.

His hands were fisted in his pockets, his long frame taut. The expression on his face was one she'd never seen before on him; a mix of indecision and fear. Those black eyes were filled with the wild look she'd noticed only minutes before outside.

"I have something more for you," he croaked.

Leaning back on the futon, she waited. She didn't know how to handle this version of Raphael Vounó. So she waited.

He jerked his hands from his pockets and opened his coat again. Withdrawing a large envelope, he placed it carefully on the table in front of her. A sudden spark of amusement lit inside her. An absurd reaction to the circumstances, still, the way he placed both items before her as if he were a supplicant was hard to take in.

Raphael Vounó. A supplicant.

Beware of a Greek bearing gifts.

The old motto rang with truth, yet her curiosity welled inside once more.

"Open it." There was a thread of arrogance in his words: an order, a command.

She straightened her spine, anger roaring back. "Your time is—"

"Please."

The hoarse plea was too much for her damn tender heart. Tam grabbed the envelope. Inside was a sheaf of papers with tons of legalese filling the pages.

"I don't understand." She met his intent gaze with her confused one. "What are these?"

"Read the bottom of the first page."

She read and read again. Her mind reeled at what the words said. The words made no sense. "What are you doing?"

"I'm signing Viper Enterprises over to you. You're the new owner."

His claims crashed into the room and filled it with a fire of stark disbelief. She felt the hairs on the back of her neck rise as if she were in an electric storm. A boom of thunder outside reinforced the sense the world had been thrown into chaos.

Or this man in front of her had gone mad. "Are you nuts?"

"No." His mouth's edge turned down in a wry curl. "I figure your money started the whole thing, so you're the rightful owner."

"How?" Shock blasted her disbelief into a thousand pieces. Her hands tightened on the papers. "How do you know—?"

"Why didn't you throw this in my face when we met again?" He frowned, a quizzical look crossing his face. "I would have."

"I'm not you." Sometimes, she wished she did have a heart as hard as steel. She could have stuck this knowledge into him like an infected dart right at the very beginning and let it eat away inside of him.

"No, you're not, are you?" The frown fell off his face. "*Dóxa tō Theó.*"

"Don't thank God. He had nothing to do with it." She let the papers slide onto her lap. "If I'd told you this at the beginning, you would have dismissed it anyway."

"True." He grimaced. "But then why not later?"

"I... I..." She hadn't wanted to hurt him. She hadn't wanted to diminish any of the amazing accomplishments he'd achieved at Viper, although he didn't belong there. Still, she didn't want to confess this tenderness and give him another weapon in this war between them. "Never mind. It doesn't matter anymore."

"It matters—"

"What matters is how you found out." Who could have told him? The only one she could think of was Haimon, yet she couldn't imagine him seeking a meeting with this man standing in front of her—the old man was afraid of him and rightfully so. Plus, the agreement she'd signed with Rafe precluded him from searching for the old man. She didn't trust this man before her, but she'd believed him when he'd stated he had no more use for her stepfather or her.

"Well, that's a bit of a story." He shifted his weight to his other leg as if he were suddenly uncomfortable.

"And according to you, I don't have much time left to make my case."

Make his case for what? For her to run his company? There was no way she'd ever go back to Greece, much less work in a company that had Rafe's presence stamped into its very being. But her curiosity kept her tied into the middle of this horrible conversation. "Tell me. I want to know."

He hesitated before stating with resignation, "I won the bid."

Blind rage wiped all her questions and confusion from her mind. That night, the memory of that night, blasted back into the core of her, dripping its toxic brew into her bloodstream. She still didn't understand what all this meant and she still wanted to know how he found out about the money. But the searing memories of what this man had done wiped away her curiosity, replacing it with fury at his betrayal of their bond. "The bid you accused me of steal—"

"*Nai.*" His hands went back into his pockets. "That bid."

She glared at him, the anger running so fierce and fiery inside she thought she'd turn into a burning fire. "Then you know I didn't betray you."

"That's why I'm here."

"Too late." Tam slapped the papers onto the table. "I don't want your company."

I don't want you.

The unspoken words hit him; she could tell when he flinched. This stupid connection between them, this stupid, wretched horrible way they saw into each other had to stop.

"Your time is over." She folded her arms in front of her in firm rejection. "I want you to leave."

"I tracked down Haimon."

Closing her eyes, she took his words in. He had broken another promise. "You told me you wouldn't search for him."

"I wasn't searching for Drakos as much as I was searching for answers."

So it had been Haimon who told him about her seed money. Why the old man would have confessed such a thing, she had no idea. Another one of his schemes, probably. "He told you."

"*Nai.*" A quiet, simple response that made her want to weep.

"You believed him." She squeezed the tears back. "Yet you never believe me."

"*Theós,* Tam." His hoarse exhalation filled the room.

She concentrated on swallowing her tears.

"You're right." Rafe's voice came at last, a rough, dark sound. "I have no excuse for that. None that's worth anything."

A sad silence floated in the room.

"Time for you to leave." She kept her eyes shut so she wouldn't have the image in her head of him closing the door between them for all time.

"Maybe I believed Drakos because I had him cornered." The words were tight and rushed.

Rafe had got his wish. He'd found his enemy and quite likely Haimon was in some Greek jail. She hated her stepfather for what he'd done in the past, ruining this man who stood before her. Ruining his ability to trust and to love. She hated him for what he'd done to her a month ago. Making her choose once more, making her lose everything she'd dreamed of her entire life. However, she still didn't want him dead or in jail. "I wish you'd let him go."

"I paid him off."

Her eyes shot open and she gaped at him. "You paid him off?"

"I paid him the exact amount he gave you." Rafe's eyes gleamed. Shone with a light she hadn't seen in ten long years. The light she'd written about in her teenage journal. The light she'd thought lost forever.

Her mind went blank. "Gave me?"

"Ten years ago."

The rush of the wind outside filled the silence with a hushed roar. She couldn't understand any of this; it was too much to take in. And more than anything else, what she saw in his eyes was too much. She wouldn't let herself dream anymore. Not about this man. "You need to leave."

"I'm not done." He shuffled his feet before planting them in a solid stance. The posture told her she'd have to physically throw him out. That wasn't an option, though. She didn't want to get near him and do something stupid.

"You promised to leave after five minutes." She wanted to strangle him for what he'd done and what he was doing now to her poor, broken heart. Instead, she grabbed her tea cup.

"You promised to love me forever." His gaze bore into hers. "We've both broken promises."

"I had a good reason." She hung on to her anger, deciding to place the cup on the table rather than throwing it at him like she wanted. "But it doesn't matter anymore."

"It matters a great deal." His gaze didn't drop, his feet didn't shuffle. "Haimon told me why, Tammy. Why you broke it off with me years ago."

Stunned surprise slid through her. "No, he didn't. He wouldn't have."

Rafe stuck out two fingers, rubbing them together in the international sign of money. "He told me quite a few things."

"He told you, huh?" The old anguish, the anguish which had woven through most of her life, causing her endless despair, rose in a howl. "Did he tell you I had to make a choice between you and my brothers? Did he tell you he banned me from contacting you? Did he tell you the only way I could guarantee you had a future was by saying I didn't love you to your face?"

Her shrieked questions filled the room with her emotions. The drum of the rain on the roof served as a pounding refrain to the pain-filled words. Something hard and cold, like a knife's blade, tore her inside.

"Not all of it." Rafe's eyes blurred with tears. "However, you just told me the rest."

Tam wrapped her shaking arms around her, wanting to take the knife inside and stick it in his heart and then use it to cut the last threads of this horrible connection between them. This connection that had cost them both too much, hurt both of them too long. "Then you know there's no need to give me your company. I did what I thought was best years ago."

"You also did what you thought was best a month ago." Closing his eyes, he leaned his head back, despair written all over his face.

She stared at him, surprised at the understanding running through his voice. Misery swelled inside. Maybe she should have told him, believed in him, yet she hadn't. Now it was too late. "I wanted to tell you Haimon was lurking around, begging for money, but...but..."

"You thought I wouldn't believe you." His head shot up, his eyes shot open and the ink black swirled with pain. "You would have been right."

Misery slinked away, replaced by the familiar fury sapping her soul. "You didn't trust me, I could tell."

"Tammy—"

"You still don't trust me."

"Really?" Bending down, he swiped the papers from the coffee table. "I trust you enough to give my company to you."

"I don't want it." What she wanted to do was slip into her bed, pull the covers over her head, and never come back out. Closing her eyes against him, she leaned her head back, hoping he'd get the message this conversation was done; they were done.

Her withdrawal filled the room with a stilted silence.

"I have something else to give you," he finally said.

God help her. His gifts were like poison. Vicious, soul-destroying poison dripping into her resolve and contaminating her future. She kept her eyes closed. "I don't want anything more from you. Other than I want you to go away."

"Look," he demanded.

The command should have shot steel down her spine. All she felt instead was weariness. She opened her eyes, ready to inspect this last gift and then he'd go. He had to go.

He slid another envelope onto the coffee table. "Open it."

She stared at it with dull horror.

"Please, Tammy."

The plea again. And exactly as before, it jolted her into doing what he wanted.

This letter, an acceptance letter, was simple to understand and impossible to believe.

"You're going to medical school?" She would have winced at her shrill cry, but she was too astounded to care.

"*Nai.*" He stared at her, his gaze resolute. "So you see, I need someone to run the company. You."

The thought of her, Tamsin Drakos, taking over a multi-billion dollar company... "You're being absurd."

"Am I?" A crooked smile twisted his mouth. "Then, let's be absurd together."

Together. She stared at him in shock.

"I'm sorry." His words were simple, yet what shone from his black eyes wasn't. It was profound. "I'm sorry I didn't trust you when we met again."

Sudden tears blinded her for a moment, the sweet words so surprising in their simplicity they caught her breath from her lungs.

"I'm sorry I didn't realize you were a virgin when we made love the first time." He caressed the word *love,* stretched the vowel and highlighted the meaning so clearly, she couldn't ignore his intent.

She wouldn't believe. She couldn't believe. There wasn't anything left in her to dream a dream about him.

A stricken look crossed his face at her continued silence, but then he stiffened, his mouth tightening. "Can you say I'm sorry too?"

"What?" She blinked, the tears clearing from her eyes. "What do you mean?"

"Can you say, I'm sorry that ten years ago I didn't trust you with the truth, Rafe?"

A gurgle of regret choked her throat. Because he was right. If she'd told him, they'd have found a way. She would have still gone to London with the boys. She would have left a man behind who loved her, though, and would have waited for her. She shouldn't have taken Haimon's deal. Rafe and his family would have been strong enough to overcome on their own.

He kept his gaze on her, a dogged look in his eyes. "Because I think if you can say that, then we can do anything, Tammy. Anything together."

No words came. The pain and memories and love were too full inside her.

Rafe sighed and his shoulders slumped.

Tam wanted to speak, she wanted to because she could see the defeat crossing his face. But she couldn't force any words out; there was too much inside.

"Okay, you won't say you're sorry, too." He gazed at her, his face grave. "I'm going to give you this last gift anyway."

"Why did you build our house?" She still didn't have all the pieces to believe. She still didn't have all the courage to leap into his arms. She yearned to, yet she still bled inside.

Shock filled his expression. "You must know."

"I don't know anything." The truth cut her. She loved him, yet she didn't understand him.

"Tammy." His Adam's apple moved as he swallowed. "I built the house because I thought it was the only thing I'd ever have of you."

His confession wrenched the hard, cold knife to a stop inside her. The stark tone in his voice told her he was telling her the truth. She took it in, the words, the look in his eyes, the way he stood in front of her, completely open for the first time in ten years.

"I built the house with the frantic hope that someday you'd walk back in my life."

"You hated me." She pushed the accusation out.

"I hated you because after you left, nothing was ever right." He brushed his long fingers over his mouth, as if he were surprised at his words. "All my work, all my days, everything was merely a ghost of what my life should have been."

"Can still be," she whispered. His dreams had died as surely as hers had. She saw the pain she felt in his gaze, heard the anguish in his voice that she held in hers. The knife slid out of her heart, disappearing in the mist of the past.

His head jerked up and his expression turned intense. Whatever he saw on her face and in her eyes appeared to give him courage. "I don't hate you, Tammy."

She held her breath.

"I love you." He kneeled in front of the futon. "I always have. I always will."

"I know." The anger and fear and rage she'd felt for years, dropped away, leaving her feeling fresh and young and alive. Layers of grief slid from her heart and washed out of her life forever. "I know."

"If you know." He gulped and reached into his pocket. A small, white satin jewelry box landed on the coffee table. "Will you marry me, Tamsin?"

The crack at the end of his voice, the uncertainty in his gaze, made her heart sing. This arrogant, demanding man was willing to risk his pride to win her hand, even if apparently, he wasn't sure of her heart. "Rafe."

"Accept me, Tam." His gaze never wavered. "I'm not perfect, and I have a lot to make up for, but if you give me a chance, I'll make you happy. I promise."

"You promise, huh?" She gifted him with a soft smile.

Hope sprung onto his face. "A promise I'll keep."

She stared at him, knowing he would. Believing, finally believing in her dreams again. "Rafe—"

"I know you might need to think about this." He grabbed the satin box and jerked it open, uncovering a dazzling, pear-shaped rose diamond. "But you can keep this with you until you decide."

"I'm not perfect either."

Her confession stopped his hands. His long fingers tightened on the box as he turned his head to look at her. What he saw made his eyes light. Light with the love she'd needed for years. "Tammy?"

"I'm sorry, Rafe." The words came now, flowing across her tongue like a long-released dam. "I'm sorry I didn't trust you with the truth years ago."

With a choked laugh, he grabbed her, yanking her to the floor with him. "Say it, Tam. Please say it."

"I love you." She beamed at him, free of the past.

His hands tightening on her arms, he kissed her. The taste of him, rich and warm and sweet, made her whole.

He leaned back to stare at her. "Will you marry me, Tammy?"

"Yes." She smiled through her happy tears. "I will."

"*Eláte.*" His fingers plucked the ring from the satin box. "Give me your hand."

She slipped her hand into his one more time. And this time it was forever.

"*T*amsin Cleary Vounó."

The announcer's voice reverberated above the clapping crowd, filling the giant hall.

Tam clutched the edge of her black gown as she crossed the stage. The Dean of Economics and Business smiled at her, his shaggy white hair bouncing as he nodded encouragement. Did she appear like she needed it? Was he worried she'd trip carrying her extra weight? Or perhaps her excitement appeared to be nerves.

She wasn't nervous.

She was proud.

Proud of what she'd achieved and proud of her extra weight.

As the scroll proclaiming her degree slipped into her hands, she barely managed to stuff down the shriek of happiness. It had taken her eight long years to get to this point. Yet it had all been worth it.

She had a MBA degree.

Smiling one more time at the dean, she strutted off the stage. The feeling of accomplishment swirled inside her along with a heavy dose of relief. Finally, she'd be able to take over the rest of Rafe's work so he could do what he was meant to do full-time.

Finding her seat among the throng of fellow graduates, she turned her head, scanning the audience behind her.

She couldn't spot any of them. She knew they were there, though. Ready to celebrate her success.

After seemingly endless minutes, the last of the graduates had their scrolls and Tam joined in the loud yell as the students jumped and hugged and laughed. She'd made many friends during these past months, even if most of the students were younger than her by a dozen years. She'd miss many of them, but there were a chosen few she planned on adding to her team at the company. Her friends would now become her colleagues.

Excitement bubbled inside her.

Breaking away from the continued celebration, she edged around the crowd and scanned the audience once more. Most of the mothers and fathers had left their seats and were winding their way to their loved one.

Where were they?

"Tam." A deep, loud voice had her turning to look in the opposite direction.

There. There they were. Aarōn laughed and waved as he walked toward her. His voice was soon joined by an equally deep one.

"You did it!" Isaák beamed his usual broad smile as he pushed his way through the last of the crowd separating them. His big shoulders crowded out the rest of her vision as he pulled her into a hug.

His twin ambled over. "My turn, idiot."

Another powerful hug enveloped her. Tam smiled, all at once wistful. She still found herself amazed sometimes that her boys were now fully grown men. They both towered above her and teased her about the fact every time she saw them. Which wasn't often. At twenty-one, they had far better things to do than hang out with a sister. Like getting their own degrees and chasing girls in their spare time.

Today, however, was different.

Today was her day.

"Where are the rest?" she asked.

"Somewhere back there." Aarōn waved a negligent hand behind him.

"They'll get here eventually." Isaák smiled at her. "But we wanted to get here first."

"To be the first to congratulate you."

Her boys. Launched into the world and a testament to the love she'd given them. If only Haimon had loved them as she had, maybe he wouldn't have disappeared from their lives forever. Instead, maybe, somehow she could have given him a slice of the twins' lives. But Rafe had confessed he'd told Haimon to leave and never come back, and for once the old man had kept his promise. In all these years, she'd never heard a word. Perhaps it was for the best.

"Rafe's going to be angry," Aarōn sniggered.

Isaák's eyes twinkled as he glanced at his brother. "Yeah, he sure is."

"Why?" She frowned, her happy emotions cut short. This was her day. She didn't want anyone being anything except happy.

"He warned us." By the expression on Aarōn's face, he didn't seem to be too worried.

"He wanted to be the first to hug you," his twin chimed in. "You should have seen the look on his face when we took off to find you."

Tam's frown disappeared. "Oh, you both are teasing—"

"No, both of us aren't," Isaák said. "He's going to be mad."

"The poor guy's saddled with so much extra baggage, though, it's impossible for him to be faster than us." Aarōn's grin was as wide as his brother's.

She knew these threats and dire predictions were merely a sham. This was only the usual between the twins and her husband. The boys loved to rib their uncle and he loved to rib them right back. Rafe might cuff both of the boys when he got here, but it would be with affection.

"Tamsin." Rhachel's shriek made the three of them turn their heads. Her sister-in-law bounded toward them, a big smile on her face. "Congratulations."

"Thank you." She smiled as she received another warm hug. "It feels great to get this done."

"You have every right to feel super great," Rhachel said. "It's a huge accomplishment."

"It did take her eight long years." Isaák's eyes lit with teasing. "That's a long time."

"Well, she did have some other things going on." His aunt stepped toward him and gave his shoulder a shove. "Like taking care of you and your brother."

"And assorted others," Aarōn said wryly.

"Tamsin." Nephele's smile was wide and bright as she walked up to the group. A line of laughing, giggling grandchildren trailed behind her.

With one swoop, she found herself in the familiar arms of someone who'd become beyond dear to her. The woman's signature scent of lilacs swirled in her nose and Tam's eyes welled with grateful tears. Nephele had given her something she'd never had.

"*Mamá*," she whispered in the older woman's ear.

"Congratulations." Her mother-in-law eased out of the embrace to gaze into Tam's eyes. "You worked so hard for this, for so long. I'm proud of you."

For a moment, she thought of Skylla, so broken and damaged she'd never once given her daughter anything but negative. Yet Tam had long ago forgiven her and now was not the time to dredge up old hurts.

Now was the time to be supremely happy.

"Tamsin." Rhouth broke through the throng of gathering relatives, her amber eyes warm, her face filled with an affectionate greeting. "You did it, girl-friend."

"I did, didn't I?" She threw her arms around the woman, laughing with delight. Rhouth had just given birth three days ago and Tam hadn't been sure she should be here. Still, her best friend had been adamant. This was Tamsin's special day and nothing would cause her to miss it.

"I'm so glad you're done." Her best friend eased back from the hug they shared.

"I am too. Now, Rafe can practice medicine full time."

"He'll finally do what he was meant to do all along."

"Yes." A wash of tears filled Tam's eyes. "He's been so patient."

"Of course he has." Rhouth's mouth curved into a knowing smile. "He'd do anything for you. Plus the distractions have been as much his fault as yours."

She laughed. "True."

"And the company had to keep operating."

Her company. Viper Enterprises might still have the guiding hand of its founder holding the reins of power, but during the last two years, she had steadily taken on more and more of the daily decisions. This MBA degree would only solidify a respect she'd been developing among the staff. She loved the business, much more than her husband. Now she'd have a chance to take complete control of it, freeing Rafe to go full-time in the fledgling pediatric practice he'd started four years ago when he'd graduated from medical school.

"Just think. Rafe will be doing what he promised his father he'd do." A deep stab of satisfaction and joy ran through her. "What he should have been doing his entire life."

Rhouth looked her straight in the eye, a grave smile on her face. "Because of you. If you hadn't walked back into his life and forced him to see what was in front of him, my brother would have been too stubborn to do it on his own."

"Well—"

"Thank you." Her best friend hugged her again with a fierce grip. "Thank you for giving us back our Raphael."

"Don't make me cry." She smiled through her tears.

"Okay, okay. I'll leave it that I couldn't be happier you'll be doing what you do best, and my brother will be doing what he does best."

"Exactly." Giving Rhouth another smile, she turned around to stare into the sea of people. "Speaking of which—where is he?"

"I'm right here."

Tam jerked around and finally spotted her husband. He strode over to the crowd of Vounós, a grin on his face for them all, but his black gaze centered on her.

"Took you awhile," Aarōn crowed.

She glanced down at the obvious reason for the delay. The child stroller Rafe pushed was filled with three of the most important people in her life. One of them was sobbing as if her life were ending.

"I'm afraid Téleia isn't the center of attention." Rafe's mouth quirked. "So she's mad."

"Té." Bending down, she plucked her five-year-old daughter out of the stroller. "Shush, now. *Mamá*'s here."

Aarōn knelt in front of the other two children in the stroller. "No temper tantrums from my two guys, huh?"

"Of course not." Isaák tugged one of the babies out of his straps and lifted him high above him. "Ben and Loukas are too cool to cry."

The one-year-old twins cried all the time. Yet today they appeared to be on their best behavior, thank goodness.

"*Mamá.*" Téleia brushed her fingers across her cheeks, the glitter of the silver and pearl bracelet that was her prized possession sparkling in the light. Her green eyes glittered with stray tears. "Let's go home."

Home, Tam knew, meant Sparti where Titus awaited to charm his favorite human being. From the moment the dog had spotted Té's dark curls bouncing in her father's grasp, he'd been a devoted slave. "Soon, Té." She kissed the wet cheeks. "Soon."

"Guess who got to hug Tam first, Rafe?" Isaák grinned as he snuggled Loukas into his big arms. The baby gurgled, the blond fluff of his head waving like a white cloud around his head, contentment filling his face as he lay in the grasp of someone who loved him unconditionally.

"It's not the first that matters, but the last." A warm hand slipped across her stomach. "How's our baby?"

"She's fine." Another child on the way in two short months. Sometimes Tam wondered whether she and Rafe would be able to handle the children, the work, the schooling, but then her strong, loving husband would take her in his arms and cuddle her fears away. And somehow, with the help of the family, the nanny they'd hired, and the loyal staff at Viper Enterprises everything important always got done.

"*Kardiá mou.*" A long-fingered hand nudged Tam's chin and her gaze met his intense one. "You did it."

"Yes. I did." Her smile felt as wide as the Aegean sea. "Aren't you proud?"

"*Nai,* very proud." Rafe's eyes held the familiar darkness mixed with the light of love. "Proud to be your husband."

"Oh, Raphael." She leaned into his hand, his palm cupping her face. "Everything's going to be perfect now."

"Now, Tammy?" A dark brow arched and a smile edged his mouth. "It already is."

ABOUT THE AUTHOR

Double finalist and winner of the Golden Heart, one of Romance Writers of America's highest awards, Caro LaFever writes timeless romantic tales as well as nonfiction advice for writers. Her book, *Heroes & Heroines: Sixteen Master Archetypes,* has been a go-to resource for writers for more than a decade. Her romantic novels have won or been a finalist in such prestigious contests as the Golden Pen, the Orange Rose, and the Emily. She lives in the Rocky Mtns.

www.carolafever.com
www.facebook.com/carolafever
www.pinterest/carolafever
twitter@caro_lafever

ACKNOWLDGEMENTS

I appreciate every bit of advice and commentary that I've received from numerous critique group buddies, workshops, classes, and beta readers. After years of honing my craft, I still find new and important nuggets of wisdom every time I put my writing out there for review.

Thanks to my developmental editor, Allie Burton, who is truly my conscience and calls me on my idiot imaginings. Thanks to Sue Viders, who always catches when a character has moved across the room, but I haven't mentioned it. And thanks to Tanya Saari, my proofreader, who diligently goes with me into the correct way to spell numerous foreign foods and phrases. Finally, thanks to my family, who taught me to love books and appreciate a story well-told.

Made in the USA
Middletown, DE
15 January 2017